SILENT JUSTICE

ALEX J. FISCHER

For my Family and Friends

1

Skye helped Ashley move the large flat screen television through the door. "He let you take this television? Didn't he buy this?"

"He did," Ashley said, shutting the door behind her with her foot. "Put it on that stand behind you. I'll connect it later. He didn't complain. All he did was offer to help me move. It's like he doesn't get how awkward it is between us now. This last week waiting until the weekend was the longest grind. He wanted to know where I was outside of workout hours. I just kept telling him I was hanging with you."

"I think you're the one making it awkward, and besides, you were hanging out here anyway." Skye placed her side on the piece of furniture in front of the bed. "You should have taken him up on that offer. With his physique, we'd probably be done by now."

You could hear the apartment's main door opening and closing, along with Jason's voice. "Where do you want these consoles? In the main living room?"

Ashley finished moving the television and walked over

to her room's door and swung it open. "Yes. Hook it up to the television in the main room, please."

"At least we got Jason's help. You'll take his help, but not Jim's. I thought you didn't like him?" Skye asked, her voice quiet enough not to alert Jason in the main room. "You must be embarrassed to choose him over Jim."

"That's obvious." Ashley left the bedroom and led Skye into the main room. "How's it coming along?"

Jason was kneeling beside the television stand with his arm behind it. He grunted as his hand groped blindly behind the furniture. "The hard part is getting behind this stand and getting to the outlet, but I'm almost finished," Jason said. "There we go." He fell back on his butt with his hands behind him.

"Thanks for the help today," Skye said. "It's refreshing having more hands to make the work lighter."

"I'm always happy to help," Jason said. "Electronics are my specialty, after all."

"Alright, Thomas Edison. Calm down," Ashley said. "It's just hooking up wires."

"Ignore her," Skye said. "I hate doing work like that, so I appreciate it. Setup is the worst part."

"Are there other devices needing moved or hooked up?" Jason asked while getting to his feet again.

"I think we got all the furniture," Ashley said. "We got my tv, my consoles, my furniture, and assorted movies. I think we've got it all."

"Good, I'm tired, and we haven't even had our workout yet today," Jason said. He moved over and leaned on one of the chairs. "What are the odds the boss goes easy on us today since we just moved all that stuff?"

"Not likely, if I know him," Skye said. "He'll say we need to be ready for rigorous activity anytime and anywhere. He's not wrong when he'll say that either, for the record. Things go wrong when you least expect them to, and you must be ready."

"Speaking of things going wrong and preparing preemptively," Ashley said, "did you ever nail down a meeting with your engineer friend?"

"Baxter?" Jason asked. "Yeah, I did. He thought I was bullshitting when I asked for a meeting, but I assured him it was for an important cause. Just don't be surprised. If you think I'm eccentric, this guy is on a whole different level."

"You're sure this guy's legitimate?" Skye asked. "Have you seen any of his gadgets in action?"

"Only in news feeds," Jason said. "I know it was him since we keep in contact via encrypted emails. He was one of my first leads when I was searching for Masked Justice. When he first learned how I found him, he was as thrilled as Ashley was when I first found Masked Justice. He quickly realized my intention, and warmed up to me when he realized I could help him."

"You helped him?" Ashley asked. "How?"

"Locating his targets mainly. He'd give me a name, and I'd get him an address. It was basic stuff, but how do you think I got practice for what I've done for you? I had to hone my skills, and he helped me do just that. I've only met him in person twice so far. He's paranoid."

"As he should be," Skye said, taking a seat beside Ashley on the couch. "You don't make it long in the vigilante game if you're not."

"Look how many copycats are getting caught every month," Jason said. "What's the number? It's like two hundred a month in the country getting locked up."

"The police are certainly trying their best, but with thousands, it's barely a dent," Ashley said. "More vigilantes are springing up every single month. It's like a rigged game of whack a mole for them."

"He's probably going to suspect you're lying if you bring up Masked Justice, but I'll back you up," Jason said. "He has a fascination for Masked Justice as well."

"Another hero worshiper?" Skye said with a sidelong glance at Ashley. "I wonder if they'd feel the same if they actually met the guy?"

"I cannot see why it'd change anything," Jason said. "The man lives up to every standard I envisioned, except maybe the lying low portion after big jobs. He's brave, in perfect shape, takes care of his own, is skilled, and defends the weak to the best of his ability."

"That is what his number one fanboy would say," Ashley said, smiling widely. "I doubt everyone else puts him on as high a pedestal as you do."

"I am not alone," Jason said. "Thousands use him as a role model. He was a trailblazer. Perhaps you can argue the merits or detriments, but it would be a fool's errand to say it hadn't happened. He's a cultural icon in this screwed up world. Saying that, it is imperative we conduct ourselves accordingly. We don't want to sully his image."

"I agree," Skye said. "We may need your help soon, but there's just one caveat."

"What's that?" Jason asked.

"Just keep it quiet," Ashley said. "We can't sit by and watch as more injustices are committed."

"You're going behind his back and working the streets?" Jason asked. "Yeah, alright."

"Seriously?" Ashley asked. "I pegged you for a tattletale to the boss man. You are his most devoted follower, after all."

"All we're doing is what he set out to do. He wants a brief

rest is all. That doesn't mean our vigilance should falter. If you are working, I want in. It'll be safer for both of you if I'm involved. I know he wouldn't want either of you two hurt."

"That was easier than I expected," Skye said. "I thought you'd run and tell him or try to dissuade."

"Are you familiar with the saying 'What the boss doesn't know won't hurt him'?" Jason asked. "That applies here. I would bring your identity concealing wear when we go to meet Baxter. Oh, and for the love of God, never call him Baxter. Call him his vigilante name."

"Which is what again?" Ashley asked.

"The name the news uses for him is The Soaring Specter," Jason said. "I would probably just call him Specter."

"That's an interesting name," Ashley said. "How did he get it?"

"You saw the news footage," Skye said. She leaned forward toward the coffee table between the three of them. Opening her computer, she logged in and opened a web browser. She navigated to a video hosting site and searched the moniker.

The page opened to reveal a shaky camera pointed down at the street. The sound of sirens permeated the video. It zoomed in to show a masked man pinned in an alleyway. He reached behind a nearby dumpster and retrieved a gargantuan device. He looked up when his figure was illuminated in red and blue lights. The device in his hand activated, shooting out a grappling hook and connected to a ledge above. A loud whirring filled the air as he was pulled up. The camera followed the movement skyward, but he quickly disappeared out of sight once he was on the roof.

"That's how they gave him his name," Skye said,

gesturing toward the screen. "It seems he can disappear at a moment's notice."

"Neat," Ashley said. "I wonder what kind of engine horsepower it has to be in order to pull his body weight upward."

"Supposedly it's a proprietary system he designed himself," Jason said. "I am not privy to its designs. I knew better than to ask. You'd do well to remember that. He's secretive for a reason. He's easy to spook, so don't push him."

"Me?" Ashley asked, placing a hand to her chest. "I'd never."

"You'd better not," Jason said. "He may want payment for the gadget too, if he doesn't believe us about Masked Justice. That will be a hard sale, seeing as Jim won't be there."

"Payment?" Ashley asked. "You mean he'll want money? How much are you talking about here? I can chip in."

"It probably won't be a monetary payment he wants," Jason said. "I hardly spoke to him, so it's anyone's guess as to what his chosen payment would be. To be safe, we should carry at least five thousand. It won't be cheap for proprietary technology like this. On the plus side, if we acquire a working model, I could reverse engineer it and make another, in theory."

"I thought you were studying computer science," Skye said, raising an eyebrow. "You think you can play at Engineer and build another?"

"I can try. It'd be a hell of a lot cheaper than buying more than one from Baxter. I'm pretty good with my hands. I'm confident."

"You'd better be if we entrust you with a gadget that pricy," Ashley said. "We don't want it ruined, and then you can't even create another."

"Just trust me," Jason said with a smirk. "Have I let you

down yet? No? I didn't think so. Just follow my lead when I bring you there and it'll all work out."

"When are we meeting him, anyway?" Skye asked, fully relaxing on the couch.

"I set the meeting for tonight at eleven. We're meeting in an abandoned warehouse."

"Ah, yes," Ashley said with sarcasm heavy in her voice. "That's where I want to meet a mentally unstable engineer with God knows what gadgets."

"It's the only place he was comfortable meeting," Jason said. "He didn't want us knowing where he lives for obvious reasons. He picked the location, not me. We'll deal with it. We always do."

"Let's research this location," Skye said. "I want to know every door, window, and entrance it has before we arrive. You know, just in case."

"You're awfully uptight for a normal meeting," Ashley said.

"We're all aware plans don't always go as planned," Skye asked. "It's best to be prepared. Jim's right."

"Fine. Let's study an abandoned warehouse for the next few hours." Ashley rolled her eyes. "It's not like I wanted any rest."

"Good," Skye said. "Jason, let's see the place in depth and devise our approach plan…"

2

"This is his place?" Ashley asked while staring at the derelict building. "I guess no one would bother us here, but it's sketchy as fuck."

"Our entire business is sketchy, if you didn't know," Skye said. "We murder people who're a lost cause. Does this really surprise you? The dude has how many kills under his belt?"

"Depends on who you believe," Jason said. "The news puts his body count at over ten victims."

"What does he say?" Ashley asked.

"No one ever asked. You'll know why when we meet him. Just don't insult him for the love of Christ," Jason said. "I don't feel like dealing with a mobile lunatic who could kill on demand. Besides, we're asking for a favor here."

"I'll conduct myself accordingly," Ashley said. "I'm always nice."

"You'd better be," Jason said. "He has no qualms about using firearms."

"A guy who can change floors on demand and has guns on him is not someone I want to make an enemy of, especially if he knows how to shoot accurately." Skye studied the building. "We're early. Are we to wait until he gets here or head in without waiting?"

"You're asking me?" Jason asked.

"You're the one who's met the dude before, so yeah."

"I'd just go in," Jason said. "He respects punctuality. I'd rather us be early than be perceived as being late. It's a pet peeve of his I found out the first night I met him. I had this exact mental conversation with myself and waited around."

"That solves that then." Skye raised her neck gaiter above her nose and made sure the covering over her eyes was secure. "Make yourselves ready, and let's get inside. Jason, you're going with us. Does he know who you are?"

"I've worn a mask every time I've met with him." He followed the same steps Skye had just done. "Let's head inside then."

Ashley was the last to obscure her identity before climbing out of the car. She jogged to catch up with the others. "You two are in a rush."

"Let me do the talking," Jason said. "He doesn't like new people talking unless he asks them a question. I realize it's annoying, but if we want a chance at this gadget, we need to play by his rules."

"Go for it, Mr. Ambassador," Ashley said. "I don't think either of us has a problem with that."

"Quiet," Jason took lead and approached a door leading inside the warehouse. "Here we go." He opened the door and left it open behind him. The interior was dark with lights shining downward in the middle of the floor space. The lights showed a line of desks filled with all different manner of objects. Seats were in front of each desk. A lone bulletin board of sorts sat behind the tables with pinned pieces of paper affixed to it. Various arrows and phrases were written between the posted papers. Aside from the tables, everything else was cloaked in nearly complete darkness.

Jason strode forward toward the tables. "Specter, are you there?" He elevated his voice without yelling. "We've done as you've requested."

"You'd better have," a deep male voice said. A whirring sound above them drew their attention upward as they glimpsed something moving above through the darkness. They couldn't spot anything with the lights shining down on them, aside from a momentary view of something zipping across the catwalks above. "Is this the pair you mentioned?" The voice emanated from a different direction, still above them.

"It is," Jason said.

There was no further response besides a grunt behind. The girls turned to see their target donned in a mask behind them. His mask was white, depicting a skull with red markings on the sides of the cheeks. It almost looked like a Halloween skeleton mask kids might wear on Halloween evening, yet obviously higher quality. "They are not what I expected." He walked past them and over to Jason. "Are they who you're with now?"

"Yes, sir," Jason said. "Did you hear about Calvin Webb recently?"

"I knew of his operation," Specter said. He pointed toward the board with all the papers placed on it. "It was too big for one man to tackle, so I focused my efforts on more attainable goals."

"That was us," Jason said.

Specter looked at Jason and over toward Skye and Ashley. "Just the three of you?"

"There's four of us," Jason said.

"Where's the fourth?" Specter looked up at the catwalks above. "Is this a fucking trap?"

"No," Jason said quickly. "He's at home. We may not have told him about this meeting."

"Which implies he's the boss and you're sneaking out." Specter glared at the girls. "Why should I deal with the side-kicks and not the main attraction? Who is this guy, anyway?"

"You won't believe me when I say this, but I swear on my parents' life it's true." Jason cleared his throat and locked eyes with Specter. "It's Masked Justice." He gestured toward Ashley. "That is Blind Justice." He pointed over at Skye. "This is Silent Justice."

"You expect me to believe that Masked Justice who was last seen in Oklahoma is now operating in Denver? Nobody's heard from him in years. I do not find this joke funny, boy."

The door flung open and an irate Jim's voice pierced the darkness. "They're not lying. They are, however, in deep shit when I get them home." His tone turned harsh. "Did you all really think I wouldn't notice? You must think I'm slipping to try this stunt."

"That's a big claim," Specter said. He looked at the group he had originally come to meet with and saw pure fear plastered in their eyes. He looked over at Jim approaching. "Am I to believe you are indeed Masked Justice? Why should I?"

"Do you want to know why Masked Justice started this whole crusade? I know the news said I did it to clean the streets. Do you wish to know why I started this crusade? It wasn't for vigilante justice or whatever they claim."

"Enlighten me." Specter came to within a few feet but kept his distance from Jim, who was now standing beside his team. "Why then? Why did you start this movement?"

"Honestly, it was a byproduct of my luring child predators online. I found a genuine piece of shit one night. I got him over under pretenses that I was a small girl. He quickly found out who I was. I had quite the social media following, you see. I've long scrubbed it from the web, but my fans ruined his life. The next night, he came over to kill me. That's what started it all. It was self-defense at first."

"I've never heard this tale on the news or the internet." Specter said.

"No one but these chuckleheads have." Jim tilted his head toward the three younger team members. "It's not a story I tell lightly. However, seeing as they've involved another entity - you, Mr. Soaring Specter - I feel you should know who you're in business with. Business or whatever they brought you here for." He looked away from Specter and toward the group. "Why did you go behind my back?"

"It was to hopefully buy some new tech," Jason said.

"That's the reason?" Specter asked. "I should have known. I'm afraid you might be disappointed at the reality of what you're asking."

"Meaning?" Ashley asked.

"I've seen the same news feed you've seen." Specter pointed down toward his belt line. "Did you imagine I pulled out some little gadget, pointed it upward, and then I fired it before it pulled me up?"

"Maybe," Jason said.

"Sorry, Junior," Specter said. "That's not quite how reality works. Do I possess a device that does what you describe? Yes. In fact, I used two copies of it just earlier. There's just one detail the sharp observer might notice."

"You didn't bring them down with you," Skye said. She pointed up at the rafter's above toward the large rifle leaning against the side of the metal bars above. "I can see them now. They're quite large."

"They have to be to carry an adult's body weight and pull him up the side of a building," Specter said, chuckling. "The sheer horsepower alone means they weigh over a hundred pounds. I possess a spare unit I might be willing to part with; however, you have to understand that these are much better suited to securing escape routes ahead of time rather than daring escapes on the fly. Are you still interested, knowing that?"

Jim paced over to the group with his arms crossed. "How much would you want?"

"It is not a matter of money," Specter said. "An equal exchange must be made if we're coming to a fair arrangement. I want a favor for this. I have no need for extra money."

"Like what?" Jim asked.

"I didn't realize you'd become the chief negotiator now, Mr. Masked Justice."

"I'm the leader of this circus, even if they don't act like it. As the leader, I apologize for their impetuous nature."

"I want proof you really are Masked Justice and company. You must do something only the real Masked Justice could. Many people can talk the talk, but can you walk the walk?"

"Who is it you want investigated?"

Specter reached down to the table and picked up a manila envelope. He handed it to Jim. "It's all in here. I've vetted his guilt already, so you need not waste time."

"I'll still make sure myself, thanks." Jim accepted the gift. "It's a general rule we have." He turned around and glared at the trio. "We're going to have a real fun conversation when we get home. You know that, right? Now let's get out of Specter's hair tonight." He turned back to the vigilante they'd just been bartering with. "I apologize for this display. Assuming this intel checks out and he is guilty, he's done."

"I shall wait with bated breath. There are droves impersonating Masked Justice. We will see if you're telling the truth or not."

Jim turned away and pointed at the door they'd entered. "Okay, everyone, we're heading home."

Later that night...

"Get ready for an ass chewing," Ashley said as their car followed Jim's onto their apartment complexes' street. "I've never seen him that mad before."

"We went behind his back and used his name without his permission," Jason said. "We deserve it, if I'm honest. At least I do."

"It'll just be stern words," Skye said. "It's not like it'll be something new or exceptionally scary. Just don't talk back. I learned that with my dad. It'll make you feel better, but almost always just makes it worse for you."

"Here we are," Ashley said, pulling into the parking lot and putting her car in park. The group exited the car and made their way up to the familiar apartment. They followed Jim inside and shut the door behind them.

Jim exhaled a deep breath and walked into the main living room. "Get in here," he said. His tone allowed no disagreement. He watched them pass by him toward the sofa. "Sit down and explain yourselves. Now. Why were you bartering for some gadget with a random vigilante?"

"It would prove useful," Skye's calm voice said, daring to look at Jim in the eye.

"I won't deny it could be, but why go behind my back?

That implies you thought I'd say no. You could have simply asked, you know."

"Are you familiar with the saying 'Better to ask for forgiveness than ask permission?' I feel that fits here perfectly."

"Do you now?" Jim asked, his voice calm. He paced in front of the group of young people sitting on the couch. "Look, this whole thing works best if we coordinate together. If everybody goes rogue, doing whatever they like, then things get messy. I'm assuming some of you didn't want to lie low any longer. That's the only reason I can conceive why you'd pull a stunt like this. How close am I?"

"Maybe we just wanted our next jobs to go smoother, whenever they are," Skye said. "I think you're inferring something that's not there, boss."

"Aren't you a smooth talker?" Jim asked. "Here's my theory. My former ward moved out to live with her best friend. They want independence anyway. They get it in their heads that without the overbearing boss figure, they can do what they like without him knowing. If you craved independence, all you had to do was ask. This sneaking out stunt isn't the way to handle it. We need trust, not subterfuge. Am I making my point?"

"You'd have said yes?" Ashley asked.

"Possibly," Jim said. "Look, I'm not here to yell and bitch." He stopped in the middle of the three vigilantes. "My point is to communicate. We're all in this together now. What you or I do affects everyone else here. Do you get it? It's only fair we all get a say."

"I'm sorry," Skye stood up. "This was my idea."

"Is that correct?" Jim looked at Ashley and Jason before turning his attention to Skye. "I can't say I saw that coming. Can I ask why?"

"I wanted to keep working, but differently. A method the grappling hook would aid with."

"Elaborate further," Jim said. "What does that mean? You mean going around rooftops and stopping little old ladies from getting their purse snatched by crooks? I ask because I suspect driving around in your getup with a bow and arrow would attract some unwanted attention. Zipping rooftop to rooftop would be much more discrete."

"You're correct." Skye did not look away. "I feel we should keep trying to make the world a safer place, not only when someone bad falls into our lap."

"Well, alright then. Was that so flipping hard?" Jim asked. "Telling the truth is all I want. Know that if you ever pull this shit again, normal training will seem like a Caribbean cruise. As it is, we are doing triple duty for every workout for the next two weeks. Is that understood?"

"Triple?" Ashley asked, jumping up to her feet before looking away from Jim.

"Do I need to make it quadruple?" Jim turned and looked at her.

"It will not happen again, sir." Jason got to his feet and bowed before Jim. "I will do as you ask as penance."

"You kiss ass." Ashley stuck her tongue out at Jason.

"If you want autonomy in heading out, you can have it. I simply want to be kept apprised of your plans. I don't want you all getting in over your heads. Call on me for help anytime you need."

"Seriously?" Ashley asked. "Just like that?"

"I ran out on a dinner date with Cynthia to watch what you were doing. Of course I knew this time would come eventually. I just want us all to be safe. That includes figuring out which of you will call the shots. We can't have bickering about authority while on a job. Any volunteers?"

"I usually end up overseeing everything anyway," Jason said. "I could if no one else wants to."

"What about Skye?" Jim asked.

"Me?" she asked.

"You were the one who spoke up and admitted fault. That takes guts. You came up with this idea. I know it. Ashley and Jason here wouldn't."

"What's that supposed to mean?" Ashley asked with narrowed eyes.

"It means neither of you took the responsibility to fess up when asked whose idea it was. Skye is taking a figurative bullet for you, or she came up with it. That shows maturity, which shows if there must be a leader of this trio, I'd rather it be Skye. I still expect you to keep me in the loop, mind you. Is that agreeable?"

"It's fine by me," Skye replied.

"Good," Jim said. "Now you three have work to do. Make damned sure you do your own vetting. I do not trust a mad engineer vigilante to do his due diligence. Is that clear? I'll leave it in your hands to decide if the intel checks out. Let me know if you need my assistance or expertise. That is all. Oh, and remember to show up tomorrow for training."

"Oh shit." Ashley watched as Jim walked away from the main room and toward his bedroom.

"Now I'm going to get ready for bed. Go plan in your apartment or whatever you want to do. I need some sleep for the inevitable bitch fit I'm going to receive from Cynthia tomorrow for dumping her mid-date."

"Come on, gang," Skye motioned toward the door. "Let's go plan this out then. You heard him." She led the group past Jim in the narrow corridor and to the door. Opening it, she turned toward her apartment's direction. She kept walking, eventually hearing Jim's door closing behind them.

"I expected worse," Ashley said from the back of the group. "I thought he'd be irate."

"He was," Jason said. "Triple workouts are going to be a killer. He was also disappointed."

"What?" Ashley asked. "How could you tell?"

"His tone," Jason said. "He wasn't mad. It disappointed him we'd go behind his back. You couldn't tell? I wish he had been pissed. That'd have been easier to take."

"Whatever," Skye said. "You heard him, though. We're clear to do this job and get our device from Soaring Specter. He could have said no." She stopped at her door in the empty corridor. Unlocking it, she motioned everyone inside before following them in and shutting the door behind her.

"Don't let the power go to your head, fearless leader," Ashley said.

"The first priority is researching the target," Skye said. "Jim's right. We can't just take Baxter's word at face value. Jason, that's your realm of expertise. How long will that take?"

"It depends if I get started right this second."

"Assume you get it done as soon as possible."

"My guess is it'd take three hours if I'm thorough."

"Get that done by tomorrow night. If it checks out, we'll get the job done and schedule a meet for afterward. I want us practicing with that grappling hook by tomorrow night," Skye said. "I'm imagining it's harder to use than simply pointing it and squeezing a trigger."

"Aim would be important," Jason said. "If you aim skyward and miss, the hook would come crashing down to earth in a hilarious display of ineptitude."

"Let's just focus on getting said grappling hook first..."

3

"I found where this guy lives," Jason leaned forward and placed his laptop on the table. Jim, Ashley, and Skye sat around it, either on the sofa or on one of the other chairs, and leaned forward. "I've also confirmed that he got out of the penitentiary on charges against children."

"You're one hundred percent?" Jim asked.

"They convicted him in a court of law, boss. I'm as sure as the justice system was. In fact, according to the court records, he's guilty of abusing not one, but three kids."

"You said you had his location?" Skye asked.

"Yes, I do," Jason said. He reached forward and switched the windows to a zoomed in digital map. The map displayed the city from a bird's eyed view. "He's worked as a fast-food employee for the past few months. I'm guessing because it was the only place that would hire him, given the circumstances."

"It's not near a school, I trust?" Ashley asked.

"No. He's smart enough to know to stay clear. The police wouldn't smile on his workplace being too close to his proclivities." Jason continued leaning forward and switched it to a house plan. "This is his house. The layout is simple, at least compared to some we've run into in the past."

"I'm glad to see we've done our research," Jim said. "Does he live alone?"

"Unknown," Jason said. "To my knowledge, he does. I wouldn't bet on it, though. I'd be prepared, just in case."

"This looks like a one-floor home," Skye said, squinting her eyes looking at the plan. "There's one bedroom, if I'm not mistaken."

"Correct," Jason said.

"Then it stands to reason he probably lives alone," Ashley said, a triumphant smile on her face.

"Just assume the worst will happen and operate under that assumption," Jim said. "It's always worked for me in the past. Who's going to do the deed?" He looked over at Skye. "It's up to you. I assume either you or Ashley - unless you want me to tag along."

"We'll be fine on our own," Skye said. "I can do it."

"You're sure?" Ashley asked. "What if he gets close to you? Your bow won't work so well in tight quarters. I'm better suited for that small ass house."

"That's true," Jim said. "I've only started training you with a blade. A week of training wouldn't cut it."

"We're going in together anyway, so it's moot," Skye said. "If he stays asleep, I kill him. If he gets close, Ashley takes him out. It works out either way. The only negative is that more people might mean a higher chance of waking him up. But that's the safest option I see. Correct me if I'm wrong."

"I'll tag along anyway," Jim said. "I won't go inside, but I'll stay out with Jason. It wouldn't hurt if I learned a little something, just in case. I've always wanted to see how he directs us inside places like that."

"You don't have a date with Cynthia tonight," Ashley said. "Do you?" she asked.

"What?"

"That's why you're coming along this time."

"Are you trying to piss me off?" Jim asked. "To answer your question, no. I don't have a date tonight."

"I knew it."

"Let's focus," Skye said while shaking her head. "We know he works a day job, we know he lives here, and we know that he's guilty. This seems to be a straightforward job. Let's execute this by the book and complete this mission."

"It means he'll be tired," Jim said. "He may well sleep with a weapon near him - don't forget that. Always be coiled and ready once you're inside. It's his habitat. He knows it better than you do. You don't want to know what it's like to be panicked, running around inside a stranger's home. I did it once when an alarm sounded, and that bruise was horrible. I was lucky that bullet didn't penetrate my vest from the short distance."

"Ashley, you'll be taking point. I'll watch your back. When we get to the room, provided he's asleep, I'll take him out. Does everybody have the plan?"

"Keep in mind Baxter might not have sent you a job as straightforward as it seems," Jim said.

"Negative," Jason said. "I believe it is. He's simply testing us to see if we kill the guilty. He was right about one thing. A lot of folks want to pretend to be Masked Justice. A lot fewer will kill. I'm betting this is all to see if we're as dedicated as we claimed."

"Whatever the case, it never hurts to be prepared. So, when are we going?" Jim asked. "I'd recommend after one a.m. People are asleep then, except those who have insomnia."

"I thought two, but one works," Skye said. "I'd like us to have some okay sleep for tomorrow, if nothing else. We have our gear ready. If you two need anything before we leave in a few hours, you need to retrieve it beforehand."

"We'll be sitting in a car," Jim said. "I'll carry my piece with me and my neck gaiter, but hopefully I won't have to use them."

"I always carry my gaiter and my laptop, but I don't have a weapon," Jason said. "Provided I charge my laptop, I'm good with what I have here." He gestured toward the laptop. "Which I'll do right now while I'm thinking about it." He grabbed the laptop and got up. He took it over to a nearby electrical outlet. Digging into his pockets, he pulled out a coiled wire before plugging it in.

"It sounds like we're ready," Jim said. "We should plan the route you're taking once you're inside. Oh," Jim said, "I should also make sure Ashley here remembers what I taught her about picking locks. It never hurts to be prepared. People tend to lock their doors now. Especially types like this who fear vigilantes coming for them. It's harder to do in the dark, so a refresher is due."

"Seriously?" Ashley whined. "I remember it fine."

"Then it won't take too long, will it?" Jim asked.

Later that night...

"We're parking behind his house," Skye said. "Does the alley behind have any cameras?"

"Not that I'm seeing." Jason stared at the monitor. "I spot two on the front side."

"Perfect." Skye turned and slowed down. She stopped behind their target's home. "Gloves, mask, hairnet, and weapon. Check."

"Check. I'm prepared," Ashley said. "I always am."

"It never hurts to be safe," Skye said. "It keeps us out of prison, after all."

"At least this place won't have random cars coming down the alley," Ashley said, staring at the empty stretch of road behind the nearby houses. "It looks like nobody comes here."

"Then take your time and make certain it's done correctly," Jim said. He leaned over, trying to find out any intel from watching Jason at his side in the back seat. "Remember - stay quiet, always be ready, and get out quickly. If you do all that without leaving DNA, we're set."

Skye gripped the car door handle. "Are you ready?"

"As I'll ever be." Ashley pulled the hoodie up over her hair net and made sure her neck gaiter was secured. "Let's get this over with."

Both girls opened their respective front doors and left the car.

Skye was the closer of the two to the property, so she immediately hopped the short chain-link fence. She surveilled the backyard, searching for anything that could prove troublesome. Her eye landed on a small doghouse in the backyard. She tiptoed over and got to a knee while she heard Ashley climbing the fence behind her. She saw nothing inside other than a water bowl, food bowl, and a blanket lining the bottom of the wooden structure.

"Is there a dog in there?" Ashley asked once over the fence.

"No," Skye said, getting to her feet again. "I think he has it inside, actually. It shows evidence that a dog used to live in there. I'm betting he brought it in at some point, so keep an eye out."

"If that dog is violent, prepare for the worst," Jim said. "Dog bites draw blood, you know."

"Oh, come on." Ashley said as the pair moved past the small structure and toward the house. "I don't want to hurt a puppy."

"I don't want you to either, but I also would rather you two not leave DNA evidence behind." Jim paused before his voice was in their ears again. "Focus on getting inside first before you focus on a dog. The dog can be dealt with."

"We should bring a steak or meat in the future," Skye said, finally reaching the back entrance. "Just in case," she said.

"Mixed with a dog friendly tranquilizer and you'd have a humane way of dealing with it too," Jason's voice said. "Now stop thinking about dogs and get inside like the boss said."

"This is your cue," Skye stepped aside, allowing Ashley access to the door. "I need to learn that myself."

"I'll teach it to you then," Jim said. "Now focus up. The entrance is the scariest part. If an alarm goes off, abort. It's not worth it. The police department isn't far. They'd be here in a couple of minutes."

"Quiet, please," Ashley said, her voice tense. "This is harder with a running commentary in my ear." The talking stopped and within a minute, she was done. "It's unlocked now."

"It's time for the moment of truth then I suppose," Skye said. She waited for Ashley to get out of her way before grabbing the doorknob. She twisted and pulled. No sirens accompanied their entrance, only the creak of the door. They both ducked inside and quickly shut the door behind them.

"Follow me and stay close," Skye said. She took the bow off her shoulder and held it in her left hand, then reached and plucked an arrow out of the quiver strapped to her back. She stalked through the dark interior with Ashley hot on her trail.

"At least it's a small damned house," Ashley said under her breath.

"Quiet," Skye said, equally as quiet. She pointed ahead. "Any of those rooms could be our target's. Let's get to work."

"Do you hear that?" Jim asked.

"Hear what?" Skye asked.

"Why do I hear sirens?" Jason asked.

"Sirens?" Ashley asked, her voice betraying a sense of panic.

"Calm down and let's finish this before it's too late," Skye said, attempting to hide any panic in her voice. She took off toward the three doors without waiting further.

She opened the nearest and readied her bow and arrow as the door was creaking open. No one was inside. She sidestepped and tried the next door, only to find it empty. She looked and saw Ashley opening the last door.

"Fire!" Jim yelled in their ear.

"To clarify the boss's point, there's a fire in the house next to our boy's house. Perfect timing, wouldn't you say? Hurry and get out. Where there's a fire department, there will be police, and I'd rather not stick around."

Ashley pulled the door open. Their target was still fast asleep in the small double bed in front of them. She stepped to the side. "You wanted to do it, do it fast," she whispered.

Skye stepped past her and gripped the arrow by the tail end, the arrowhead pointing toward the ground. She raised her right arm and made her way over to the bed. She brought the arrow down into the neck of her target.

His eyes snapped open and reached up to grab the arrow.

"I wouldn't remove that," Skye said.

Her target didn't follow her advice, choosing instead to yank the arrow out of his neck. Expectedly, blood spurted out of the wound with every heartbeat. His left hand covered the hole in his neck while his right swung toward Skye, trying to pierce her with the very implement she had used on him. He growled with every swing of his arm. He had a hateful glare leveled in her direction, trying to take her down with him.

Skye jumped back from the arrowhead, avoiding any grazing or injury. His movements grew slower as blood gushed out in lower amounts. He stood, still clutching the puncture wound in his neck. Stumbling, his eyes fluttered closed, and he collapsed in a heap on his bedroom floor. "He's dead. Let's leave."

"You're sure?" Jim asked. "Let's leave. We need to call the fire department now, just in case. We can't risk that fire next door spreading to anymore houses and innocents dying."

"Agreed." Skye brushed past Ashley in the doorway. "Come on, we're leaving."

The pair hurried as best they could through the dark interior until they found their way to the door.

"Hurry," Jim said in their ears. "We just called the fire department on our burner, so we need to leave like two minutes ago."

"We're moving as fast as we can." Skye gripped the doorknob and threw it open. She let Ashley exit first before moving through and closing it behind her. She watched as Ashley jogged past to the fence and hopped over.

Ashley threw open the passenger door, then reached over and opened the driver's side in time for Skye to climb inside and slam the door shut. The car lurched forward. A crunch met their ears.

"What was that noise?" Skye asked.

"The phone being crushed under the tires," Jim said. "Burners are only good when they're untraceable. Let's pray the firefighters get here soon. That fire is concerning."

"What fucking luck," Ashley said. "You all nearly gave me a heart attack when you shouted fire. What are the odds of a fire erupting while we're inside?"

"It happens," Jim said. "It could be wiring, it could be an electrical fire, or something else entirely. The reason isn't important. What's important is we were awake and there to call it in. Imagine if we hadn't. There could be children in homes nearby. No one was awake to call it in. Ironically, we might have saved quite a few lives tonight when you think about it."

"That is true." Ashley tilted her head and eventually broke out in a smile. "It's not nearly so bad when you say it like that."

"I wonder if Soaring Specter will want proof of the man's death," Jason said. "I never even thought about it. We should have taken a picture for proof."

"He'll know he's dead," Skye said. "The news will jump over a murder committed with an arrow. If he doesn't find out, then we can point to the stories ourselves."

"I hope he'll believe that," Jason said. "He's not known to be trusting. That's all I'm saying."

"There is no honor among thieves," Jim said. "Still, he'd better hold up his end of the bargain for this gadget. What does it do anyway?"

"Oh," Ashley said. "You weren't there when he was using it. That's right. We'll use that to grapple to building tops like in the movies and comics."

"That device must weigh over a hundred pounds. You'd have to stash it away for a getaway. There's no way you could carry it with you. The sheer size of the motor alone would require such bulk."

"A little planning is precisely what you espouse, correct?" Ashley asked. "To use it, we'd have to use planning. I don't see a problem there."

"I suppose so," Jim said. "You need a ton of practice with it before I'd want you to use it in a live operation though."

"That's the plan," Skye said. "I don't want to go flying through the air without knowing exactly what I'm doing."

"By flying through the air, you're talking about walking or getting dragged up the side of a building?" Jim asked. "Because that's probably what would happen. You'd need to practice, so you didn't scrape and cause bleeding. That'd defeat the purpose."

"If we go horizontally, it'd be gliding," Skye said. "You are correct on the verticality argument."

"Horizontally would mean you'd slam into walls," Jason said. "It seems like you'd have to only use it on handrails where you would slip under."

"You'd best learn how to roll properly to alleviate the horizontal momentum," Jim said.

"You two just want to ruin all our fun, don't you?" Ashley asked.

"I'm just realistic is all," Jim said. "Which reminds me, we'd need a place for you to test this thing. Does anyone have any ideas? We obviously can't use it at our apartment complex. We'd need somewhere where you wouldn't be disturbed by the public."

"An abandoned warehouse would fit that bill," Jason said. "It wouldn't have too large of a drop. It would have handrails so they could practice their little sideways glide and no one would bother them."

"You could have to deal with squatters," Jim said.

"Homeless flock to any structure to protect them from the cold. Still, it's an idea."

"We could just bring food and water," Ashley said. "Homeless would keep quiet then."

"I wouldn't count on that," Jim said. "I don't care if you're homeless, a millionaire, or somewhere between. If you saw a masked young woman flinging herself everywhere using some weird gadget, you'd tell anybody that would believe you."

"We'll figure that part out once we actually get the gadget," Skye said. "We should focus on acquiring the device before figuring out where to practice. It's a moot point otherwise."

"I was just trying to be helpful," Jim said.

4

"I'll be damned," Specter said. He had a handheld device in his hands and swiped across its glass screen rightward before looking up at the small group. "He is dead."

"About the fire. We weren't responsible for that," Skye said. "It scared the piss out of us when we heard sirens after we did the deed."

"I'd imagine so," Specter said. "A deal's a deal." He pointed to the large rifle looking device on the nearby table that had a grappling hook sticking out of the end. "You can take that model. I made sure it still works and did maintenance on it today. In fact, you can practice with it here before you leave. I'd recommend putting out the cushions I have stashed away somewhere here first if I were you, though."

"You have cushions here?" Ashley asked, inspecting the vast interior of the warehouse. "I don't see any."

"Do you think I'm stupid enough to test out my own inventions without at least some safety features?" Specter asked. "Of course I have cushions. I didn't want to break anything while testing this fantastic gadget. Would you like me to show you all how it works?"

"I would," Skye said, stepping forward. "More than likely, I'll be the one using this baby."

"Fair enough," Specter said. He guided her over to the large, hefty climbing aid. He went on a technical rant about its specificities in great detail before picking it up. "The motor itself is a technological marvel. To lift a fully grown human, it is without a doubt the bulkiest and heaviest weighing aspect of the design."

"How much does it weigh?" Skye asked, inspecting the behemoth.

"Approximately one hundred and forty pounds. That was as lightweight as I could make it and be totally capable of pulling me upward. For you, a smaller engine would no doubt work, but unless you pay me, I will not make one specially for you. Go ahead, see if you can lift it."

Skye reached down and grabbed it with great care. She lifted and, while it was a struggle, she barely lifted it off the table and held it in her arms. "This isn't too bad."

"That device must weigh more than you, little lady," Specter said with a grin. "You're quite strong. Honestly, I thought you wouldn't be able to lift it. That is the hardest part of this. Once you aim, fire, and the hook is attached, you just hold on for dear life. So long as you can support your own body weight, you're fine at that point." Specter looked at Jason and Ashley. "You two," he pointed at a nearby door they had never entered. "Go inside and drag the mattresses outside."

"You just have a bunch of mattresses in an abandoned warehouse?" Ashley asked, walking her way over with Jason. "Aren't you worried some homeless might sneak in and sleep on them?"

"Why would I care?" Specter asked. "If someone in desperate need gets use, that's not the worst thing. Now if they stole it, I'd be miffed, but I can afford replacements."

"I should help them move them," Skye took off after the pair who had just pulled open said door.

"Hold on," Specter said. "I'm sensing you're the de facto leader here since Masked Justice isn't present. Is that right?"

"Maybe." Skye stopped and looked at Specter. "Why?"

"Between you and me, extra people are almost never worth having on the job," Specter said. "It's just additional avenues for one of you to be caught or make a mistake."

"They keep me alive; I keep them alive," Skye said with a shake of her head.

"Did you ever consider if one of them gets caught?" Specter watched and noticed the pair each dragging a mattress out of the doorway. "Will they keep your secret? I doubt it."

"I don't know what you're trying to pull, sir," she said. "With all due respect, you don't know us that well."

"Don't say I didn't warn you." He pointed to a nearby spot on the floor beneath the catwalk above. "Drop one there and create a line across." His finger trailed over across the way to another catwalk above. "That way there's cushion and not concrete while you're learning and adjusting. I also expect after every training session you'll keep this place tidy. I don't want to enter and see mattresses scattered everywhere. Is that clear?"

"Crystal clear," Ashley said, dropping the mattress where he directed. She looked over at the pair. "What were you two talking about?"

"Nothing you need to concern yourself with," Specter said. "Keep bringing them out."

Ashley didn't immediately oblige, choosing instead to

look at her friend. She saw Skye nod before finally heading back to work.

"She's a willful one," Specter said, crossing his arms and watching the pair work. "At least I know Jason is reliable. He's helped me in the past. You should watch out for him. He follows orders to the letter, and it can get him in trouble."

"Noted," Skye said. "He's certainly helped us out a lot. He's a master on that laptop, to put it mildly, but he doesn't talk much."

"I think he's just shy." Specter stopped talking as Jason approached and set down his own mattress before immediately heading back for another. "Watch out for him, for me."

"You must like him," Skye said.

"He's helped me on jobs before, but he's too nice for this business. He came to me asking about Masked Justice out of the blue. I shunned him and told him he did not know what he was doing. He, of course, found out what I was doing and showed he was serious. I used him for my benefit at first, but quickly relied on him. Obviously, I cut him out for his own good. It seems he finally found his Masked Justice after all this time. I just want the best for him. He's killed no one. He deserves better than this life we've chosen."

"Exactly how many jobs did he help you with?"

"Twelve," Specter said. "I won't elaborate further, seeing as it's none of your business."

"True," Skye said. "I'm just trying to learn more about him. He is my partner now and all. Whenever I try to talk to him, he clams up unless it's about the job."

Specter let loose an uproarious laugh before containing himself. "That's obvious why, dear. You're just too young to realize, or maybe just dense."

"Excuse me?"

"I'll tell you later if you still haven't figured it out. It's not my place to reveal that secret. Besides, it's just a hunch I have. I have no proof."

"Help us out already, will you?" Ashley plopped another thick mattress in the line.

"I should do just that. A good general suffers alongside his troops, right?" Skye asked before immediately following Ashley back to the supply room.

"Music to my ears," Specter said with a smile. He looked toward where he first watched Jim, images of him busting through the door. "God knows how he has such patience in dealing with this many teenagers and keeping them in line. The man's a veritable saint dealing with these kids," he said to himself, watching the teenagers work. "Hell, I guess I should help this along. It'll be quicker that way..."

A little while later...

"There, that should be sufficient," Specter said. "Now, who shall be first?"

"Me," Skye said while raising her right hand.

"Then pick it up and do exactly as I instruct." Specter walked over to where a catwalk was above. "Aim at that handrail upstairs. Once your aim is ready, all you do is squeeze the trigger. Once it's connected, let go of the button. Then, when you're ready to ascend, press and hold the button."

Skye hefted the beast upward and walked over as fast as she could, with the device weighing more than her body weight. She aimed up as best she could and followed the directions to the letter. The hook shot out and grasped onto the handrail above. It was silent for a moment before the unmistakable sound of a whirring motor reached their ears.

To no one's surprise, Skye was pulled up. Once she was high enough, she rolled onto the catwalk and unhooked the hook. It went back into its original position with a pop.

"Wasn't that easy?" Specter asked. "When you're ready, why don't you try to zip across to the catwalk across from you? Double check that you line up with the mattresses. Horizontal jumps are more difficult than going vertical. In fact, I'd recommend aiming at the bar above the catwalk. Straight horizontal is probably too difficult for now. I'd hate for you to slam into it and fall."

Skye adjusted her aim above the original target and fired. The hook missed the bar hanging above the catwalk.

"It's good this happened now," Specter called out from below. "Just press the button again and it will retract the hook. Make sure you hold the button to retract it if you're climbing something. Keep your hands clear. It's fast at returning."

Jason placed both hands around his mouth to amplify his voice and looked up at Skye. "Your last shot was low. Aim higher."

Skye held the button, and the grappling hook snapped back in place like a tape measure being retracted.

"She's got a kick on her, doesn't she?" Specter asked. "Try again. It'll take a few days of practicing to get aiming down."

Skye didn't wait after the hook returned to her. She adjusted her aim and tried again. This time the hook clasped onto the metal bar hanging above. It pulled her up and over the handrail in front of her, banging her knees into the metal bar as she went.

Ashley winced as she saw the contact. "That's got to hurt."

"I should've instructed her to start on the other side," Specter said. "I forgot about that little caveat."

Skye zipped through the air, swinging over the gap, holding onto the device for dear life until she reached her destination on the other side. "How do I remove the hook from this while I'm in the air?"

"Do you see the dial that you can turn?" Specter asked. "Just turn it to the left. It will give you more slack and lower you to the ground. You can then climb up and unhook it manually if you must. Worst case, you fall onto the mattresses we put out."

Skye twisted the dial on the side of the device until she lowered slowly to the walkway below. She placed the gadget down before climbing up on the handrail. Skye looked down and steadied her feet on the relatively thin handrail before focusing on the hook. She undid it from the metal bar and hopped backwards. She fell a few feet until the clatter of landing on metal grating echoed across the warehouse. "That was fun, except for the hitting my legs thing." She reached down and rubbed where her leg had slapped the handrail.

"Are you satisfied?" Specter asked.

Skye didn't answer immediately. She looked above where the group stood and saw a spot she could grapple. "Move a bit, will you?"

The group looked above and backed off until they were out of her path.

"That's an advanced jump," Specter said. "You may have to adjust the line distance if you want to make that."

"I'll be fine. I've learned a lot these past few jumps," Skye said.

"On your head be it," Specter said.

"Be careful!" Ashley yelled.

Jason did nothing except bite his lip as he saw her prepare for her next jump. He held his breath as he watched her climb up and over the handrail. "I see she learned from her last jump."

"Move to the side, not just backward. If she adjusts properly, she'll swing forward quite a way," Specter said. He led the group to the side and out of her potential swinging zone.

Skye didn't wait after they moved. She adjusted her aim and fired. It hit its mark. She jumped off the walkway and pressed the button down. She swung forward and immediately twisted the dial, shortening the rope as she was in motion. The result being she didn't slam her feet into the ground, instead swinging just above it before landing where they had just been. She moved to the side and pushed the button. The hook grated against the metal, but moved until it dislodged and snapped into position.

"Nice move," Jason said.

"Quite," Specter said. "That's better than my first attempts at jumping. If you keep practicing, you'll be proficient in no time, if you're not already. Just remember to always be careful. Keep physics in mind so you don't slam into a wall or railing, and you'll be fine."

"I learned that the hard way." Skye gingerly placed the grappling gun down and kneeled. She rubbed her leg. "Nothing's broken. It's just a bruise." She stood up. "Thanks for letting us practice here."

"Better than getting yourselves killed doing it somewhere else. I'm not going to ask what you wanted it for. You didn't get it from me. Do you understand?"

"We know how to keep a secret," Ashley said.

"So I noticed," Specter said. "If we're finished, I have work to do. I must ask you all to leave for tonight. Remember to clean all this up before you leave." He pointed at the mattresses. "That was part of our deal, remember?"

"Come on, everyone," Skye said. "Let's get these put back."

"Aw man," Ashley said.

"Blind," Skye said.

"Alright, fine," Ashley said.

5

"I hear you had a fun night recently," Cynthia said before taking a bite of the casserole on the plate in front of her. She swallowed and looked at Jim across the table.

"You heard that, huh?" Jim asked. "I meant what I said before, you know."

"That you wanted to scale back your minor operations?" Cynthia tilted her head. "What were you doing, then?"

"If you must know, I was overseeing as Skye and Ashley went inside. I stayed back with Jason in the car. I wanted to see if they still needed Masked Justice to accompany them inside, or if they were ready to go alone."

"What did you find out?" Cynthia asked.

"They did fine without me. I'm still mad they went behind my back and took that job, but teenagers will be teenagers, I suppose. It's not like I can point the finger in good faith."

"They did fine without you, you say?" Cynthia leaned forward, placing her elbow on the table between them. "Does that mean you're stepping away from that dirty criminal life?"

"Possibly," Jim said. "I will still help them if they ever get in trouble, though."

"I know," Cynthia sighed. "You can't help it. You always stuck up for people you liked if they were in trouble. Besides, you got them into it. I just wish you were out permanently. It's been nice the past week. You're free to hang around and chat."

"I, too, have enjoyed our dates."

"Who said they were dates?" Cynthia asked.

"I did," Jim said. "Why? Do you not consider this a date?" Jim mirrored her movement and placed his elbows on the table, locking eyes with her. He gave her his best suave look. "Do you not enjoy this flirting?"

"Let's not mix fantasy and reality here," Cynthia said. "I know it can be hard for you."

"You always play hard to get. That tactic only works so long. Most admirers would've quit already."

"Not you though," Cynthia smiled. "You're too stubborn and hardheaded."

"That's precisely what you need in a partner," Jim said. "I love your mannerisms and all, but most guys wouldn't."

"Let's not start throwing the L word around, yeah?" Cynthia looked away, trying in vain to hide the flushing of her face. "It's not my fault guys give up too easily. That, or they get hurt when I tease them a little. When we grew up, it was called being manly."

"If only there was some idiot who hung around. Someone that received your constant needling and kept returning," Jim smirked. "Who'd be crazy enough to endure?"

"Crazy is the proper term for you," Cynthia said with a giggle. "At least you're self-aware enough to realize that."

She snapped her fingers. "Speaking of crazy, I have a question."

"Here we go," Jim said with a fading smile. "Yes?"

"You mentioned they snuck out behind your back before. Why did they? They had to have a reason."

"They met with another vigilante. You've probably heard of him. His name is the Soaring Specter."

"That guy on the news?" Cynthia asked, wide eyed. "Why on earth would they?"

"You know that grappling hook device he used to escape?"

"They wanted that thing? They'll kill themselves with something that dangerous. It's not like he'd give it away. What happened?"

"He gave them a job as a sort of price for his spare," Jim said. "As one might imagine, he didn't believe them when they introduced their alter egos. He wanted to see if they were for real, so he gave them a lead he'd gained. They researched it, not taking his word for it, and finished the job once they were sure. Last I heard, they were out at the warehouse practicing with it."

"You're not there with them? What if he's a crazy man?"

"I already know he's crazy," Jim said. "He's in the same business as I am. However, in a three versus one, I doubt he'd be crazy enough to harm a group that did him a favor. I have to trust them if I want to step back."

"They sneak out behind your back and you immediately jump to trusting them with a known wild card? Thank God you're not a father yet. You'd be a shitty one. Look, you need to keep them in line. Don't slack off chaperoning simply because you want to be here instead."

"Seriously?" Jim asked. "I'm trying to inch away from that violent life in your honor, and you tell me to jump in?"

"I also don't want young kids trying to do something they're not ready for yet and then getting caught. Then we're all in some shit. I appreciate that you're trying to stop for me, but be careful. That's why I'm here, isn't it? To help you out? I've always had to ever since we were kids." She reached across the table and flicked his forehead with a playful giggle. "Remember when you got into a fight in second grade?"

"No, I don't. I'm sure you're about to remind me though."

"You saw that shy girl, Lily, getting bullied and walked off from our friend group. I watched you march over and immediately knew what was going to happen. I had to rush over and tell the teachers they attacked you."

"You lied," Jim laughed.

"I lied," Cynthia said. "It kept you out of detention and from your parents getting wind of it. I couldn't let you miss my birthday party later in the week, could I?"

"Fine. I get it." Jim looked down at the empty plate in front of him. "I'll keep them in line. You can't blame a guy for trying to spend time with the woman he loves." He looked up with a wink at Cynthia.

"They are still showing up for your workouts, I assume?" Cynthia asked, ignoring the casual flirtation. "You can't give them any slack or they'll take a mile, just like we did. They're trapped in a deadly world we never had to navigate, and you're the only guide they have."

"Sounds like I'm receiving on-the-job training on how to be an exemplary father," Jim said. "I also worry about being overbearing. We both know from experience that an adult trying to teach can be annoying. They tune out after that. It's a thin line."

"One you must tread for everybody's sake though," Cynthia said. She reached across the table and laid a hand over his. "Keeping them safe keeps me safe. You remember that for the future. I'd rather you not be involved with that anymore than you must. I'd be thrilled if you took a more back seat role."

"That's what I've been doing." Jim looked down at the comparatively dainty hand covering his. "They're adults now. It's sort of hard to tell them they still need guidance. You know how headstrong teenagers can be when their autonomy is questioned. I don't want them to rebel. Then we're in an even worse situation."

"You'll be fine. Assert your dominance. You are the leader of your little group, right? Act like it. They'll listen."

"Speaking of the group, Ashley still refuses to even speak to me." Jim looked up and past Cynthia.

"She'll get over it." Cynthia reached up with her free hand and brushed a stray hair out of her face. "She's a moody teenager who just got rejected. She'll learn how to be an adult, eventually. Just be patient and don't make it awkward. She'll get the message eventually that you two are still working together for good and to treat you kindly."

"Right," Jim said. "At least I don't have to worry about Jason. He sends me reports before, during, and after the operations."

"That's how you knew where they were going when they met with that lunatic vigilante," Cynthia smirked. "Then why did you let them go?"

"To see what they were doing. I knew trying to stop them outright would just make them sneak around. I couldn't let them go in alone, so I followed. Jason is loyal, keeps a level head, and he's essential to them, so they've no choice."

"The perfect informer," Cynthia said, removing her hand from Jim's. She placed it on her chin in deep thought. "You'd best hope they don't figure that out. If I were them and I found out, I'd feel betrayed. You're putting the kid in a tough situation."

"What would you have me do?" Jim asked, his voice betraying his weariness. "I want to take a step back. Why do you think I've been coming over so much lately?"

"There are no simple answers. My best advice is don't let them figure it out. You should also treat Jason to something special if he's your little rat in there. It doesn't matter how, he'll appreciate it. He nearly worships the ground you walk on. It'll mean the world to him."

"I'll come up with something. For now, I'm monitoring them. They haven't done anything catastrophic yet. Now let's move on from my life and move toward yours," Jim said. "How's the lawyer life treating you lately?"

"There're always innocents in need of a skilled defense. There's always work. It's not as glamorous as the Hollywood movies depict. We're not allowed to yell at the witnesses for a dramatic reveal of crucial evidence. I always wonder if my clients tell me the truth. I can't go into specifics of cases for obvious reasons."

"Well, aren't you succinct?" Jim asked. "Here I thought you'd have all kinds of interesting stories."

"You need a hobby," Cynthia said. "All you do is work and play ghetto superhero. Visit an arcade like you used to in high school or get a game console. Hell, buy a new computer. I don't care. You need some kind of entertainment before you burn out or go crazy, if you haven't already. Try out one of those virtual reality devices or something. I know you used to love those in the arcades we went to. You can buy those now."

"I was kind of going for the Zen master lifestyle. You know, dedicating my life to the pursuit of training and bettering myself."

"Now that you've played that role," Cynthia said in a sickeningly sweet tone. "You should be yourself. That's an order."

"An order is it now?" Jim asked with a raised brow.

"You heard me."

"If you insist," Jim said. "I never thought I'd have a potential girlfriend telling me to play video games. I thought this was like a unicorn."

"You certainly are a special case. I mean that in every sense of the word special." Cynthia burst out laughing.

Jim smiled despite being the butt of the joke...

6

Skye looked at the scantily clad women standing on the street corner before the stop light flashed green. She pressed the gas and spotted what she was looking for - an abandoned multi-storied building. Judging by the signs still on the front window, it used to be a furniture shop. Pulling into a nearby alleyway, she exited the car after making sure her hoodie was up over her hairnet covered hair. She pulled up her neck gaiter, went to the back door, opened it, and hefted out the grappling device. She placed it next to the car before reaching back inside and taking the quiver out, slinging it over her shoulder along with the bow. "This will become easier," she said to herself. "That's what I keep telling myself."

She took the hulking tool and entered the abandoned building, climbing the nearby stairs. It was an agonizing climb. She raised one foot before gingerly putting her weight down. "The last complication I need is to fall down these dark stairs. Be careful," she said to herself.

Her arduous journey was complete when she reached the top of the building. She opened the door and emerged outside again. "Ashley should be here soon. If there's a location for a crime to be committed, it's this part of town. I'd rather not do this by myself." She placed the hefty accessory down on the roof. "My arms are burning," she said, shaking her arms.

She stayed low on the roof, barely able to overlook the short raise near the edge. She saw Ashley's car pull into a different, albeit nearby, alleyway. "There she is." She reached up to her ear and started a call. "Do you hear me?"

"Yeah," Ashley's voice said. "Sorry about being late. Why are we here anyway? Surely there are better places to use that grappling hook for the first time."

"Why not?" Skye asked. "It has plenty of multi-level buildings and, historically, prostitutes aren't treated well by their bosses or their clients. It's this or hope we can catch some mugger. Do you know the odds of catching one? People would rather steal identities and credit card information online nowadays."

"Good point," Ashley said. "Where do you want me?"

"Go to the alley beside the furniture shop," Skye said. "I'm on its roof already. I figure if we can cover ground and upper level, we'll have everything accounted for."

"You expect something to happen on the roof?" Ashley asked.

"Not necessarily, but I'll get an angle quickly. You'll have cover regardless of where you are with me up here."

"Is there a reason we didn't bring Guardian along with us on this?" Ashley asked.

"We don't need him for this. We're unsure if we're going to find anything. Besides, he has homework. You remember what that's like. He needs all the free nights he can get."

"Oddly considerate of you," Ashley said.

"What's that mean?" Skye peeked over the parapet over-looking the street. "I'm always considerate."

"It sounds like you just wanted to ditch him if you ask me," Ashley said. "Speaking of which, I have a theory. Do you want to hear it?"

"We have nothing else to do unless something happens, so go ahead," Skye said. She looked at the ladies on the street corners. One took a drag from her cigarette before blowing a faint cloud of smoke.

"Don't you find it odd that Masked knew where we were before? He had no way of knowing. We didn't bring phones to track, we didn't tell him, and he just shows up. There's only two ways that happened, if you ask me."

"Go on," Skye said. It was hard to tell if she was bored or genuinely interested with the lack of emotion.

"Either he followed us there, or someone told him where we were going."

"You think it was Guardian?" Skye asked. "Is that what I'm putting together here?"

"You can't tell me you don't think it's odd." Skye could hear Ashley sigh over the line. "Maybe I'm wrong, but is that why you didn't invite him?"

"No," Skye said. "Honestly, it's immaterial even if he told Masked. It's not like we're doing anything we're to be ashamed of. If he told him, it was for our own safety. There's no sense assuming malice where it was probably done for our own safety."

"We can take care of ourselves, though," Ashley said.

"Can we?" Skye asked. "You can't tell me it doesn't give you some manner of comfort having an old hat in the party to supervise us. It did for me anyway. Answer honestly. I know you're still embarrassed after your little rejection."

"We're fine on our own."

"If you say so," Skye said. "We'll see tonight."

"Looks like a client has shown up," Ashley said as a beat-up, decades old car stopped near one lady.

"He has a thing for blondes, apparently," Skye said. "Let's confirm if this is business as usual or something sinister."

"I doubt the first stop will be anything besides a quickie."

"Ew," Skye said. "She's just giving him an old-fashioned. I wish I could forget that memory." She ducked back under the parapet.

"Old-fashioned? Did you mean a hand..?"

"Yes, now be quiet. I'd have thought they'd at least head to a damned alley or something, but no," Skye was now audibly annoyed, "they do it on the street."

"This is a seedy part of town," Ashley giggled.

"Don't even point out the dirty joke. I wish I didn't get it."

"Talk about a quickie. Yikes," Ashley said. "He's done already. What was that, like two minutes?" The sound of an engine starting and the fading sound of a motor stressed her words.

"Can we focus on something else, please?" Skye asked.

"How about the guy walking toward the ladies further down the street? He's got his hands in his jacket pockets. Who knows what he'll do? Maybe he'll pull out a gun or knife."

"He could walk past," Skye said, peeking up and over again. She spotted the man. "I can't see his face. Who would walk this area late?"

"We're about to find out. He's approaching the women now," Ashley said. "Oh, he's just old school it looks like. He's leading her off to a nearby alley - thankfully not mine. That'd be awfully awkward."

"We knew this would happen," Skye said, exhaling. "Women of the night work at night. Who'd have imagined? Maybe this whole excursion was a massive mistake, and I was overzealous thinking this would succeed."

"You're not giving up already, are you?" Ashley asked in a teasing tone. "It's only been like ten minutes. We need to give this attempt at least an hour."

"You're right."

More cars passed as seconds turned into minutes before Ashley spoke up again. "At least you don't have to smell these dumpsters down here. You get nice clean air up on the roof."

"At least you didn't have to lug one hundred and forty pounds up two flights of stairs."

"Touché."

A piercing wail, undeniably feminine, rang out in the city.

"I'm moving to get a view of the alley that guy brought her to." Skye reached down and lifted the grappling device. "You get over there and intercept. I don't want him getting away."

"She could just be vocal, but yeah, better safe than sorry." Ashley's rapid footsteps could be heard as she spoke.

Skye took aim at a nearby rooftop's antenna. She fired the grappling hook. It hit its mark as it affixed itself to the metal. She pressed the button and, after stepping up onto the elevated parapet, she was pulled over as she jumped. The combined forces were barely enough for her to cover the gap and not smack into the building. She approached the ledge and could see Ashley already near the alley's entrance. She spotted a man and a woman covering her face further into the alley. "Shit, it's too far. Keep him talking if you can. I can't get an accurate shot from here." She looked across the road toward the buildings they were standing between. "Perfect," she said to herself.

"Easy there, big guy," she could hear Ashley say as she fired the grappling hook across the street.

"This will hurt," Skye said to herself. She stepped up onto the parapet and pressed the button, swinging through the air until she bounced off the building. She kept the button pressed and kept her wits about her. Her feet kept moving, giving the illusion that she was running up the wall. Once she reached the top, she tossed it down and readied her bow and arrow. She looked down at the group. Ashley was still a fair distance away. The prostitute and client below were trapped in a dead end.

She could hear the man below. "Get out of my way, little girl. I'm leaving with or without your permission."

"My face!" The prostitute had her hands still covering it. "He poured acid on my face!"

"Sick son of a bitch. I'll take care of this. Keep him still as best you can," Skye said.

"I won't do anything, buddy. Just why are you doing this?" Ashley asked.

"Why the fuck do you care?" the man growled. He held the canister, still half-filled at his side.

"Too late, fucker," Skye said. She had the arrow nocked and ready, focused on the perpetrator. She released the arrow.

The man stumbled backward with the newfound wooden arrow piercing his chest with a thunk. "What the fuck?" He brought a hand to the offending protrusion and grasped it.

"I wouldn't do that if I were you," Ashley said.

"Who cares what you think?" The man yanked the arrow clean out of his chest, tossed it to the ground, and covered the wound with his hand. "Where the hell did that come from?" He looked all around.

"Upstairs," Skye said, loud enough to be heard below. She let loose another arrow, this time penetrating his throat as he looked up at her. The arrowhead pushed through the back of his neck, causing a blood splatter to appear behind him near the prostitute's feet.

"Yeah, you're not surviving that," Ashley said.

Skye wasn't done yet. She nocked yet another home-made arrow and fired once more. This time she hit the arm holding the canister, causing it to drop to the ground. The caustic material inside seeped out onto the black pavement underneath. "He's disarmed. Do what you will down there. She needs a hospital, fast. We'll leave when you're finished. I'm heading out now. It'll take me longer."

"Got it," Ashley said.

Skye watched her friend below charge at the man as she drew her short sword. She placed the bow over her shoulder and looked down at the grappling hook as she heard metal sliding along with a woman's sobs below her. She picked it up with a grunt and looked at the street below, spotting the alley she'd pulled her car into. A nearby streetlight illuminated the street below. "That's my ticket down."

She took aim and fired as she heard Ashley say something below her. Hitting the mark, the grappling hook clung to the pole. She gave a powerful tug to make sure it was secure before hopping and pressing the button on the device's side. She flew through the air, seeing vehicles below her passing by. A lone horn blared as she passed above. She made it across the street and lost momentum. She twisted the dial, and it lowered her to the ground. Guiding the hook off the curved pole, it snapped back into place. She ducked off the street and into a nearby alley. She went halfway down the alley before taking a turn and finding her car.

Hopping inside, she inquired, "You're out of there?".

"I just called an ambulance. After this call, I'm destroying the phone."

"Good job tonight. Make sure you don't leave the same direction you entered. Preferably exit via another street. See you soon," Skye said, ending the call. She turned down another winding passageway between buildings before pulling out near the end of the street they were on. She pulled out onto the road and let out a large breath. "Just get home and prepare for work tomorrow morning."

7

_____

Skye stopped her car and let her passenger exit. "Thank you for choosing Oover. Please use us again next time for your transportation needs."

The passenger said nothing in recognition of her words and simply exited the vehicle.

"He paid with a credit card, right?" Skye pulled her phone off the dashboard and checked the app for her company. "Yeah, alright. It's quitting time already? How time flies when you're listening to people bitch and moan while you're driving. At least his destination's near my apartment." She reached up and touched her nose. "Ah shit. It feels like it might be broken. I knew I'd be lucky to not have anything broken after last night's building climbing incident. I'm lucky nothing else important was broken."

She checked her rear-view mirror and pulled back onto the road before turning right again onto a familiar road. "Being an adult sucks. Working and returning home to sleep sucks. No wonder my dad complained all the time." She pulled into the parking lot and made her way up to her apartment.

She dug through her pants pocket and unlocked the door to find a surprise waiting for her inside. It wasn't a beaming and happy surprise either.

"Look who showed finally," Cynthia said, watching her enter.

Skye entered and quickly shut the door behind her.

"If it isn't public enemy number one." Cynthia slowly clapped with an obviously fake smile.

"What?" Skye asked.

"Oh, you haven't seen the news yet?" Cynthia asked. "Here, let me show you."

Ashley sat on the nearby couch, looking defeated. Doubtless she'd already been yelled at for a while already.

Cynthia changed the channel to a local news station. Commercials showed on the television. "They've been replaying your superhero moment over and over on the evening news. You didn't think to check if you were by traffic cameras?"

"No one saw Silent or Blind Justice entering any cars or even know our license numbers. It's fine," Skye said in a calm voice.

"It's fine, is it?" Cynthia's sugary sweet sarcastic voice asked. She pointed at the television. "Do you see that?"

Skye looked over at the screen.

"In case you've missed it," a cheerful female news anchor said, "last night traffic cameras caught sight of what authorities are speculating to be one of the many vigilantes currently operating in the Denver area. Look for yourself." The camera shifted from the news anchor behind the news desk to a grainy video of the street they were on earlier.

The video showed a masked figure wearing a hoodie, firing the grappling gun and tugging at the cord before jumping and swinging over traffic. It also showed the figure eventually descending and freeing said device from its grip before disappearing into a nearby alleyway.

"That's not all the footage we've received, though," the same female reporter said, excitement clear in her voice. The camera shifted to a different point of view. This time it faced the opposite direction, showing the hook already mounted on top of a nearby building. It showed a masked figure slamming into the building before running up the side of the building out of the camera's scope.

"Judging by that broken nose, I'm assuming you know exactly what I'm talking about." Cynthia planted both hands on her hips.

"Why are you here?" Skye ignored Cynthia's tone and sat down beside Ashley. "Are you here to just yell? If so, go right ahead. It won't be anything worse than dealing with ungrateful clients. I'm used to it."

"I'm here because I knew this day would eventually arrive. It's not like you can run around doing what you do forever before you eventually slip up, even if it's just a slight mistake. As a lawyer, I don't think there's anything telling on these clips."

"Make this quick. We have a workout," Ashley said. "God knows what Jim will do to us. No doubt he's seen this already. If it's to punish us, don't worry. He'll do that soon enough."

"I know that," Cynthia smiled. "That's considering I talked to him earlier."

"Oh shit," Ashley shook her head. "What did you tell him exactly?"

"I told him his apprentices were busy last night and made the news - basically, exactly what happened. He didn't seem surprised. I gave him some advice, though."

"I'll take a guess and predict you didn't tell him to

reward us," Skye said. She laid her head back on the couch and stared up at the apartment's drab gray ceiling. "You told him to make us miserable? Big loss there," she said with sarcasm. "We're always miserable after his workouts. No big change there. Try a little harder."

"Is that right?" Cynthia tilted her head. "I guess I'll up my game then."

"I have to sit here and wonder," Ashley said. "Do you think we rubbed our hands together last night and decided 'Tonight we'll be caught on camera just to piss off Cynthia'?" Ashley asked. "Tell me, because from the way you're acting, you seem to think it was intentional."

"No, I think you two didn't take all parameters into account," Cynthia said. "You didn't check for cameras, obviously."

"No one has any clue who it was aside from us anyway," Ashley said. "What's the big fucking deal? Or do you just want to yell at us for your date going bad?"

"Keep making light of this," Cynthia said. Her voice was eerily calm. "Go ahead. Do you have any more wise cracks?"

"Why?" Ashley asked. "You going to run back to Jim and have him take care of the big, mean teenage girls?" She stood up and moved right up to Cynthia. "You're too much of a coward to try anything. That's why you're pissed at us. You're afraid while we're doing good, you're going to get in trouble. It's pathetic."

"Are you finished with your jealous rant?" Cynthia held a straight face the whole while. "I have to assume it's jealousy, because otherwise it's straight ignorance spewing from your mouth with no discernable logical reason. He turned you down, sweetheart. Accept that into your heart. Jealousy is an ugly thing on anybody."

Skye jumped up at Cynthia's last words and caught

Ashley's balled up fist that was preparing to strike Cynthia. "Hold it."

"How childlike." Cynthia gave a haughty laugh. "Refusing to take responsibility for your own actions and then trying to assault the one trying to help. That'll get you far in life. Fine, I can see you two don't want to listen to me." She brought out her cell phone with a wicked smile. Her next words were full of fake concern. "Oh, no." She looked at the pair. "It appears you're late for your workout. I'm sure he'll be totally fine with you being late after being lazy and careless last night. You two stay here and calm down. I'll go tell him your demeanor." She quickly left the apartment.

"How did she even get in here?" Ashley growled, looking at the door leading outside.

"Jim has a key," Skye said. "I gave him one just in case."

"Which means she's wound him up more than likely," Ashley said. "What do we do now?"

"What can we do?" Skye asked. "We go to Jim's and see what happens. I'm betting the longer we stay here and stew, the worse it'll be."

"Then why are we standing around letting her pour more poison into his ear?" Ashley grabbed Skye's hand and dragged her toward the door. "Let's go already."

At Jim's...

"I hear you two had an entertaining evening last night," Jim said. He was sitting on his couch with Jason on the other end. "The entire state heard it, as a matter of fact. Well, I say heard. I guess I meant saw."

Jason stared at the textbook he had open nearby while writing in the notebook in his hand. "I doubt Soaring Specter would be too happy either. Now police know he's met with someone else and given them one of his inventions."

"No one asked you," Ashley said, glancing at Jason.

"On the contrary," Jim said. He stood up and stretched. "I asked him this morning why you all went out on a job. Do you know what he told me?"

"I can imagine," Skye said.

"He said he wasn't aware there was a job last night," Jim said. He was smiling, but his tone made it obvious he wasn't happy as he spoke. "Do you know why I require overwatch? Do you have the slightest inclination why? Obviously you don't, or you wouldn't have forgotten it." He brushed past Jason and now stood in front of the two girls.

"I take it you've spoken to Cynthia?" Skye asked.

"Does that matter?" Jim stopped in front of Skye. "Does it change my point? With a tech specialist, you'd have known there were cameras and never been on the six o'clock news. Hell, Jason could've disabled those cameras temporarily before your daring stunt."

"I suppose it doesn't change that. Would you like to know what we accomplished given what you already know? The news hasn't told that part."

"Is that right?" Jim crossed his arms and continued pacing. "What did you accomplish? Did you stop a mugging, rape, or assault?"

"Kind of," Skye said.

"What does kind of mean?" Jim asked. "Be specific."

"We heard a woman scream. When we rushed over, we found a guy had splashed acid on a prostitute's face. We took him out."

"I see." Jim momentarily looked at the ground and back at Skye. "You stopped a man who assaulted women, presumably multiple, either in the future or in the past. I'll admit that's an admirable goal."

"You do?" Ashley asked.

"I'm not condemning why you went out," Jim sighed. "I'm mad at the secrecy and leaving a vital team member out of the loop."

"She was afraid he'd not get his homework done," Ashley gestured toward Skye.

Jason turned and looked at this revelation. "What? Me?"

"Apparently," Jim said. "She was worried about you, to hear Ashley tell it."

"I appreciate that, but you know I get my work finished as soon as I can after school. Don't worry about me. I take care of my schoolwork so I can be ready anytime."

"There you are," Jim said. "Now, is this going to happen again? I'm not trying to be a dick just for fun, you know. I'm genuinely worried here." He frowned and faced away from the group. "Is it?"

"We won't leave Jason out again," Skye said. "I promise."

"Alright then," Jim said. "Now let's get working out. The sooner we start, the sooner we finish."

"That's it?" Ashley asked.

"What? Did Cynthia put the fear of God in you earlier?" He chuckled. "Sure, she told me to teach you the folly of your actions. Did you get it? Or do I have to use more drastic measures? I'd assumed you both were smart and weren't going to argue. If you insist, I can be an ass. Quadruple workouts are always available."

"No, we're good." Skye stood up.

"Aside from that broken nose, I believe that." Jim approached. "Was that from the building stunt I saw on television earlier?"

"Yes," Skye said. "I didn't even feel it when it happened. Didn't even notice until I woke up this morning."

"I'm surprised, with that bump. You played it off well, though. The average person thought it worked perfectly. The news reporter recounted how you ran up the side of that building. I will admit, it looked cool. You still need to practice so you don't give yourself a concussion. Those are more dangerous than a simple broken nose," Jim said.

"I should practice with it too." Ashley stood up. "You never know when it could come in handy having more than one person able to operate it."

"It is true," Jim said. "Jason," he said, "how difficult would it be to reverse engineer the grappling hook?"

"For my skill level? Impossible. I regret to say, sir, I don't know where to begin."

"Fair enough," Jim said. "I just thought I'd ask. Now," he clapped his hands together, "who's ready to sweat? Mind you, I'm going to make it rougher, or I'll get yelled at myself. So don't blame me. You have only yourselves to blame."

"You can't take it easy on us just this once?" Ashley clasped her hands together and made her best puppy dog eyes toward Jim.

"No," Jim said. "I'm not getting yelled at for your actions any more than I already have. I'm trying to be nice here as it is."

"We appreciate that," Skye said.

"Sometimes I wonder if you're too friendly, boss." Jason placed the laptop beside the book on the coffee table. He stood up and raised his hands above his head with a yawn and a stretch.

"You be quiet." Ashley shot him a dirty look.

"I promise it won't happen again," Skye said.

"It better not, or I'll follow Cynthia's recommendations. I doubt you want that."

"What were those, pray tell?" Ashley asked.

"I'm glad you asked. Are you familiar with running suicides?" Jim asked. "You know, where you run to markers, run back, then run to a further marker multiple times. It tests one's mental fortitude, physical conditioning, and speed. That was just one such exercise she recommended. Shall I show you?"

"We'll be good," Ashley said.

"I trust so..."

8

"You two were busy," Specter said after he closed the door to the warehouse. He spotted Jason sitting in a fold-up chair. "I see you're training with it. That's probably for the best. That looked painful on the television. I'd only ever tried from firing directly below. I thought it'd be dangerous doing what you did. It probably was not the smartest idea."

"We were on a timetable," Ashley said. "A woman was assaulted. We didn't have the luxury of time and deciding how to best use our advantage."

"A woman you say?" Specter asked.

"A prostitute, to be specific." Skye lowered herself to the concrete floor of the warehouse. "The guy splashed acid in her face. Since I was across the street, I improvised."

"I figured as much when I saw what part of town you were in. I know you succeeded from the dead body with an arrow that showed up. Well, multiple arrows. Those are untraceable back to you, I trust? If not, get out and never return."

"I craft them while wearing gloves and making sure no

DNA gets on them." Skye placed the grappling hook gently on the ground before wiping her brow of sweat.

"Impressive." Specter circled around Skye. "May I inspect one?"

Skye reached over her shoulder and pulled out an arrow to hand over.

"I see." Specter held it close to his face. "Minimalist, but effective. Who taught you to make these?"

"My father," Skye said. "He was a hunter. We were too poor to buy arrows regularly, so he taught himself and then me."

"I don't know him, but if he taught you, he was a natural. The fletching is exquisite. These arrowheads are primitive but effective too."

"It's amazing what you can find when you go walking in nature. Feathers and certain rocks chief among them. Nobody ever questions when I want to go walk in nature. Now I need a few modern tools to create them, but they're untraceable. I didn't want to go to prison when I started, so I practiced caution."

"Wonderfully elegant, yet primitive. I like it." Specter gave the makeshift deadly ammunition back. "How did your boss like you appearing on television? I imagine he was not happy."

"Don't remind us," Ashley said.

"He wasn't the angriest, but he wasn't happy," Skye said. "We thought you might be pissed off."

"Me?" Specter asked. "I knew the risks when trading. That's why I wanted to see if you're serious before I handed an experimental prototype over. Just know if you're ever arrested, I will be most displeased if you throw my name out there. So displeased, in fact, an accident may befall you two. Please don't make me do that. I like you three."

"That's not threatening at all," Jason said with a sarcastic inflection.

"It was meant to be, computer man. What was your title again?"

"Guardian of Justice." Jason looked up with a visible frown. "I keep them safe by being the overwatch."

"Sounds like a coward's job."

"Is that right?" Jason got up from his seat and walked over. "You'd do well to have someone watching over your every move on jobs."

"It seems I struck a nerve," Specter said.

"I'm not here to fight with you. Just know I keep them alive by guiding them while they're in unfamiliar places, telling them where patrols are, and messing with cameras."

"Unnecessary, but quite the luxury," Specter said. "Tell me, Guardian. Can you handle yourself in a fight if it came down to it?"

"It wouldn't be my first."

"I can tell from your stance, tone of voice, and determination you're telling the truth," Specter said. "No hard feelings."

"I hold no ill will toward you. Just don't call me a coward again, please and thank you."

"My bad, young man." Specter paced to the side. "Speaking of your little television adventure, I hear a big player is coming into town tomorrow morning at eight a.m."

"Big player?" Ashley asked. "What do you mean by that? How's it related to last night?"

"One question at a time, young lady," Specter said. "You attempted to save a woman of the night, shall we say?"

"Yeah," Ashley said. "If you want to be fancy about her job title, I guess."

"Quite," he said. "Well, an infamous big name is coming

back to this town. She was here a few weeks ago, but she left in a huff after some guy named Calvin Webb screwed up the job she gave him twice."

"Was her name Martha Henderson?" Jason asked with quickness.

"Ah," Specter said. "You know of her. That makes this easier."

"How could you know that?" Jason asked.

"I keep my ear to the pavement. Also, I have my contacts in the criminal underworld. Just because I hunt down some of them doesn't mean I don't have friends in their ranks. Word on the grapevine was that she was supposed to capture women for some Saudi oil baron's harem. He got quite pissed at her failure and fired her. It was the first time it had happened to her, and it was monumental news in the international criminal sphere."

"At least we got her fired," Skye said. "That's something. Who's she working for this time?"

"I don't know. All I know is she's returning to town tomorrow."

"Why would she return to Denver?" Jason asked, his brow furrowed. "We screwed her over last time. There're dozens of cities to find young women, like any college town stocked with a bar. Why here?"

"If I had to hazard a guess," Specter said, "I'd think it's because she has connections to this town. By that I mean she knows the players in the underground. You know, people who acquire what she needs. If she went to a random college town, it would force her workers to do the dirty work, and that means risking exposure."

"More syndicates?" Ashley asked. "Just another Tuesday it looks like."

"You all should know that Calvin Webb and his son were

the smallest outfit in town," Specter said. "They were on the decline when their leader died of mysterious causes." His eyes wandered down to Ashley's sword and over to Skye's bow over her shoulder. "Though I'm sure you two know all about it, judging by the method of his death. My point is, they were just the tip of the iceberg. They were cruel and effective, but small. Their competition is just as malevolent but even larger. I have three guesses who she's going to hire for this next job. It depends on what the job is."

"There's no way of knowing before we get ears on her," Jason said.

"Good luck," Specter let out a hearty laugh. "Her head of security doesn't fuck around. The guy's used to guarding high profile political figures in the UN. Getting any kind of bug on her will be nigh impossible."

"She's just a concierge, isn't she?" Skye asked. "Why does she have such high-powered personnel?"

"Would you want some wimp keeping you safe when you lead that kind of life? She had tens of millions of dollars with more coming in with every job. Money is no object."

"Good point," Skye said. "You're sure she's coming back?"

"As sure as intel from lieutenants in different syndicates can be." Specter reached up and scratched under the bandana adorning his face. "Mark my words. I wouldn't trust them with my life, but I know them from my past."

"We appreciate the information," Skye said. "We'll take care of it."

"Will you now?" Specter laughed. "On your head be it. You fuck with Henderson, you piss off high powered crimi- nals the world over. Are you sure you want to stick your pinky toes in that ocean of sharks? Remember, this is the woman who gets powerful players whatever they desire. She can get women, weapons, houses, drugs, and every other vice you can imagine. She's prized for her ability and ingenuity."

"Sounds like she needs to go," Ashley said. "While I enjoyed watching her embarrass Calvin, we can't let her go around taking people."

"It would inconvenience the big players around the globe," Jason said. "Which means if we do, we may be on the international wanted list if they ever figure out we're involved. That's if, as I suspect, some of her criminal clients are actually in law enforcement."

"A worthy list to be included on. Hope we're front and center," Skye said.

"Well put," Specter said. "I watch your careers with great interest. Do not disappoint me. Now, I have more work to plan. Surely you understand."

"Thanks again for letting us use your warehouse," Skye said as Specter turned to walk toward the exit.

"Make sure you calculate your jumps in the future," Specter said while looking over his shoulder. "Broken noses are the least of your worries if you keep winging it." He slammed the door shut behind him.

Jason inched closer to Skye. "Speaking of which, how is that feeling?"

"It hurts," Skye said. "How do you think it feels?"

"Fine, it was a dumb question. I was just concerned is all."

"I appreciate that, but let's focus on the job ahead of us," Skye said. "We should report to Masked Justice and see what he thinks."

"Agreed," Ashley said. "He's not going to like it if we hide information after our latest screw up."

"Fine." Skye handed the hook to Ashley. "Now you need

more practice. Don't make my mistakes. Who knows if you'll ever need to use it? You need to be familiar with its use and confident."

"Fine..."

Back at the apartment complex...

Jim turned off the television and stood. He moved to the nearby lamp and leaned down to turn it off when he heard the doorbell. "Who is it at this hour?" he asked himself. He opened the apartment door to see Skye, Jason, and Ashley. "I might have known." He moved to the side, allowing them entry. "Come on in then."

The group funneled inside and stood around in the living room.

"Sit and tell me why you're all here at almost midnight." Jim leaned against a nearby wall. "Did something happen?"

"Not really happened, boss," Jason said. "Moreso, we learned something interesting we thought you'd want to know."

"Go ahead," Jim said.

"Do you remember that haughty businesswoman that was lecturing Calvin Webb a few weeks back? The one who pissed him off royally?" Skye asked.

"Henderson?" Jim asked. "Was that her name? Jason said she was a ghost and concierge to the ultra-wealthy scumbags, right?"

"Correct, boss." Jason reached inside his hoodie's pocket and retrieved a tape recorder. "I think it's better if you hear it straight from the source."

"You had that recording the whole time?" Ashley asked. She slapped Jason's arm. "Why didn't you tell us before we went?"

"I thought if you two knew you were on tape, you might act wooden and be suspicious," Jason said. "Am I wrong?"

"I don't know, but it's creepy. Who just records conversations at random?"

"Recording a vigilante we don't know is not random," Jason said. "It's smart."

"He's right," Skye said. She laid a hand on his shoulder as she stood next to him. "Good work. I wish I'd thought of that."

"Seriously?" Ashley asked.

"Let's hear it already." Jim sat down in the only free seat, his recliner.

Jason placed the device on the coffee table and pressed play. The entire conversation with Specter played out again.

Jim's right hand stroked his stubble laden chin. "Sources? Why the hell does he know members affiliated with the forces he fights against?"

"Keep your friends close, but your enemies closer," Jason said. "It's wise. How better to gain intel than bribing old acquaintances with dinner or football tickets? He'd receive news on what's happening long before we would. I suspect that's why he's been so active lately. He's always preparing to do some job."

"Possibly," Jim said. "It just leaves a nasty taste in my mouth. His methods aside, I assume by your rushing over here you want to take her on. Am I correct?"

"She is no stranger to arranging kidnappings, drug deals, and straight up murder," Ashley said. "She's no different from our other targets."

"Except she's rich as fuck and connected across the globe to high-ranking scumbags," Skye said. "Which is even more reason, if you ask me. You take her out, and you inconvenience all sorts. Pissing those kinds of people off is worth it."

"She's rich," Jim said. "That means she'll make Calvin Webb's security look like amateurs. We'd need to be careful, and our strikes pinpoint accurate. Also, we'd have to be creative in how we approach them. Luckily for us, we received something we can use."

"That thing's hard to use," Ashley said. "Plus, it's scary as hell. I felt like I was going to slam into something whenever I tried to use it."

"That's probably because you did," Skye said. "I'll show you a few tricks next time we practice. I just thought you should be familiar with it, just in case. Not to mention, I'm not an expert with it yet, but I have learned to not bash my face into walls anymore."

"Let's focus," Jim said. He looked at Jason. "What do you think? Is it possible to take her on and eliminate her business? Would it be suicide to deal with the backlash from her allies?"

"I don't know. I'm not familiar with how deep her ties go, sir." Jason stood and walked over to the window. He stared out at the buildings. "I would say go for it personally. This is a soul who spreads misery at the behest of her clients and has ruined God knows how many lives pursuing cold hard cash."

"I say we do it," Ashley said. She didn't ever meet Jim's gaze and looked past him. "If she kidnaps young girls and sells them into slavery, I have a bone to pick with her. Calvin was just the whipping boy compared to her."

"Yes, I'm happy to hunt her," Skye said. "What about you, boss?"

Jim took a deep breath. "Fine, we'll take her down. That means no more rogue operations. If it's unrelated to her, then fine. If it could come back to her, I expect you to come to me and we plan out the operations together. Deal?"

"Deal," Skye said.

"Then let's get figuring how we're approaching this," he said.

"I have an idea," Skye said. "It would just require a little acting from you, boss."

"Acting?" Jim asked. "What's that mean? I never was good at acting."

"You don't need Broadway skills. It'll be fine," she said.

"You have me intrigued," Jim said.

"For this to work, we'll need you at the airport at seven-thirty tomorrow morning," Skye said. "You think you can wake up that early, boss?"

"I'm not sure what I'm supposed to do in the damned airport that early."

"What you do doesn't matter. All that matters is you're there and ready to enter my car," Skye said. "Can you do that?"

"I get up regularly at six, so that's not a problem," Jim said. "Fine, I'll be there."

"Excellent..."

9

"Can you hear me?" Skye asked.

She could hear Jim's shushed voice on the cell phone. "Yeah," he said. "How do I know when to move? I can't exactly tell when they're going to head outside."

"You can head out now," she said. "Just act like you're waiting for your ride. Let me know when to move. I can't sit there and wait."

"Right, airport rules. I see." She could hear a door opening over the line, along with his footsteps. "I'll be outside in a minute. Where are you, anyway?"

"Where all the other drivers waiting for their fare are. I'm nearby. Don't worry. I can see the exit where you'll be coming out. Tell me when you see the entourage. She's rich, but she's flying public. She's probably too cheap to have a private jet."

"Those who are rich became rich because they didn't waste money," Jim said. "Alright," he said. "I'm outside."

"I see you," Skye saw Jim standing by the curb. He had on a formal suit and a suitcase hung at his side. "You look handsome in a tie," she said.

"Don't get used to it," he said. "I hate wearing this." He reached into his suit's pocket and retrieved a pair of sunglasses before putting them on. He turned to look inside the sprawling building before turning around. "I see a large group. Looks like bodyguards."

"I am nearly there, sir," Skye said in her best plastic friendly tone. "Please wait outside and I will pick you up as quickly as I can. Goodbye," she said. She started the engine and pulled out onto the busy road beside the airport. She waited in line as limos, busses, and various vehicles were in front of her. The line moved quickly, but not as fast as she'd have liked. "Come on." She tapped the steering wheel in front of her with a finger. She looked at the controls beside her left arm and pre-emptively unlocked the back door.

Eventually, she made her way up to the airport loading area. She rolled down her window so Jim could see her. A crowd of muscled men wearing suits were surrounding someone beside Jim a dozen feet away. She couldn't tell who was behind, but she concocted an idea. "Your ride is here, Mr. Benning."

Before Jim could move, the back door flung open and an altogether different middle-aged man hopped inside. "Take me to Mile High Stadium."

Skye looked at the crowd of bodyguards and their client entering a limo directly in front of them. She turned and noticed an innocent interloper with a smile. Her voice was raised but decidedly polite. "I'm sorry, sir. This is a privately scheduled transportation vehicle. I must ask you to exit so the paying customer can enter."

The man's eyes went wide. "Seriously? Fine," he said. "Fucking hell," she could hear him say under his breath.

She looked back at the window. "Sorry about that, Mr. Benning. If you'd enter, we can exit right away."

Jim gave the exiting man a funny look as he slipped by and climbed aboard. He slammed the door shut. "Let's get out of here. Good timing, by the way."

Skye rolled up the window before following the limousine in front of them out from in front of the passenger loading area. "The pedestrian made it difficult. Do I look like a damned taxi?"

"The definition seems to match what you do," Jim smirked.

"I don't have a bright yellow car, sir. I am a service that taxis, not a taxi. Why am I arguing semantics with you? The hard part will be following them without them realizing they're being followed."

"No need to worry," Jim said.

"What?" Skye asked.

"While you were busy causing a scene, I used the distraction to help."

"Oh, come on," Skye said. "That was not a distraction. That was me trying to be nice and him being rational. How is that a distraction?"

"It got the bodyguards to look. I noticed they were hypervigilant. Jason gave me a tiny device that enables me to track its signal. I attached it to the back of the limousine while I walked over to your car. No one batted an eye. You can sit back and not draw suspicion." He opened the briefcase on his lap and pulled out his laptop. "He even taught me how to track it. Aren't I just the most useful?"

"You've certainly been surprising me lately," Skye said.

"I'm not a computer wizard, but I know a few things." The pair fell into silence as Jim logged in and typed. "Here we are," he said. "I see the signal now. So long as you stay within a couple miles, it'll be good. Its signal is kind of crap, but it was cheap, so we can't complain."

"It was a stroke of luck you found him," Skye said. "He's an invaluable part of the team."

"It's not so much I found him, more that he found us. To be more specific, he found Ashley. I agree though. He's taught me a fair bit about computers, and he's far more advanced than I will ever be. He knows all the shortcuts, intricacies, and mysteries that I can only dream of. The man built a robot to cut power to a house inside of a day. Who can do that?"

"That's why he went on that anime rant when he was drunk before?"

"What?" Jim laughed, keeping his eye on the screen.

"Just what I said. He claimed he always wanted to build a robot. Went on about how you helped him make it a reality."

"Vastly overstated, I'm sure," Jim said. "All I did was go shopping and hand him tools when he needed it. When was this, anyway?"

"When Ashley was confessing to you. You took her to her room and put her to bed. That was when Jason woke up, and boy was he ever talkative. It was eerie hearing him talk so much at a single time."

"I know he doesn't seem it, but he's just a young man. He has all the same emotional needs as the rest of us. I think he's just shy," Jim said. "Ashley treats him like crap. Hopefully you two are getting along better. He deserves to have someone treat him with respect besides me and Cynthia."

"I treat him fine," Skye said.

"So fine, in fact, it's showing," he said.

"What are you going on about? I know you have to watch a dot move for God knows how long, but you're talking nonsense."

"It's either that or you were lying before," Jim said. "You

said you didn't take him along on your tv adventure because he had homework. That implies you pay enough attention to him to know he had homework. It also implies you care enough about him that you try to help him out."

"Why are you only observant at inconvenient times? It's annoying," she said. "I assume you'll tell me if they turn. We're so many cars back on the street, I can't see them anymore."

"If they turn, I'll announce it," he said. "I'd be a terrible leader if I didn't notice how my colleagues were treating each other. Look, I'm not saying it's a bad thing if you like him enough to care about his education. Not at all - quite the opposite. We need to protect each other. All for one and one for all."

"He keeps me alive. I keep him alive as best I can," Skye said. "That's how it works."

"Turn right on the next street," Jim said. "I'm not sure that correlates to homework, though. That seems closer than business associates."

"Are you trying to imply something?"

"Far be it from me. Turn left up here."

She slowed and turned the wheel left. "I think I know where they're going. See that huge hotel? It's the biggest one in Denver. My money's that they're staying there."

"It's either that, or she'll stay somewhere she trusts. A hotel isn't exactly private, but I guess when you're professionals, you can dance around that issue with proper operational security." Jim watched the dot stop moving. "They stopped moving in the hotel parking lot. Pull around somewhere near, but don't be obvious."

Skye pulled into a parking lot across the street, facing the fifteen-floor hotel, the front of the car facing the building. "How about this?"

"That's perfect," Jim said.

"How's this going to help us, anyway?" Skye asked. "We know she's staying in a big ass hotel. It's not like we can do anything while she's inside. There're too many cameras everywhere."

"I can't do anything about it, but our friend Jason's another story no doubt. He should be able to find the room they're staying in, how long they're staying, and a slew of useful details. This is a great first step. Not to mention we know what car they use, or in this case, limousine."

"That's assuming they use it for everything. Smart money says they use another vehicle," Skye said, staring at the towering building.

The group exited the limousine and slammed the doors shut. Four men surrounded a middle client on all sides. The group moved inside the hotel and the automatic doors shut behind them.

"What now, leader?" Skye asked. "What's our next move?"

"What would you do?" Jim asked.

"Excuse me?"

"I want your opinion. Consider it a test to see how well you can lead in the future. What would you do next?"

"I'd task Jason to see what he can find. Then the plan shifts, depending on what he finds."

"Good," Jim said. "Haste gets people killed, and not always the ones we want. Anything else?"

"I'd like to keep them under surveillance until then. You know, see if they go anywhere. Find out who, if anyone, she's hiring to fill her quota. I doubt her men are going around kidnapping people for their order. She has to have someone doing the dirty work for them. That's their MO."

"I know you're not expecting me to sit here all damned

day, are you?" Jim asked. "Besides, my car's at the airport. You need to escort me back so I can retrieve it."

"You work from home, boss," Skye said. "If anyone has the time, it'd be you." She started the engine up again and pulled out of the parking spot.

"You don't think they'd notice a guy just sitting in a car across the street? These are professionals trained in counter-intelligence."

"How would you know that?"

"If I hired bodyguards for my international crime dealings, that's who I'd hire. You'd want talent who know to keep secrets and are always on guard. This woman is not stupid, so I'd bet anything she's the same."

"By that logic, won't she also have a tech specialist that will watch for intrusions?" Skye asked as she slowed down for a stoplight. A horn erupted behind her, causing her to place her left hand out the open window and show them a solitary finger.

"That's a risk we'll have to take. Jason's not unstoppable, but we need information. We can't just let them act with impunity. I'll tell him to be careful and that he might have a cyber opponent on his next assignment. He'll have to see and test his abilities."

"If he fails, it's likely she'll send a hit squad after him and, by extension, us. I don't see their outfit calling the police for any reason."

"It's always a game of cat and mouse. Usually, we're the cat. We need to ensure we don't become the mouse in this iteration. If we don't try, we're blind. If we do, at least there's a chance we succeed."

"We'll see where they go tonight," Skye said. "That should give us an inkling of how they're going to accomplish whatever they're hired for."

"While my ass gets to sit in a car for over twelve hours looking suspicious. I'll be lucky if someone doesn't call the police about a suspicious person."

"Then don't be suspicious," Skye said. "It's easy."

"Is it now? How do you propose watching a hotel?"

"Walk while keeping the property under surveillance. Hell, I know there was a café we just parked by across the street. Sit out and enjoy a cup of coffee. I don't know. Be creative. Blend in. You can manage that."

"At least they'd allow me to charge my phone and laptop, I imagine," Jim said. "Fine. Just know I'm not doing this every job. I'm only doing this because I'm the only one who's able to during the daytime."

"We appreciate the sacrifice,"

"You'd better..."

That night...

"How nice of you all to finally show," Jim said. "Move." He waited for Jason to scoot aside before opening the door and climbing in. "I haven't seen any movement all day. They've been in there doing God knows what."

"I'm checking for them now," Jason said. "It might take a while. Every room has a cell phone, many possess laptops. It's like searching through the haystack for a singular needle."

"Check the records and see which room they're occupying," Ashley said. "That'd be faster, wouldn't it?"

"That's assuming this hotel keeps live digital records," Jason said. "I imagine they do, but it's also risky. It's much safer to just do it the old-fashioned way. Are we in a big hurry?"

"I'm certainly not," Jim said. He rolled his neck, eliciting a loud crack. "I've watched this hotel for over twelve hours now."

"Then we can be patient another hour. The more rooms I check, the higher the chance I find them."

"Take your time," Jim raised a large cup of coffee to his lips and took a drink.

"How many coffees have you had today?" Jason asked.

"This would be my third," Jim said. He finished the drink.

"He'll be fine," Skye said. "Don't worry about it," she said.

"I just don't want you having a cardiac incident, boss. You should drink some water. Goodness knows you're probably dehydrated now with all that caffeine."

Ashley remained quiet during this entire exchange in the front passenger seat, listening intently.

"You've been quiet, Ash," Jim said.

"One, do not call me Ash."

"Don't like the name?" Jim asked. "Is there a reason?"

"It's a morbid name is all," she said. "Think about it. When you get cremated, you're turned into ash. Who chooses to be named after human remains?"

"I didn't picture you being bothered," Jason said without turning away from his work.

"You don't know as much about me as you think, Guardian."

"Perhaps so," he said, still typing away and checking different numbers and names on his screen. "One thing's for sure. They're not using her real name, as expected."

"It'd be nice if we knew who her client was," Ashley said. "Then that way we'd know who she's targeting. It could be any group."

"We'll know soon enough," Jim said.

"I've hit pay dirt," Jason said. "They are on the ninth floor in room 914."

"Excellent," Skye said. "Can you find anything else?"

"I see their room has a television. Give me a minute. I'm trying to tap into the microphone inside it."

"Excuse me?" Ashley asked. "Televisions do not have microphones inside them."

"They do now," Jason said. "There's been a filter salesman yelling about conspiracies for the last decade. Do you think smart tv's can hear you with fairy dust? When you command it to switch to channel twenty, it turns the channel. Now, if they're used to spy on you on behalf of the government, it's a conspiracy. What's not is that any competent computer AI can tune in and listen. Now be quiet. We should get an audio feed here shortly."

"Your ride is ready, Ms. Henderson," a male voice could be heard over the laptop's speakers.

"Finally," a female voice said. "It took you long enough."

"My apologies," the first voice said. "Our associates insisted we wait until evening. They did not go into specifics why."

"Those idiots better not try anything stupid and reckless," she said.

"I am sure they were just busy, Ms. Henderson," the male voice said. "If it is otherwise, we will deal with their audacity."

"This guy's a real mixed bag," Ashley said. "Weirdly calm and gracious, but vicious."

"Whatever," Martha said. "Let's start this ball rolling. My client insists I get this done before the week is over."

"He always was an impatient man."

"He's also the most successful sex slave trader in the world today," Martha said. "We do not argue and pontificate on why people choose their paths. We deal with it. You and your men know the job. Stay quiet and let me do the talking. Let's head out."

"Yes, ma'am."

"What timing," Jim said. "At least that specified they have another group they work with locally. How many human trafficking rings do you think a big city like this has?"

"Too many, apparently," Skye said.

"It should be easy enough to follow them," Jason said. "I've pinpointed which cell phones belong to her and her entourage. We can follow those all the way to wherever they're meeting their associates."

"You're thinking sabotage?" Jim asked.

"It's an option, or we can cut the middleman. Ignore the associates and go straight for the prize. If we know where they go, we can prepare accordingly."

"I think that'd be difficult with bodyguards of that caliber. No doubt they'd have bullet resistant windows. Anything short of an explosion and I'd doubt they would be affected."

"Sir, it's a limousine. A run-of-the-mill limousine doesn't have such tactical modifications."

"Normally you'd be right," Jim said. "Around my third coffee today, I noticed they replaced that limo with the one you see across the busy street there." He pointed ahead out the front of the car.

The same telltale crowd of bodies surrounding one in the middle emerged from the hotel's automatic doors.

"I'd bet anything they replaced the real limo with one they've had prepared beforehand. If we're going to strike at her directly, we'd have to do so when they're on foot. That means either at the location or before they leave. I don't know about you, but I don't relish the idea of entering a hotel and killing. There're too many cameras."

"Then it sounds like you're saying we can only fuck with her partners," Ashley said. "Don't you think they'd have some sort of backup this time around? They're not wanting two straight jobs ruined in the same city. If she's as smart as you say, she's bound to have backup plans for just that."

"They're moving," Skye said, watching the limousine pull out of the hotel's parking lot. She waited until they were a few blocks away before pulling out and following.

"Let's just focus on our next move and not try to pre-plan the entire war at once," Jim said. "We follow them, find out their muscle in the city, and then we proceed from there. Agreed?"

"It's a decent plan," Jason said. "Now turn right on this next street."

"If we take down this Henderson character," Ashley said, "don't you think your friend in Congress might take offense?"

"Charlie?" Jim asked. "Possibly, I don't know. He's in the PHR. I don't think they give two fucks about regular trafficking. Their only priority is kids. I imagine he holds a grudge against me for scarring him for life."

"Especially in politics," Ashley said. "Their face is their money maker."

"Did he know any of your names, besides the boss's?"

"He knew mine," Ashley said.

"Then there's a solid chance he already knows where we all are, if he cares enough to," Jason said. "You never changed your name and can be looked up from anywhere. It'd be child's play for a politician to find such information."

"There's no use fussing over what ifs," Jim said. "Focus on this job, not the fallout from it, or we'll never get it done."

"Jim's right," Skye said. "Our focus is keeping whoever their future victims are from being kidnapped. Failing that, it's rescuing them before they can be shipped overseas. Once they're out of the country, they're gone for good. We get one chance at this with multiple lives in the balance."

"Turn left two streets up," Jason said.

"I'm not familiar with this portion of the city," Jim said.

"It's where affordable housing is built. I wouldn't quite call it the poor side of town," Jason said. "That's because I try to be nice."

"Do you have knowledge of which crew runs this turf?" Skye asked.

"I am not up to date on all the street gangs in my city. Sorry. I'm certain there are power hungry types trying," Jason said. "Once we know who, we're able to ask someone familiar with the underworld."

"You're referring to Specter, I assume?" Jim asked. "I don't like him having any more access to our plans than he already has."

"I'm pretty sure he's one of the good ones," Skye said. "He's never struck me as malicious."

"Not to you," Jim said. "He may be one of the good vigilantes. He might not. That's all I'm saying. Don't trust this guy so easily."

"Noted," Skye said.

"He has done nothing for us except give us one of his toys. He's killed no one that we know of. For all we know, he's some crazy ass who longs to be a vigilante and is living vicariously through us."

"He could be legitimate," Ashley said. "It doesn't matter right now. What concerns me is how we're driving further into, for lack of a better term, a ghetto. People are watching us."

"We're just having a pleasant evening drive," Jim said, keeping his cool. "We're not doing anything illegal."

"They're turning right. It's a dead end though, so don't follow. There are two warehouses down that way. We can track their location. Find someplace we can stop for a few minutes, and we'll have our answer."

"Not quite," Ashley said. "All we know is where they operate. We need to be proactive if we want to know their identities, not sit in a car a mile and a half away. We need to get closer. It's the only way we're going to stop them ahead of time, if you ask me."

"Make the turn, but don't approach the warehouses. Ashley, when she stops, you're with me. We're going to move a little closer."

"Me? Why not her?" Ashley refused to turn around and speak to him directly.

"Because I need my bodyguard if I'm going out in a hostile environment. You didn't abdicate that title, I hope?"

"Fine," she said. She shook her head and exhaled.

Skye brought the car to a stop behind a nearby billboard facing the warehouses.

"That's our cue," Jim said. He opened the door and waited for Ashley. "Hurry, lazy bones. There's no telling how long before they backtrack. We can't allow them to see us, or this entire operation will be moot."

"Why'd it have to be me?" Ashley hurried behind him as they made their way down the desolate road. She looked up at the light above and shielded her eyes. "You know things are awkward between us right now."

"Are they?" Jim asked, pushing forward. "I don't feel awkward. This seems like your problem. Besides, it's imperative we're able to work together or innocents will die. Think of this as me trying to help you overcome your shyness, or awkwardness if you prefer. I'm not making it awkward - you are. Besides, I needed a cover story if someone saw me."

"What does that mean?"

"Hopefully you won't find out. Now hurry." Jim got off the sidewalk and onto the grass. He found a nearby bush and kneeled behind it. "Come over here. You can see both warehouses perfectly."

"I'm getting my jeans all dirty, but fine." Ashley kneeled beside him.

"That wasn't so bad, was it?" Jim asked with a slight elbow into Ashley's ribs. "I'm not the boogeyman. I just want us to be normal again. Friends, comrades in arms, and possibly even a father figure."

"You don't want much, do you?" Ashley asked, an obvious mocking tone to her voice. "Fine, you want to clear the air? Let's do it. Just give me one minute," she said. She pulled out her cell phone and turned it off. "There, now we can start."

"Afraid Jason might get curious? He could be jealous, you know. He could assume all kinds of scenarios. You both are about the same age."

"No chance in hell," Ashley said. "The dude worships the ground you walk on. He stalked me home, and I still don't fully trust him."

"That's awfully harsh. Without him, we'd have had a tough time on past jobs. Look, I'm not saying love the guy, just be nicer. He's a good kid, if a little socially awkward."

"He defended me while I was drunk, I guess." Ashley looked away and then finally faced Jim. "Fine, I'll be nicer to him. Just know if he tries anything else, I'll not dance around the issue."

"I wouldn't expect you to." Jim paused for a few seconds

before he continued with a smirk. "It's a real shame, though. You two would make a great couple."

"Oh fuck off." Ashley reached over and slapped Jim's shoulder, hard, but this was undermined by her near manic laughter. "We'd never get together. The very notion is outrageous. Besides," her laughter died down, "I think he likes Skye better, anyway."

"Maybe because she's nicer to him than you were," Jim shrugged. "It's just a thought. If you want people to like you, always consider how you treat them. That's some regular sage fatherly advice right there. I should charge you for it."

"I think my parents would agree I've learned too much from you already," Ashley said. A frown replaced her fading smile. "God, I hate them."

Jim rested a hand on her shoulder, keeping his view ahead. "I know, and I realize I'll never be a replacement. I just wanted to help you. That's all I've ever wanted. It's the same for them in the car. I'm a broken man," Jim continued his monologue. "I can't help anyone else, but I keep trying. Some help I am, dragging all of you into this messy, blood-soaked life."

"Stop feeling sorry for yourself already," Ashley said. "It looks like their hosts are coming out to greet them, so pay attention."

The pair watched the limousine open and the group walking in formation toward the warehouse. They were greeted by the warehouse's door opening and a group of men wearing suits.

"They have fancy suits," Ashley said. "I also see all different races and genders, so they're equal opportunity."

"That's one interpretation," Jim said. "Mine would have been evil people are evil, no matter the race or gender."

"That's not very progressive of you." Ashley stifled a

laugh. "They look well to do, judging by their apparel. It means their business model is profitable."

"If they're working with her, that much is obvious. She's the big time, even for a group working in this vast city. I wish we'd brought a directional microphone. That would have been smart, so we could hear what they're saying. We have no clue if they're accepting a job or hashing out details. If we knew who they're targeting, we'd have a step up."

"Moaning about it won't help," Ashley said. "There's only one avenue where we can figure that out if you're up for it."

"You're not serious?" Jim asked. "There's no cover between here and the warehouse. We'd be spotted inside of a minute, and there we'd be, trying to explain to a bunch of slavers why we're eavesdropping."

"I'm just telling you how we could get that information you desperately desire."

"They seem to be having a pleasant enough exchange," Jim said. "It's nothing like when we saw her talk to Calvin Webb."

"That was after we fucked them both," Ashley said. She heard a noise at her side. "What are you doing? Oh," she saw Jim with his phone out, taking pictures of the meeting. "Can you actually make anybody out with that phone camera?"

"Zoom is a thing, you know. The cars lining the parking lot may make it difficult to see, but maybe those license plate numbers could help just the same." Jim kept taking pictures of the two groups. "Not that I'd call these professional quality photos, but they're something to show your little friend, Specter."

"I don't trust the dude," Ashley said. "Having said that..."

She brushed a stray piece of shrubbery away from her face. "He's helped us. He's given us no reason to suspect him yet."

"It's always safer to be paranoid. You never know who's trustworthy other than the people you vet. In our case, that's our group, no one else."

"Looks like their meeting is over. We should move." Ashley tried to get to her feet.

"Wait," Jim said, stopping her in her tracks and pulling her back down by the hand. "There's no chance we'll reach the car before they drive by. They'd see us running back and be suspicious. We're going to have to hide and hope they don't see us."

"If you say so," Ashley said. She turned back and saw the group enter their limousine and pull out onto the road, heading toward them.

The pair ducked down, hiding as best they could. The sound of an approaching engine got louder until it eventually passed by.

"Wait until they're out of sight," Jim said. He still had his hand holding Ashley's as he spoke. He released her hand. "Alright, now we can head back."

The two scrambled to their feet and ran toward the car, only to stop behind a nearby tree at what they noticed. "Oh shit," Ashley said in a quiet voice.

"Skye will figure something out," Jim said. He looked at the police cruiser parked near her car. He could see a uniformed officer standing at the driver's side window and speaking to Skye.

"What do you think they're talking about?" Ashley asked in a hushed voice.

"If I had to guess," Jim said, matching her volume, "I'd say they're admonishing her for taking their spot behind the billboard. Sometimes cops sit behind these things and try to catch people speeding. He's probably giving her the 'This isn't a suitable parking spot, and you need to leave' thing."

They weren't close enough to hear anything clearly other than their voices speaking indistinctly. Suddenly the officer's voice became loud enough to make out. "Alright then. I'm letting you off with a warning, but make sure I don't catch you a second time. Is that clear?"

"Crystal clear, officer," they could hear Skye say.

"Alright. Leave, and quit loitering," the officer said with a smile. He walked back to his cruiser and got inside before taking off back toward the city.

The pair left their cover and jogged over to the car before climbing inside. "That scared us," Ashley said. "He didn't issue a ticket?"

"It's amazing how far a little manners and cooperation go," Skye said, starting the engine. "Apparently, it's a no-no to park behind one of these billboard things. Good to know for next time."

"What did you two find?" Jason asked.

"I got some pictures on my phone," Jim said. "I'm hoping that'll lead to addresses or a solid start on who they are. You're going to ask your friend Specter about them, I assume. Personally, I'd recommend doing some good old-fashioned research, but I suppose more avenues to find them is a worthwhile effort. Here." He handed his phone to Jason. "Look at these pictures. I doubt you'll get any good mugshots from it, but maybe there's a clue."

"I'll see what I can find," Jason said, accepting the device. He looked at the pictures. "Oh, nice job, boss."

"What did he do?" Ashley asked.

"He got some viable license plates I can check out. They're probably just grunts, but it's a good starting point."

"We know she has a job of some sort she needs done,"

Skye said. She pulled out onto the road and drove away from the warehouses. "We know she's hired that group in the warehouse, otherwise I'd imagine it'd have been a lot nastier. We know our goal. Find out who they are and sabotage their operation. If we can nab Henderson, fantastic. If we're careful, we may save any they end up kidnapping."

"Odds are we won't get to them before they get caught. You're right." Jim tilted his head in thought. "We'll deal with it as it comes. Who has work early tomorrow morning?"

"You know my schedule," Ashley said. "I get up at five thirty most mornings. You have to love the clients that book you for six in the morning."

"Why are you asking?" Skye asked.

"Because my ass can't be missing work every morning. Jason, if you find anything, send me an encrypted email with everything. I'll try to plan some operation tomorrow night. Just be sure to be ready. Odds are we'll need to move quickly after your working hours if we want to get anything of meaning done. Agreed?"

"I'm game," Skye said.

"You know I'm in, boss," Jason said.

Jim reached ahead and poked Ashley in the shoulder. "What about my fearless bodyguard, Blind Justice? Is that alright with you?"

"I'm fine with it," she said. "I'll just need a shower beforehand."

"We'll see how that timing works out," Jim said. "Let's just focus on getting a good night's sleep before our next big job."

10

———

"Did we learn anything?" Skye asked as the group finished entering Jim's apartment. Jason placed a bag in the hallway leading outside. They all took seats in the living room, leaving Jim's beloved recliner for him to sit in as he spoke.

"We know a few of the low-level enforcer types," Jim said. "In large, thanks to Jason's hard work. How he did that while at college is beyond me. Sometimes I worry about your ever finding a girl if you're so busy, buddy, but I'm not arguing with the results."

"Did we ever figure out the gang's name?" Ashley asked.

"I don't know that they have a name," Skye said. "I asked Specter, and he said he knows who leads that group."

"When did you ask him?" Jim asked.

"On the way here, I stopped at his warehouse. He had just arrived. I told him where we went last night, and according to him, those warehouses are owned by Mr. Frank Patterson, son of Patrick Patterson. Their naming conventions are truly revolutionary."

"Enough with the jokes," Jim said. "Did he say anything else about his group?"

"He said they were competing with Calvin just a few short weeks ago. Word on the street was he was crushing Webb until he got the job from Henderson. It gave his group a boost in street cred and an influx of cash - until we ruined that, anyway." Skye looked at her partners. "His group's bigger than Calvin's ever was, according to him, but there is one saving grace he said."

"Enlighten us," Ashley said. She leaned to the side on the sofa's arm.

"They're not nearly as regimented and disciplined as Calvin's little criminal enterprise was. Apparently, this Patterson is laxer. That's why Henderson chose Calvin's little group. She must be desperate."

"That, or they owe her favors," Jim said. "Maybe she grew up in Denver and has connections locally. Regardless of the reason, we're certain of the group. We have a few of the henchmen's addresses. Now we act. The only question is, doing what? Kidnapping and questioning, or killing as per usual?"

"They say information is power, and I'd agree," Jason said. "I say we grab a street guy and question him."

"Where are we going to do that?" Ashley asked. "It's not like we can grab a dude and bring him back here past God knows how many neighbors in the hallways. The only location I can feasibly think of is taking him into the wild and questioning where no one usually wanders."

"I love camping," Jason said without pause. "Don't you? We need to go camping soon."

"Then the question becomes, would a piss ant actually know anything?" Skye asked.

"He'd know the new orders issued from on high," Jim

said, leaning forward. "He'd know if they're running around picking up girls or not."

"Unless he's just warehouse security," Skye said. She looked over at Jason. "How many names did you piece together?"

"I have three names to choose from," Jason said. "Hold on. Let me get my laptop, and I'll show you the different case files I've made. It'll be a lot easier than trying to remember verbatim." He stood and walked to the bag he put in the hallway leading out of the apartment. Kneeling, he unzipped the bag, extracting the laptop before making his way back. He sat down, logged in, and opened three different files before placing the laptop on the coffee table between them. "Have a look."

Jim picked up the laptop and placed it on his lap. "Here's hoping," he said. He was quiet for a few minutes as he read the different files Jason created. Once he was done, he handed the device to Skye. "Here, you see what we're dealing with. We can decide on the target together rather than me deciding everything."

"Really?" Ashley asked.

"You are my partners, after all. You shouldn't be surprised that I trust your judgement."

"I know you trust us, but I didn't think you trusted us in this aspect of the business."

"I won't be around forever," Jim said. "You need to learn this aspect. Picking targets is crucial if you want to stay alive and succeed." He glanced at Skye. "Pass it to Ashley when you're done. Then we decide which of the targets we want."

"Don't start talking like that," Ashley said. Her normal tone was replaced by an obviously annoyed one. "It's like you just raised your own death flag."

"I don't understand what that weird phrase means," Jim said with a look of bemusement.

"I didn't know you liked anime and manga," Jason said. His eyes sparkled with excitement. "Which one is your favorite series?"

"That isn't a conversation we're having now. As far as what it means, I thought it was obvious."

"Here." Skye handed over the laptop. "That's a tough choice."

"I thought so too," Jason said. "There are merits and risks associated with going after any target."

"Quiet," Ashley said. Her brow furrowed as her eyes danced left and right.

"Talk about rude," Jim said. "I know who I think would be a good start, but I'm eager to hear everyone's thoughts."

Ashley quickly placed the laptop down on the coffee table. "I'm done."

"Jason, what do you think, buddy?" Jim asked.

"Me?" Jason looked genuinely surprised.

"Yeah, you," Jim said. "Your insight has been invaluable so far. You did the investigating. I want to know your thoughts."

"If I had to pick a target to chase, it'd be Milo Grant. He's their tech specialist. I'd bet he'd know about every dirty dealing they're involved in. He's the one bringing in a good portion of their money by less than legal means online. He's not just helping traffickers, but he's also stealing identities. If we want info, this is the ideal target."

"Interesting," Jim said with a smile. "You're analytical. That's good." He looked at Skye. "What about you?"

"I say we go after Kyle Graham. His rap sheet reads that he allegedly kidnapped over five women. That's just what they could charge him with. He got off on a technicality. If we want answers about where and how they operate, then Kyle's the obvious choice. We can catch them before any innocents get taken away to God knows where."

"That is the direct approach. Nothing wrong with that. Now, Ashley, who do you think?"

"We go after Willard MacDonald," Ashley said. "His history shows he's been hired by security firms. The dude knows professional security measures. None of his clients have ever been killed. He was a marine before that. We get him, we increase our chances by a factor of ten in the long run. He can tell us how their patrols work, how much personnel they keep at each location, and the best method of infiltrating. It would also be useful to knock him out of the picture to make everything easier."

"The pragmatic approach has its merits," Jim said. "You've each heard each other's arguments. What do you say? Has anybody changed their minds?" He watched the group stare at each other, all of them shaking their head. "Alright. I guess I'll have to be the tiebreaker then."

"Don't make us sit in suspense," Ashley said. She rocked forward and backward, awaiting the decision. "Who are we going after?"

"There are two sides," Jim said. "On one hand, I want to keep innocents from getting kidnapped. On the other, I want to raise our chances for subsequent operations. Odds are we'd make more of an impact if we go after Milo. Kyle Graham is only one of many kidnappers they employ. If we take him out, it won't really matter all that much. As far as Willard MacDonald, he wouldn't be useful or practical to acquire. I say we go after Milo first. He'd give us intel we can use to make the next operation easier and safer."

"He'd also be easier to get to talk," Jason said. "Most geeks aren't too tough when push comes to shove."

"Shall we test that on you?" Ashley asked, a smile on her face.

"You already know my resolve, lest we forget the night we first met," he said.

"It was just a joke," Ashley said. "You should get used to them eventually."

"We're going to let Kyle Graham run rampant?" Skye asked.

"For the time being," Jim said. "Let's play the situation out if we chose him. What would happen? We'd get rid of one of their kidnappers - that's it. The others would still be working and kidnapping innocents. We'd be no closer to knowing how, when, or where to strike next. If we pick the tech specialist, he'd give us plenty to go on."

"I see," Skye said. "It makes sense. It just feels wrong to leave a kidnapper free to do as he pleases."

"For the moment, not permanently," Jim said. "It's a better idea to know where to strike next than to save someone immediately. It would take a few days for her to be shipped out, I'm assuming. If they get kidnapped, there's a very high chance we could get them out before they're shipped. Bottom line is this way gives us the highest chance of success, if you ask me."

"No arguments there," Skye said. "What you said makes sense, but I have another idea I think we can swing to maximize our impact." She clasped her hands together and looked left and right at everyone before continuing. "Why not split and go after different targets simultaneously?"

"Because multiple targets are difficult to pin down and successfully kidnap," Jim said without pause. "Unless our security officer is nearby inside the same building as the tech specialist, then maybe that'd work. Even then, I'd prefer three people focusing on them alone."

"What if I told you we could send two operatives after Milo and two bodies chasing another target?" Skye asked.

"You're asking Jason to go out in the field?" Jim asked.

"Not quite."

"Oh, don't tell me." Jim brought a hand up and facepalmed.

"Soaring Specter," both Skye and Jim said together.

"I do not want that man involved in our plan," Jim said. "He cannot be trusted."

"He hates these guys as much as we do," Skye said. "We'd be dumb to not use a resource at our fingertips."

"Who gets the short straw of partnering with Specter? Me?" Jim asked. "I wouldn't want you accompanying that unknown. He could dip at the first sign of trouble, and then you'd be high and dry."

"If you'd want to be his partner, sure. I don't mind volunteering myself, though," Skye said. "He could be useful, and he wants to take down these guys. I don't see a negative unless he flakes out or is a sham."

"You're proposing we follow both home from the warehouse and have two simultaneous operations going at once? Are you proposing kidnapping them while they're at work in the same location or at home?"

"Either way would work."

"Specter's already involved, boss," Jason said. "He's complicit in our adventures as it is. He'd be charged the same as we would if they ever linked the device we control to his first use of it on television."

"Come on," Ashley said. "We can use all the help we can find. We know he can handle himself from his news escape, and we know he goes after the same people we do. Why are you so distrusting?"

"Because I'm responsible for all of you," Jim said. "One

wrong choice, one wrong move, and all our lives are over. Now maybe this guy wouldn't fuck us over. Maybe I'm wrong. Or maybe I'm right. We won't know until we try, and by then, it's too late."

"Two targets for the price and time of one seems like a worthy test of Specter's integrity," Skye said.

Jim looked at the floor for a long minute, silent, before looking at Skye. "Fine, but I reserve conditions."

"Which are?"

"I'm the one partnering with him, and we're the team going after Willard MacDonald. If he says yes and wants to work, he'll get a rigorous test. I don't want anyone else going with him, and I don't want anyone else going after the more dangerous target. Kidnapping is a whole different game to straight up murder. It's much more difficult, to put it mildly. I'd know."

"Where would we take them, anyway?" Ashley flopped back on the couch and stomped her foot. "We need to figure that shit first. Are we just taking them out into the middle of nowhere and doing our best mafia impersonations before burying them? That's risky since anybody could camp out there."

"Ninety-eight percent of campers camp near or in a campground," Jason said.

"Did you just pull that number out of your ass?"

"Maybe."

"Shut up," Ashley said.

"If you have a smarter idea," Jim said, "tell us. We need information, so we need to take one of them. I'd prefer just Milo, but if we can nab two, that's obviously better. Where else would we question them?"

"An obvious answer springs to mind here," Skye said.

"You are volunteering this guy for a lot right now," Jim

said. "You really think he'd allow questioning of prisoners in his warehouse? Did you ask him any of this while you visited?"

"You think I'd just volunteer someone else in a highly illegal activity if I didn't?" Skye smirked. "Yeah, of course I did."

Jim glared at her. "We need to talk later in private," he said. His normal tone was gone, replaced by an angry inflection. "The damage is already done. Fuck it," he said. "Fine. We'll take them to the warehouse and conduct our questioning. I guess we're headed to the warehouse to get our last member involved."

"Already ahead of you. He's waiting there already."

"Yes," Jim said, getting up. "I bet he is."

At the Warehouse…

"We meet again, Masked Justice," Soaring Specter held out his right hand.

Jim grabbed it and returned the handshake. "Soaring Specter, always a pleasure to see you."

"Quite," he said. "Now shall we talk shop?" Specter gestured toward the tables. "We can plan everything out over here."

Jim looked to his side at Skye before returning his gaze to Specter. "That's fine. We'll need more space for this. Quite the base and prep area," Jim said, looking across the warehouse's spacious interior, searching for anything out of the ordinary. "It's refreshing to meet someone in this line of work who values prep. There're entirely too many imbeciles who fly by the seat of their pants and commit mistakes."

"The feeling is mutual," Specter said. "Planning is key. Too many young vigilantes worship the killing itself and forget how to go about it safely. It leads to a lot of good intentioned fighters learning harsh lessons on the first offense."

"Youth is wasted on the young, they say." Jim stood beside Specter and snapped his fingers.

Skye, Ashley, and Jason all pulled out folders. They placed them on the table before opening them.

"Did Silent Justice inform you of any details of what we'd be doing tonight?"

"All she said was that you were going after Frank Patterson and his outfit. I know little more than that. I know that they're into some nasty business," Specter placed both hands on the table, leaning while reading. "Kidnapping, blackmail, grifting, identity theft – basically anything that can make money. It's rare they kidnap though. Too risky."

"They're back in the business, more than likely," Jim said. "I have good reason to believe that. Have you heard of Martha Henderson?"

"Yes," Specter said. "However, I keep up to date with this city, nothing beyond it."

"Think illegal concierge to the stars," Jim said. "This woman gets women for rich foreign princes, drugs for whoever can afford her services, etcetera. She's paying Patterson, and her last job was for a lot of young women that she hired Calvin Webb to take."

"This makes sense. I knew of Henderson, but only what my informants told me. You think she's here to kidnap more people? What do we plan on doing? I assume this must be a bigger job to bring me on?"

"You could say that," Jim said with a momentary side glare at Skye. "We want to kidnap their tech specialist, in addition to their head of security, Macdonald."

"That's an awful big job just to get one of them, Mr.

Justice," Specter said, looking over at Jim. He stood up straight and pointed down at the picture of Willard MacDonald. His finger rested on the bearded chin of the large man. "He won't be easy to take alive. You'd be better off killing him and taking the geek."

"They can replace the security man," Jim said.

"I doubt they have anyone that experienced to deal with their security. You'll permanently weaken them while gaining untold information through the twig boy. Now I assume with Guardian doing his overwatch thing, we're splitting into teams of two?"

"That was the plan, I think." Ashley looked at Skye, who was avoiding Jim's glances.

"You and I will go together," Jim said. "We'll leave the two girls to get Milo. We'll get MacDonald. Are you good with that?" he asked.

"Wanting to judge my abilities?" Specter asked, fully turning to Jim with a smirk. "Or my loyalty? Regardless, you'll soon learn. It's fine by me. Protect your group however you like. I will do my job to perfection."

"That's music to my ears," Jim said. "Do you know anything about the warehouse beyond these floor plans Guardian found?"

"Only who owns them, I'm afraid." Specter shook his head and wiped his masked face with his hand. "We know MacDonald and Milo work at the warehouse."

"We were going to wait until Milo went home to sleep," Skye piped up, drawing Jim's attention. "That way, we wouldn't deal with security."

"Odds are you'll still have to deal with an alarm," Specter grunted. "No personnel, but you'd require Guardian to get you inside. That leaves us. According to these files, we don't know where the security specialist stays. Yes, former military men are usually ghosts. Our only option would be the warehouse or outside."

"We're lucky to even gain a photo of them when we did," Jim said.

"If all three were present, then the job was accepted. I guarantee."

"How do you know that?" Jim asked.

"Did you see shots pop off and people die?"

"No."

"That's how I know. That was him putting his best foot forward with those he trusts the most. They know the stakes. They're going to be on guard. The girls have an easier job. We have our work cut out for us, friend." Specter backed up and raised his hands to massage the sides of his head.

"How good a shot are you?" Jim asked.

"With a firearm? I don't know. I never fired one before," Specter said.

"If you don't mind my asking," Ashley said. "What do you use then?"

"I'm glad you asked." Specter reached down to his belt line and pointed to the various containers held in a specialized belt hanging at his side. "These are homemade concoctions, explosives, and various drugs in aerosolized form. All it takes is a good toss, and you're in business."

"Drugs?" Jason asked. "What drugs? Barbiturates or benzodiazepines?"

"You're on the nose, Guardian," Specter said. "They're downers. It helps an aging man like me get an edge if they're woozy or not at their full potential. Slowing reaction speeds is useful if nothing else."

"I trust none of that can be traced back to you?" Jim asked.

"No more than one of your victim's being traced by your blade or her bow and arrow," Specter gestured toward Skye. "I keep my DNA off my creations. I also can get to high up places; you know how already."

"I have an idea how we're going to approach this," Jim said. He brought a hand up to his covered chin and rubbed. "What do you think about this?"

11

"Let me know when you're in position," Jim said. He heard no reply in the earpiece besides static. "I'm in position below. Nobody's out here, but I don't want to hang around outside."

"Just hold your position and stay quiet. I've been on the roof for an hour. Your MacDonald always exits at the top of the hour to indulge himself with a cigarette. Never underestimate the regularity of a nicotine addict. He'll be there soon. Just focus on dealing with him when he gets out there. I won't be able to descend quick enough to help. I'm just here to curtail anyone that gets curious inside and heads out to investigate, since I have a perfect vantage point to drop some surprises. They don't make a habit of locking the window on top."

Jim pulled the blade hanging at his side part way out of its sheathe and rested a hand upon the handle of the blade. He took a deep breath, standing beside the door behind a nearby smelly dumpster. The rancid smell of God knows what stayed in Jim's nose. "How many hostiles are in there?"

"If we'd just let Guardian come along, he could tell us,"

Specter said, a hint of annoyance permeating his voice. "I see four inside, but I can't see everything from my position."

"I want them to be safe when they go after Milo. That's why I sent him with them. Alarms are just as dangerous as men."

"Your priorities are a thing of mystery, Mr. Justice. We need aid here, not there. They'll be fine against a single combatant or his lack thereof. We conversely are outgunned and outnumbered, with only our wit and cunning to our advantage."

"Just focus, please," Jim said. "Is Willard still patrolling the lower level?"

"The last I saw, he walked under a grated walkway. He should be near your end of the warehouse soon, if he's not already." He paused for a few seconds. "At least a getaway driver would have been nice. It's going to be a tight escape."

"Not if we play our cards right," Jim said.

"Yeah, nothing ever goes wrong on jobs like this, right?" Sarcasm was clear in Specter's voice.

"That attitude is not productive. Let's focus on doing this quietly. We can leave the body here. Worst case, officials find this place and do our job for us."

"Agreed. I see him. He's headed toward the southern door you're posted up outside of. Get ready down there."

Jim fully took out the wakizashi at his side and held it, blade pointing down at the ground. He heard the door pushing open behind his cover, along with a male voice and footsteps.

"Lower level is clear. We're checking the outer perimeter now. Stay alert."

"With all due respect, sir," another unfamiliar male voice said. "Do we predict we're going to be attacked?"

"We don't know. That's why we're prepared, you fool,"

Willard said. "Now come on. The sooner we patrol, the sooner we get back inside."

"Why haven't you taken him out yet?" Specter asked in Jim's ear.

Jim waited until the pair's footsteps faded away as they circled around the building the other way. "There were two. We're going to have to coordinate. I can't take out two targets before they know I'm there - not quietly anyway."

"Fair enough. What do you need?"

"You mentioned they patrol in a circle and enter back inside via this door, correct?" Jim asked.

"From what I've seen the past hour, yeah."

"Then before they turn the corner to come to my side again, I want you to drop one of your creations on their heads."

"I don't believe explosives would be quiet, but I might drop an aerosolized downer on them."

"You can grapple hook out of the immediate vicinity, yes?"

"Yes. I can hit that streetlamp if I must."

"Then use an explosive," Jim said. "I don't want to take chances on either target surviving. The girls should be moving. Milo left just as we got here. As soon as I hear the explosion, I'll turn the corner and finish them. We run, or swing in your case, like hell after that. Are we clear on the plan?"

"If you believe it's our best course, I'll do as you say. Be aware, this will be loud. Cover your ears," Specter said into his ear. "I'll just have to guess on the fuse delay."

"You do that," Jim said, moving toward the end of the warehouse where the men would approach soon. He peeked his head around the corner to see a lone stationary guard looking through the city streets. He ducked back behind cover with a curse under his breath. "Shit," he said.

"Something wrong down there? They're not close yet."

"There's a guard that sits stationary." Jim's voice was barely audible, barely a whisper.

"I can drop two if that helps."

"It couldn't hurt," Jim said. "God knows these people aren't innocent. I don't like indiscriminate killing, but he's joined with their organization. That's close enough."

"There's no feeling guilty about these gentlemen on my end. I'll adjust," Specter said.

Jim reached up to his shoulder holster and brought out his handgun. He made sure it was loaded by ejecting the magazine before reinserting it and pulling the slide back. "Fuck being quiet on this one," he said before sheathing the blade.

"Do you make a habit of talking to yourself? You know your microphone is open, right?"

"Focus on your own job," Jim said. "I'm just making sure this will be quick," he said.

"They turned the corner. They should be visible if you peek around. Once they're near the still guard, I'll drop the packages. I'd recommend staying behind the corner until they explode. They do have nails and such you'd rather not have pierced into your flesh."

"Listen to Mr. IED," Jim said. "Wish I knew how to make those."

"Maybe some other time. Now pay attention. It's game time."

Silence replaced the hushed conversation as Jim waited just around the corner. He wiped a bead of sweat off his face and looked at his shaky hand holding the pistol. "Just like old times," he said under his breath.

"Dropping now." Specter's voice was barely audible. "Take cover down there."

Jim leaned away from the corner when he heard two distinct noises, along with indistinct male voices yelling.

"Oh shit," Specter's voice could be heard.

The next moment a loud blast erupted around the corner. The surge in noise left Jim temporarily hearing a loud ringing in his ears. He shook his head and sidestepped around the corner. He saw one man laying slumped against the warehouse. His eyes were closed, and numerous puncture wounds could be seen perforating his torso. The door flew open and their target came out brandishing his own handgun.

Jim opened fire immediately upon confirming his target, firing three times in rapid succession.

His target took cover behind the still open door. Jim saw a gun angling around the corner before quickly hiding back behind cover. "Oh fuck me," he said.

"You need to leave now," Specter said over the earpiece. "His men are already mobilizing."

"Working on it," Jim yelled. Once the shots stopped, he pivoted around the corner and fired. More men funneled out of the warehouse. His shots struck one after another, some falling, others seeking cover behind nearby vehicles.

"I'll take care of them. Prepare to run if you know what's good for you."

Jim could barely hear any of Specter's instructions, but he made out the word run above all else.

"Grenade!" a male voice cried out.

"Open the door!"

That was the last phrase Jim heard before another blast rocked his ears. Inhumane screaming met his ears, along with whimpering.

"I'm leaving now. I suggest you do the same," Specter said.

Jim holstered his pistol and took off into a sprint out of the warehouse's parking lot. He heard shots as he exited his cover. He ducked his head, keeping as low as he could while maintaining speed. Above him, he could see Specter swinging in the same direction. "What did that shit mean before you dropped them?"

"As I dropped them, our primary target and his partner switched up their patrol route. I think all we got was one of his men outside."

"I shot him, but it wasn't a head shot. Three body shots are all I had. If he's as good as we think, he was wearing a vest."

"It's not like you could've run up there to finish him," Specter said. He paused as Jim looked up mid run and saw Specter land on a nearby roof. "His men inside were mobilizing as soon as the blast went off."

"All we did was alert them," Jim said. "Perhaps we scared the piss out of them."

"Fear causes mistakes in even the greatest of minds. We may have sown the seeds of victory and not yet even know it."

"Be careful getting back." Jim finally reached his car and flung the door open. "I'm heading back now. Will you be alright?"

"I'll be fine. I took the scenic route in, and I'll be taking it out. Don't start the festivities without me."

"Right..."

Half an hour earlier in a different part of town...

"He really doesn't like Specter," Ashley said. "Does he?

How do you think they're doing? I don't know how they plan on killing the chief of security, of all things."

"She's quite the chatterbox when she's nervous, isn't she?" Jason asked.

"I am not nervous." Ashley turned around and slapped Jason's leg. "I have an active imagination is all."

"They'll be fine," Skye said. "They'll either come up with something or come back empty-handed."

"Those are the optimistic choices," Ashley said. "We all know the other option. It's not like this is a safe hobby we have. Plus, they are at their base for lack of a better term."

The cabin went quiet at the implication of her statement.

"Let's focus more on our job than theirs," Skye said. "Worrying about them won't aid us. We can't allow ourselves to be distracted."

"Quite right," Jason said. "Now, our target is inside that house over there." Jason pointed toward a nearby backyard.

"The guy must make bank to live in a luxurious house by himself," Ashley said. "One hundred bucks says he has an alarm system."

"Maybe," Jason said. "Maybe not. I'd bet not because his employers wouldn't want the police anywhere near him. If an alarm goes off, the neighbors would call them, and there he'd be. It's not like I can tell if he has one on such short notice, anyway."

"You can't tell?" Ashley asked. "What's the good of you being here then? Can you shut it off if there is one?"

"I am not magical. The answer to your outlandish question is a resounding no. I cannot work miracles of that magnitude. What I can do, however, is shut off all the recording devices he possesses in his house. He has quite a few. There's a laptop, a television, a virtual reality headset with a camera, and, of course, quite a few audio recording devices disguised as convenience items."

"What good will that do?" Ashley asked.

"It will make sure his friends won't know who kidnapped their boy genius. It will also leave no evidence of your being present should the police see the recordings. I'll also be backup should you two need it."

"Let's hope it doesn't come to that," Skye said. "Do we have the handcuffs?"

"Do not ask about how many fucking weird looks I received when I bought these. I'm sure I can never visit that store again," Ashley said. She pulled out a pair of handcuffs.

"I'd love to have been a fly on the wall of that store when you bought those babies," Jason said. "Those will be helpful in securing Milo. I'd recommend putting those on his hands, not his ankles. You'll want him able to walk."

"No duh," Ashley said.

"Let's move, folks," Skye said. She made sure her neck gaiter was secured and donned the covering over her eyes. She reached into her hoodie pocket and retrieved a roll of duct tape before placing it back inside. "Ashley, you'll be the muscle here. I'll watch your back."

"Me?"

"Yeah. I'm more of a ranged intimidator, not melee. That's your domain. You're good with that blade. Just don't cause any fatal damage. We'll convince his ass to come along."

Ashley secured her identity concealing garments. "Let's do this. We're sure his bedroom is upstairs?"

"That's according to these floor plans and his laptop camera." Jason flipped the laptop so they could see it. He pointed toward the window showing a dark room and a bed, along with a distinctive human shape lying in it. "He's in there alright. Someone's downstairs inside a bedroom too. Oh, here's one more piece of advice before you head inside. Open the back gate. You don't want a nerd trying to climb a fence while his hands are tied. It'd take forever and would make a lot of noise."

"Good idea," Skye said. "Let's go."

"Right behind you."

The pair got out and made their way to the chain-link fence surrounding the multi-story house and climbed over it. Skye quickly unlocked the nearby gate and pushed it open. They jogged through the backyard to the backdoor.

"Once we're inside, the stairs should be on our left," Skye said. She tried the door, only to find it locked. "Pick this, would you? You learned that, I think."

"Damned right I did," Ashley said. She pulled out her lock-picking tools and got to work.

Skye kept a look out while her friend worked. "What are the odds this guy comes in easy?"

"I'd give it a one in three chance," Ashley said. "He's not going to want to appear weak if he lives through this, or else his group would disown him and kill him."

"I'd say more one in two," Jason said. "He'll recognize he's outgunned and outmaneuvered."

"Done," Ashley said, lowering her voice. "Let's pray there is no alarm or we'll be on a ticking clock. Ready?"

"Hurry. This is a middle class neighborhood," Jason said. "If there was ever a location for a peeping Tom nosy neighbor, this area fits the damned bill."

Ashley stood up and filed away her lock-picking tools before opening the door to no alarm blaring.

Skye slipped inside first. She looked over her shoulder and kept her voice hushed. "Get the handcuffs ready. It will be our first order of business when we find him."

"This place is a nerd's paradise." Ashley reached into her pocket and pulled out the handcuffs. She looked at the fifty-inch flatscreen hooked up to multiple game consoles on top of a nearby desktop. "What is that headset looking thing?"

"Can you focus?" Skye asked.

"It's probably a virtual reality headset," Jason said.

"Is that why it's spartan inside? It's just a sofa and a wide gulf between it and the screen."

"The last scenario you want is to knock stuff over while you're immersed in virtual reality."

"Focus," Skye said. She reached out and grabbed Ashley's hand. She dragged her away from the door and past said electronics, heading toward the nearby stairwell.

"I was just wondering is all."

The pair stalked through the dark interior and climbed up the stairs. They crept through the hallway and stopped in front of the bedroom's wooden door. They heard snoring behind it.

"You get his hands. I'll cover his mouth." She pulled out the duct tape and ripped a large piece off. She stuffed the roll back in her pocket and used her now free hand to open the bedroom door.

They walked shoulder to shoulder into the room. Ashley took the left side, closer to his feet, while Skye took the right, inching closer to Milo's top half.

Ashley reached the bed first, then waited for Skye to get in position before nodding at her. She reached down and enveloped Milo's left wrist with the handcuffs and then his right. She closed them together with a satisfying click.

Without waiting, Skye shoved the tape over Milo's mouth.

Predictably, his eyes opened. It was slow at first. He blinked slowly and rolled his head from side to side. His eyes went wide, and he struggled to move his hands. Muffled speech erupted from behind the tape.

"Easy now," Skye said. She reached down and grabbed an arm. "You're coming with us."

"You should be happy," Ashley said. "This is the only instance your geeky ass will ever feel a woman physically touch you. You should savor it and thank us. Get up." She punched him in the ribs. She grabbed a leg and pulled it off the bed.

"If you stand up, put your jeans on, and walk, this will go faster and easier. If you make it hard for us, well, you don't need all your fingers, right?" She looked over at Ashley. "You can still type with nine or eight fingers, right?"

"Probably," she said.

Milo squirmed under their hands, trying to evade them any way he could.

"Really?" Skye asked. "You're going to do this? Recognize when you're at a disadvantage and take your loss with grace, sir." She placed her hands on either side of his shoulders and pinned him on his back. "Fine, have it your way. Get your blade out, Blind Justice. He wants it rough. Oblige him."

Ashley pulled out her short sword and raised it above her head. "Foot or hand?"

"I don't know." Skye looked over at Ashley before turning back to Milo. "Do you want me to choose?"

He shook his head no.

"You'll be a good boy and come quietly? It's that, or we cut off body parts to make you lighter for us to carry. We're delicate after all, as you've put together."

He allowed himself to be pulled to a sitting position and swung his legs over the side of the bed. Eventually, he relented and followed their orders with a smirk adorning his face.

"There, see?" Skye asked. "All he needed was a little persuasion."

"Uh, guys?" Jason's voice was in their ear. "I think you should hurry and exit."

"Come on, then." Skye pulled him up to his feet. "We're not staying here all night. You're going to meet our boss. Surely you've heard of him? Masked Justice is quite famous at this point."

Ashley pushed him forward, toward the hallway. She kept her hand on his shoulder, helping guide him where they wanted. "What is it anyway, Guardian?"

"I think you might have set off an alarm."

"There's no alarm," Skye said as the trio entered the hallway leading to the stairs. "We'd hear it if we did."

"You wouldn't hear a silent alarm. I didn't find it earlier, but ever since you two went inside, I've caught a signal that wasn't there before. It's safe to assume he had a silent alarm rigged. He wouldn't want a noisy one where people could call the cops. He'd easily rig it to alarm the Patterson family, though. I'd assume reinforcements are incoming, so get out of there," he said.

"Hurry," Skye pushed him forward toward the front door after she hopped down the last step. "You're going to see a car with an open back seat. You're going to hop inside, or we're going to stuff you in the trunk. Do you understand?"

Milo nodded, coming to a stop in front of the backdoor they led him to.

"Good." Skye stepped forward and opened the door to the backyard.

"If you try to make a run for it, she'll shoot your legs and we'll still take you. Don't test her aim." Ashley forced him to follow Skye by shoving him with most of her strength. She shut the door and followed behind Skye and Milo.

Skye saw the back door of the car was already open. Jason was visible with his neck gaiter up over his nose.

He scooted over and exited the car, standing beside it. "Is he riding up front, or is he being difficult?"

"He's up front." Skye shoved him inside. "Now move over." She looked over at Ashley. "You're on the other side. I want both of you sitting on either side. Keep your eyes on him. I don't want him anywhere near Guardian's laptop."

"We're on it," Ashley said. She circled around the car and flung open the driver's side back door and disappeared inside. She looked over at Milo inspecting the vehicle. He constantly rotated his focus from each of the three and the car itself.

Skye got in the driver's seat and closed the door. "Keep a low profile. Get him blindfolded. We can't drive around with masks on all over the city this late."

Ashley reached down toward the floor and picked up a folded piece of cloth. "You nearly lost it, Guardian. Don't be sloppy," she said. She tied the makeshift blindfold over Milo's head, making sure it covered his eyes totally. "You've been well behaved," Ashley said. "Keep that up and you may yet live."

"Really?" Milo's muffled voice asked.

Jason leaned forward and looked at Ashley. He shook his head but remained silent.

"Sure. I'm not the one you'd have to convince, though. You'll meet him later. If I were you, I'd be helpful. He's not a real patient kind of guy," Ashley replied as she removed the tape from his mouth.

"Why are you taking us on?" Milo asked. "I don't remember us ever screwing over you vigilante types. We don't touch kids or anything like that. Why are you doing this?"

"That's not for us to explain," Skye said from the driver's seat. Her hands were firmly planted on the steering wheel, having already removed her masks. "Nor is it your business to know. You focus on staying agreeable, and maybe I'll put in a good word for you."

"I don't think he'll be much good." Jason spat on Milo. His spit spattered on Milo's cheek. "You make money for those who spread misery. Your skills are wasted, and you've built your career on the destruction of others' lives."

"You realize they'll be coming for me, right?" Milo asked, his voice shaky. "They need me. They're going to kill all of you."

"I'm sure they will try," Skye said.

"That's assuming they ever find you," Jason said with a sneer. He rifled through Milo's pants pockets before extracting a cell phone. He rolled down the nearby window and tossed it onto the road. "No more phone for you. It may have had valuable intel, but it'd be too easy to track. I doubt you removed anything that could be tracked. You don't strike me as smart enough."

"Think what you like," Milo said before taking a deep breath. "It's not like you'll ever like me anyway."

"He's got more sass in him than I thought he would," Ashley said. "I thought he was supposed to be timid."

"That is the stereotype after all, right?" Milo asked. He leaned as the car turned.

"Intimidation without ability won't earn many points," Jason said. "Talk it up now while you can. You'll tell us what we want. That I guarantee."

Milo turned to Jason. "We will see, you loudmouthed simpleton..."

12

"Do you find the accommodations lacking?" Ashley mocked Milo. She looked down at him, tied to the chair under the oppressive light shining on him. "Too bad."

"This is your first time questioning prisoners," Milo said.

"Is that right?" Jason asked, circling around the seat. "Why does the tech specialist say that? It's not like you'd know the kidnapping protocol of your group." He stopped in front of Milo and bent down to get to his eye level. "Would you?"

"He's trying to appear tough," Skye said. "Let him have his fun. The boss should be back soon."

"The boss," Milo snorted. "I'm waiting for another psycho in a ghetto ass mask to waltz through that door."

"Ghetto?" Ashley asked.

"Yeah, you look like wannabe gang members with that mask covering your mouth."

Ashley lashed out with an open palm to slap Milo's cheek. "You're lucky I can't really hurt you until the questioning starts. You have no decorum, insulting a lady's choice of dress. Didn't your mom ever teach you how to talk to a woman?"

"Take it easy," Skye said, walking over to Ashley and placing a hand on her shoulder. "As for you..." She looked back at Milo. "The tough talk and the bravado aren't doing you any favors."

"Fuck you."

"Alright then." Skye took a few steps forward and stood in front of their prisoner. As she looked down at him, she heard a door opening nearby.

"I see you all were successful," Jim said, walking over. "Is this him?"

Skye backed up, allowing Jim access to Milo. "It sure is. He's being stubborn about answering our questions."

"Maybe I can persuade him then," Jim said. He got closer, replacing Skye's former spot. "You want to survive today?"

"Obviously," Milo said. "What kind of question is that?"

"He's been smart mouthed for a while now," Skye said, her tone bored. "We figured we'd let you two handle it from here. How did your job go?"

"Let's not talk about it," Specter said, coming up on Jim's side.

"You are going to tell us every minute detail," Jim said. His tone left no room for disagreement.

Milo didn't get the hint. "Am I now?"

"You sure are. I can tell from looking at how you're sitting that you think you're tough. You think you're hard. You work for one of the worst, most heinous criminal groups in the state; but that doesn't mean you are immune to consequences. Now if I were you, I'd give up that combative rhetoric really quick." He looked to his side. "Specter, get the tools ready."

"With pleasure." He walked over to the multitude of tables and picked up a toolbox before returning and plopping it down beside Jim.

"You wouldn't," Milo said.

"Is that a question or a statement?" Jim got to a knee and opened the box. He rummaged around the toolbox while talking to himself. "Should I use the hammer, screwdriver, or something altogether different? Tell me your preference. You aren't talking and will be loyal to your crime family, yes?"

"Come on, man. If I talk, they kill me."

"They're not here currently," Jim said. "We are. I guess I'll pick the hammer. I always wondered if breaking a kneecap was as easy as the mob movies made it look."

"Wait a minute. You haven't even asked questions."

"What's the point if you're going to play tough guy?" Jim got to his feet, clasping the hammer in his right hand in a tight grip. "I'll release some pent up anger instead. Do you want to answer my questions?"

"Ask your questions."

"That was a quick turn," Ashley said. "A little show of force and you crack? I'm a little disappointed."

"Guardian, ask him your questions," Jim said.

Jason moved over to stand by Jim and Specter. "What's your network passwords? I want them all."

Milo looked between the group of masked vigilantes, searching for any option to not answer. "It's a complex string of numbers, mixed capitalized and lowercase letters, along with special characters. You'd need to write it down. That's just for the main warehouse's network password. That's not getting into how many passwords you'll need to access all the files within."

"We'll come back to that later," Jason said. "What are you all doing for Martha Henderson?"

"Martha Henderson? You're familiar with her, I assume?" Milo asked. "She tasked us with swiping young women for some international guy who runs a brothel in international waters."

"How would you know this?" Jason asked. He moved behind Milo.

"You strike me as the tech guy in this outfit. Surely you know everything that happens with your crew. My job is encrypting, securing, and making sure our deeds never go public. I know everything. It would be such a waste to kill me afterward. I can make your job easy if you want to take them down."

"He's singing like a canary now," Skye said.

"Tell us where your muscle are scouting for the merchandise," Jason said. "We can't let them be taken to a private island to be abused."

"Aren't you a knight in regular shining gaiter? They go to a local college. It's not like this job is a huge rush job. They attend every weekend. Drunk girls are much easier to corral to hear the men tell it. It's a wonder what you hear when they think no one else is listening. I would assume that's where they'll go. Check the bars and you'll find some activity. It's not like you'll be able to stop them all with this paltry number you all have."

"What do you know about Willard MacDonald?" Jim interrupted Jason's interrogation.

"I don't know shit about the dude, and I don't want to. To say he's dedicated is an understatement. Hell, he'd kill me if he knew what I've said already. Why? Was your other job to kill MacDonald? I'm guessing you failed from your earlier response."

"What does he oversee?" Jim asked.

"He's security. He deals with security breaches, keeps people doing their jobs, and keeps unwanted civilians and wannabe superheroes out."

Jim swung the hammer down on Milo's knee.

Milo's head snapped back with a yell. "What? I answered the question!"

"So you did. Less sass, more class," Specter said.

"Specifics, Milo, we want specifics."

"He tells the guards where they'll patrol, when, and when they can eat, sleep, whatever. Think of him as the defensive specialist overseeing the group. They rely on him to keep the operation up and running. He has his right-hand man he's been training. Anything else you want to know about the guy?" Milo jerked against his bonds, trying to free himself.

"Allow me, if you please," Specter gently pushed Jim to the side. "How many are in your department?"

"The tech division? There's only three of us. I'm training the other two. Why? Do you want to know how valuable your catch is worth?"

"Wishful thinking that we're going to sell you back," Jim said.

"Now, now," Specter said, shaking his head and patting Jim's back before his partner moved behind Milo. "How do you all transport the women to Henderson?"

"You expect me to know that?" Milo asked with a roll of his eyes. "That's not my department. All I know is that when they have them corralled on one of these jobs, they ship them via truck usually. At least, that's what happens when we work with Henderson. I don't know what type of truck. I don't know where they head, and I frankly don't wish to learn. Knowing too much can get you killed."

"Knowing too little has that same effect," Jason said, crossing his arms behind Milo. "How do we disrupt your boss's plans?" Jim returned to the front and knelt.

"Seriously?"

"He's quite serious," Jim said. He lowered the hammer and placed it on the concrete below, then looked at the white sneakers Milo wore. "Nice shoes. What size are they?"

"Thirteen, why?" Milo asked.

Jim untied them and removed them from Milo. He placed them to the side before picking the hammer up again. "Just wondering. Are you going to answer the question?" He lowered it until the business end of the tool rested atop Milo's feet.

"Heading to the bars would disrupt the kidnappings, but good luck. You'd be better off causing a disturbance in the area that evening."

"Elaborate," Jim said, never wavering, still holding the hammer ready to crush his foot.

"I don't care what you do. Go around in your getups and cause a ruckus, go in plain clothes and start a bar fight - the sky's the limit. If you disrupt the area and get a lot of kids to go back to the dorms, it'll stifle their efforts."

"Talk about a temporary stop-gap measure," Skye said.

"You didn't ask for a long-term solution. You asked how to disrupt them. I answered to the best of my knowledge. Don't crush my foot, man. I look after my little brother at home, and he's in a wheelchair."

"A likely story," Ashley said.

"Fair enough," Jim said. He stood up and rested the cold steel on his chest. "This will just break a rib. You'll still be able to walk with enough willpower. You can muster that for your little bro, right?"

"I'm going to go retrieve a notepad," Jason said, still

standing directly behind Milo. "When I return, you're going to tell us the network passwords and any outstanding folders I need to find. If not, you know the consequences of your stubbornness." Jason walked to the nearby tables and grabbed a notepad and a pen before walking back.

"You expect me to remember over a dozen symbols and their capitalization, under pain of torture?"

"Yes," Jim said. "Now list them off."

"I honestly don't remember. Now don't -"

Jim swung the hammer, not giving his full strength but hard enough to elicit a scream of pain from their prisoner. "That's broken. Now, did that jog your memory?"

"Oh, God!" Milo grunted, sweat pouring down his face. "It's Five, one, capital H, lower case u, six, asterisk, zero, comma, capital q, lower case k, eight, two, and ends with capital J. Are you happy now? Are you going to take me to the hospital for medical help? I think my clavicle is broken."

"That would be trusting you don't rat to Patterson or MacDonald," Jim said. "Why would I think you'd stay quiet? That'd be stupid. You may think us simple, but we're anything but."

"Come on, man," Milo said. "Surely you're not animals. We're all civilized here, right? Like you." He looked up at Specter.

"Do I look civilized?" Jim asked. "Look, kid, there's one way out of this where you're alive."

"There is?" Ashley asked.

"There is," Jim said. "You're not going to like it."

"I'll do it. Just don't kill me, man. My brother relies on me to survive day to day."

"Is that so?" Jim asked.

"I don't want you anywhere near Steven."

"I'm not going to hurt the kid. Do you think I'm a

fucking monster?" Jim used his left hand to slap Milo across the face. "That was for insinuating I'd harm a child, chuckles. We're just going to confirm you're telling the truth. After all, if you're willing to lie about your brother, you're willing to lie about anything under the sun to escape your punishment."

"Dude, he needs me to even get ready for school in the mornings. You can't keep me here all night."

"I don't think you're in any condition to help right now anyway," Skye said. "Do you have anyone else who could fill in during your recovery?"

"Maybe my aunt could."

"Perfect," Jim said. "Here's what's going to happen, Milo. We're going to confirm the existence of your brother. Assuming it all checks out, we're going to give you one phone call from a burner cell phone to call your aunt and set that up. If you try to tip her off or try to fuck us over, you're dead. Do you understand?"

"So long as you honor your word and don't hurt my brother, I get it. Do what you will to me, not Steven. Please. He's only eight years old."

"Guardian, you're coming with me. Blind, Silent, you're staying here to monitor our guest. Make sure he doesn't get himself into trouble. We'll pick up a burner phone on the way back."

"We'll have to move him before the call," Jason said. "Just to be safe. Wait."

Jim paused at hearing Jason. "For what?"

"What about that alarm?"

"What alarm?" Milo asked.

"The silent alarm alerting your syndicate," Jason said. "I noticed a signal erupting when we opened your door before."

"That wasn't an alarm. That was probably my webcam I placed in my brother's room. I installed it to ensure he goes to bed on time. You simply didn't notice it I'm betting. They wouldn't waste precious resources on me."

"Regardless of this alarm, we're agreed on moving him," Specter said. "I don't want any traceable signal anywhere near here."

"That's fine by me," Jim said. "Now don't cause trouble while we're gone, Milo." Jim nodded toward the warehouse entrance and walked off.

Jason followed Jim over. His voice was low enough so Milo couldn't hear as they walked further away. "Do we really believe this guy?"

"He knows he's dead if he lies. If he was lying, he'd have made some attempt to correct himself. He's either telling the truth or trying to waste our time in the hopes Patterson sends a rescue team. Since you destroyed his phone, they won't be able to find him to mount one." Jim pushed the door open and let Jason exit before letting it close behind him. He removed his mask and took a deep breath. "God, I hate wearing that thing. It feels like I'm being smothered a little."

Jason followed suit as they approached Jim's car. "That could be fixed with a different material, sir. Something breathable wouldn't be nearly so bad."

"Just focus up," Jim laughed as he opened his door and climbed inside.

Outside Milo's house...

"This feels wrong, sir," Jason said. "If he's telling the truth, it's a kid facing disabilities in there. It feels like we shouldn't go inside."

"I'm not going inside to harm anyone, buddy." Jim put his mask on, along with the one over his eyes, and raised the hoodie over his head. "I'm not going to even unsheathe a weapon. I'm just going to confirm the guy's story. If he's willing to lie about a disabled sibling, he's willing to lie about anything. That would put you, Ashley, Skye, and me at risk if we act on his intel. You get me?"

"I understand," Jason said. "It doesn't help me shake that feeling."

"Push through it, Jason," Jim said. "We're doing this to make sure all of us remain safe. Think of it that way. Besides, I'm the only one going in."

"May I go in too, sir?"

"Pardon me? Why? Who's going to watch over me while I'm inside?"

"This is in case it's a setup, sir," Jason said. "You never know. He could be lying and sending us into a death trap." Jason raised his shirt, revealing a loaded pistol. "I would watch your back inside to keep you alive. You need someone in there with you."

"Fine, if it makes you feel better. Just stay quiet in there and stay behind me. I cannot stress that enough. On Ashley's first job, she snuck off and killed the target without me. You will stay behind me."

"Got it."

"Alright then. Get your masks on, put on your gloves, and raise your hoodie - just to be safe. We don't want the kid seeing our faces if he's awake."

"I don't believe a disabled eight-year-old would be up this late, sir," Jason said.

"Wouldn't you? Imagine this scenario. You're eight, you live with your brother, and he's not home. What would you do? You'd stay up, whether that's because you're scared he hasn't come home yet, or because you always wanted to stay up past midnight playing video games. I can certainly see that possibility."

"Good point, sir. I'm ready when you are."

"Then let's move." Jim opened the door and spotted the house they were infiltrating across the street. He led Jason over to the small wooden fence lining its backyard and hopped over. Hurrying to the nearby backdoor, he placed his back on the brick wall and looked toward the fence to see Jason finally landing on the grass. He waved him over silently. When he got close, he spoke in a hushed voice. "The inside looks dark. That's a good sign. The kid probably went to sleep." One hand went into his jeans pocket and pulled out his lock-picking tools. "Watch for me. I'll unlock this."

Jason's head was on a proverbial swivel, constantly on the lookout for threats. "What do we do if he's telling the truth, boss?" Jason kept his voice low.

"We'll cross that bridge when we come to it," Jim said. He kept fiddling with the lock. His voice grew softer. "I'd rather not leave a disabled kid all alone in the world, Guardian."

"If we let the brother go free, he could squeal to the Patterson family. Then the entire operation is screwed proper."

"I am well aware of that possibility," Jim said. "We'll figure that out when we see if Milo's telling the truth. Now quiet. I almost have this." He twisted the skinny metal tools, and the lock clicked. He stood up and pocketed the lock-picking tools, then opened the door and entered quickly.

Jason followed him inside. He reached a hand out, grasping, fumbling in the darkness when he felt Jim's shoulder.

"This way," Jim said. He led the pair further inside, going slow. Multiple times Jim stopped suddenly along with a grunt of pain or the faint sound of an impact. "Shit," Jim hissed.

"Do you hear something?" Jason asked, his voice barely audible.

"Quiet, or I never take you inside again," Jim said. He led the pair around a nearby corner, out of the kitchen and toward a hallway. One door was closed, but unlike others, a faint light was visible from the cracks on the sides and bottom. Faint sounds of explosions and gunfire could be heard.

"Come on," a distinctly young male child's voice could be heard. "I hit him first. I can't believe this." The door popped open unexpectedly. The pair stood dead center of the hallway when it opened.

Jim pushed Jason backward. They backed up around a nearby corner into the living room. They pressed their backs to the wall. The ticking of a nearby clock hanging on the wall filled the room, along with the sound of a squeaky wheel rolling.

Jim could make out a wheelchair moving past them over toward the kitchen. "When is he getting back? Mom and Dad never made me wait like this. Why does his job make him go back in when it's late so often?"

They could hear a cupboard drawer open, followed by the refrigerator door opening. Pale light from the open refrigerator poured over Milo's brother. The sound of pouring liquid and the closing of the device filled their senses. The light flicked on afterward, followed by an audible gasp.

"Easy now," Jim said, trying to keep his voice filled with authority, but gentle. "We're here to help."

"Who are you?" A young child, around eight years old, sat upright in his wheelchair in the doorway leading to the tiled kitchen. A glass was spotted clutched in his dominant hand. His scraggly brown hair was going every which way, an obvious result of not combing or brushing it. His eyes danced back and forth between Jim and Jason. "Why are you in my house? I better call 911."

"Have you ever heard of superheroes?" Jim asked, ignoring the threat.

"You're a superhero? I don't think they sneak into people's houses at night."

"Normally, no we don't," Jim said. "We heard your brother was in trouble, though. We came here to save him."

Jason stared at Jim for a full minute before turning to the child.

"What's your name, mister? Are you going to hurt me?" The child rolled the chair backwards, away from the men, toward the phone mounted low on the nearby wall.

"My name is Masked Justice. We won't hurt you or your brother. We heard your brother is involved with some wicked men. Men that hurt people, and we're here to help him get free."

"You're not going to hurt my brother?" The kid's voice was gentle, almost brittle in its questioning.

"Just the opposite," Jim said in his best soothing voice. "A kind lady told us he was in trouble. We came to ask him questions so we can take him away from the evil criminals."

"My brother would never work for criminals," Steven said.

"First thing's first. What's your name?"

"My brother said to never tell my name to strangers."

"That is smart advice," Jim said, getting to a knee, trying

to bring himself to his eye level. "I'm Masked Justice." He pointed over his shoulder. "This is Guardian of Justice."

"You can call me Tyrol. It's my favorite game character's name."

"Okay, Tyrol. Do you know where your brother has ever worked?"

"Before Mom and Dad's accident, he used to work at a local mall. He was the nice employee at the gates that said hello to you when you entered and said goodbye when you exited. It was always fun when he was working. It forced him to be nice."

"Accident?" Jason asked.

"Mom and Dad died in a car accident. That's what made me crippled," Tyrol said. "My brother took me in and has been taking care of me ever since. He never acted like anything was wrong, but I'd catch him late at night staring at letters on the kitchen table talking to himself."

"Is that why he found a different job? For money?" Jim asked.

"Uh huh," Tyrol said. "Brother told me that money wouldn't ever be a problem again. He said my therapy could continue, and I might walk again."

"He's a fantastic brother, from the sounds of it," Jim said. "Say, are you alright here by yourself?"

"My brother should be home by now." Tyrol looked over toward the front door and the closed curtains covering the nearby window. "He's sometimes out late like this. It's been more often lately. I hate it. Is that why he's gone? Is it because he's in trouble?"

"We don't know, little buddy." Jim stood up. "We thought he'd be here. I'll tell you what, we're going to go find him. Do you ever have anybody else watch you?"

"Sometimes Aunt Leslie does. Oh, oops," Tyrol covered his mouth.

"Don't worry," Jim said with a laugh. "Aunt Leslie is safe. We'll make sure she comes over until your brother comes home, safe and sound. Now she'll be here tomorrow morning. You should go get some sleep. We'll go get your brother back."

"Okay then." Tyrol wheeled toward them a few feet. "How did you two get in, anyway? I locked the doors before I went into my room."

"Locked doors do not stop heroes. You should probably lock up again after we leave, which is momentarily. Come on, Guardian. Let's let the young man have his sleep."

"Is he your sidekick?" He watched the two masked vigilantes pass him as he turned around and followed them to the backdoor.

"I suppose he is, isn't he?" Jim said. "Did you hear that, Guardian? You're my sidekick."

"That's fine by me," Jason said.

"Alright, we probably won't meet again, Tyrol, but farewell. I hope you make a full recovery, and your brother can be happy again."

"Okay." Tyrol watched them open the door and step through into the backyard. "Please help my big brother!" He cupped his hands around his mouth. "He has a big mouth. Please try to be nice to him, even if he is mean. Okay?"

"Sure," Jim said before the pair ran toward the fence. Jim heard the door close. He and Jason climbed the fence and got back into the car.

"Superheroes?" Jason asked as Jim started the vehicle's engine. He buckled up and looked at Jim. "Do you think the kid believed that? Steven? Was that his real name?"

"It was," Jim said, tearing off the mask over his mouth.

"The kid wanted to be called a fake name, so I did. I didn't want him to panic. Steven will be fine. Now let's make sure we stop and get a burner phone. Then we can start planning on Milo's release plan."

"The guy is a jackass," Jason said.

"He is, but even jackasses have loved ones," Jim said, glancing at Jason. "He won't squeal to his bosses."

"How do you know that?" Jason asked. "The guy's as slimy as they come."

"We know where his brother stays. He knows we can deliver on any threats we make. We know we'd never hurt the kid, but he sure doesn't. We can threaten Steven and get him to help us. At the very least, we could guarantee he doesn't run to his boss. It's enough with what he's already given us."

"My money's that the kid is calling the police as we speak," Jason said. "He was way too calm."

"That would be fine too," Jim said. "I noticed you didn't like Milo much."

"Says the man who broke his kneecap and possibly a rib."

"I don't condone his work choices, but I don't have a problem with the man personally. He put on a brave front and then spilled when the pain started. I dangled the carrot above his head about letting him leave, and he took it. What's so bad about that?"

"Just because he has good reason to work with Patterson doesn't mean I'm forced to excuse his actions."

"Fair enough…"

13

The warehouse door opened and in marched Jim and Jason before it slammed shut, masks obscuring their faces. "We're moving him."

"His story checked out?" Skye asked.

"Are we escorting him to the middle of nowhere, to fall off the edge of the earth?" Ashley asked.

"I'm interested to hear as well," Specter said. "Was he lying? He didn't seem like he was. It's always hard to tell with these types."

"These types?" Milo asked, still tied up to the chair between all of them. "I just work with computers. I'm not a bad guy, really."

"He has a kid brother in a wheelchair. He's a nice kid. Now there are conditions for your release. You remember that part, right?"

"You didn't go into specifics," Milo said. "Yes, I remember, perfectly clear."

"We're about to get into that. Now help me get him in the car. Put the blindfold on him, and we'll get started."

"Must we?" Milo asked in a nasally, whiny voice. He

kicked his feet out in vain with a shake of his head. "I don't care where we are, so long as we get home."

"We have procedures," Jim said. "Take it, or we leave you with a dirt nap. Which would you like? I imagine Steven wants his big brother back, so let's just not complain about trivial things." Jim leaned down close to Milo after securing the piece of cloth that Skye handed him around Milo's eyes. "If you try to run or try anything stupid when we untie you from that chair, Steven will have a harder life. None of us want that, so act smart and keep calm. You'll be back home before you know it. Do not test me. You already know what happens if you do."

"Silent, untie his legs. Blind, keep your weapon at the ready in case he does something stupid." He gripped Milo's shoulders with an iron grasp. "Guardian, undo his arm restraints. Now, who's coming with me on this little escort besides Guardian? We don't need anyone else, but more is safer."

"I'll go with you two," Skye said, taking a step toward them after the leg ties were loosened.

"I will too. It might be tight, but whatever." Ashley held on to Milo's arm after freeing it. "Now let's get you up. Stand up and wait."

Milo stood up and fell to a knee with a groan.

"Right, the whole knee thing. I guess you can't." Jim said. "Guardian, you take his left side. I'll take his right. We'll put him in the back. On my mark, go." He put Milo's right arm over his shoulder as Jason did the same to Milo's left.

"You all be careful," Specter called out after them as they walked away. "I'm going to work on my project."

"Good luck," Jim said back over his shoulder.

"Be careful out there," Skye said.

"Don't do anything I wouldn't," Ashley said.

"That goes double for you all!" Specter yelled as the door was swinging shut.

The group carried him over to Jim's car and dumped him in the back seat. Skye and Ashley got on either side of Milo, while Jim entered the driver's seat and Jason sat in the passenger seat up front. Jim started the engine. "Double check the blindfold."

"We just put it on him," Ashley said with a scoff.

Skye didn't object, and did the routine check. "It's on tight."

"Good." Jim lowered the neck gaiter and lowered the hoodie before bringing the car out onto the city roads. "We're taking you somewhere where you can do us a quick favor, and you'll be home before you know it."

"I already gave you the location of where they hunt, their network's password, and my advice. What more could you want?"

"That's for Guardian to say."

"You're going to show me every backdoor into that system. I want to know how to get inside without Patterson's other techs noticing. I want to know every little trick."

"That will take a while."

"That's fine," Jim said. "You'll do that and move into our good graces."

"You also want me to never head into work too, I assume? They'll kill me for going AWOL." Milo bit his lip. "You know what I mean?"

"That's just the thing," Jim said. "We don't want you to cause a fuss. You're going to be our inside man."

"It just keeps getting better," Milo said, obviously not amused. "You said nothing about playing spy for you. That's a deadly game."

"It's still better odds than pissing us off," Skye said. "We're still able to go to the wilderness if you prefer?"

"It'd be a shame about poor Steven, though," Jason said. "He loves his brother. I'd hate to disappoint him."

"You'd get over it," Ashley said.

"You're right."

"There's also the fact that we know where he lives. We know his babysitter, and we're awful petty, if you catch my drift, Milo. Don't make us do that. We're not even asking you to sabotage them. All we're asking you to do is send us messages when you catch something on the proverbial grapevine. Surely you all have some kind of water cooler chatter?"

"I wouldn't have to do anything they'd notice?" Milo asked.

"You're the boss of your department, right?" Ashley asked. "Just use your own good judgement. So long as we don't get blindsided due to you, you're fine."

"He wouldn't let that happen," Skye said.

"Where are we even going?" Milo asked.

"Near your workplace. Not anywhere they could spot us, but close enough to get into their network. We told you that you're going to show Guardian the ins and outs of it."

"Chill, it was just a question," Milo said. "It's disorienting being tied up in a car. More than they make it seem in the movies. You take for granted how you lean when you see a turn coming."

Ashley leaned away from Milo as they made a sharp turn. "Lean the other way."

"Children," Jim said. "Please, behave yourselves back there."

"You'll be lucky if Willard isn't frothing at the mouth," Milo said. "If you really tried to kill him earlier, he's whipped into a frenzy. I guarantee it. I wouldn't be anywhere near that place if I were you. He'll have men and women roaming the streets for anybody suspicious. A parked car with us in it is going to be suspicious."

"Then I suppose it'd be in your best interest to make sure that doesn't happen."

"It's not like I can countermand his orders, even if I were there at my post. In fact, I'd be relaying the messages and encrypting them to his soldiers. If you're hell bent on this, then at least stop at an electronics store and get a signal booster. It'd give you another block or two of range."

"We already have one," Jason said. "It's almost like I know what I'm doing."

"Whatever you say," Milo said. "Guardian, was it?"

"Yeah? What about it?"

"How much knowledge do you have of cyber security? I'm asking if you have basic knowledge, a few classes, or are you a full-blown expert? It will help to know your skill level in how I'm explaining all this."

"Think of me between knowledgeable and expert. I know enough to know if you try to lie to me or double cross us. You will not be touching a keyboard here anyway, for safety's sake."

"How the hell do you expect me to show you anything without being allowed to touch the keyboard, you idiot?" Milo asked. "Look, I'm not so stupid to call for help while in your company. Let me work my magic. It'll go faster."

"Fine."

"We're ten minutes out," Jim said.

Skye spoke. "Blind and I will leave the vehicle and be an early warning system. We'll watch for any of Patterson's men. He mentioned that he'd have men searching the vicinity after all."

"Good idea," Jim said.

"Let me claim an elevated position. I hate standing next to dumpsters."

"More than likely you'll be at street level," Milo said. "There are not a lot of buildings. You'll be lucky to be out of their line of sight."

"We hid behind a sign last time, but a police cruiser interrupted us," Ashley said.

"Use the parking lot nearby. It has a few buildings for cover and it's out of the warehouse's line of sight. Police don't patrol there. It's quieter."

"How would you know that?"

"That was orientation. We were told to park nowhere near that sign. It was by Willard himself. He's realized the cops use that as a speed trap and that we should be on our guard."

"He's paranoid, tough, and tenacious from the sounds of it," Ashley said. "Is there anything else to this guy?"

"It's plain to see you guys have no idea how far Willard goes for his job." Milo shook his head and bit his lip. "Think military trained bodyguard with a personality reminiscent of a sea of razor blades, and you get the idea. Conversing with the man is not pleasant. Fighting him is worse. If I could pick any living soul to have by my side in a heated fight, it'd be MacDonald."

"Aw," Jim said with a sarcastic bite. "After all we'd been through, I thought we'd grown closer."

"I've never seen any of you in a fight," Milo said while shifting in his seat. "I have seen him beat the ever-loving shit out of a guy for slacking off on duty. The guy accidentally fell asleep on guard duty, and a homeless guy sneaked in. I found out when I reviewed the cameras and relayed which guard it was. Right after I'd told him," Milo audibly gulped, "he spotted the guy taking a coffee break and dragged him outside."

"Naturally you followed to watch," Skye said.

"Not just me," Milo said. "A crowd of men did. He beat that man within an inch of his life. He used brass knuckles, creatively used his lighter, and shoved the guy's own rings up his -"

"I don't want to hear the nasty details," Ashley said. "Skip that part."

"I'm pretty sure the only reason he didn't kill him was because he wanted to punish him more. That theory was backed up a few weeks later. I noticed he would always give that guy the shit jobs. You know, the dangerous ones. He never got a cushy gig ever again, to my knowledge."

"Okay, the guy's possibly psychopathic," Jason said. "That's not an enormous surprise, given who he works for with such fervor."

The car came to a stop. They parked on the opposite side of the warehouse from earlier, across a playground park, behind a tree line, obscuring the warehouse. "We're here. Let's hurry this up in case Milo is correct about Willard's zeal and willingness to waste working hours."

"You two, get out and keep watch. Join our call, and we'll keep you informed on how it's going. Be sure to speak up the moment you spot any hostiles approaching," Jim said.

"Let's go. Guardian, I assume you'll be moving back here to do whatever this is you're doing."

Skye and Ashley exited the car.

"Where are we posting up?" Ashley planted her hands on her hips and studied the nearby tree line and children's park nearby. "Is that a playground?"

Skye looked over at the sandbox, swings, slides, and assorted children's activities. "Looks like it. I think I'll post up in one of those trees between us and their warehouse." She pointed at the tree line. "It should give me good sight-lines. You have your choice. Just watch this park area and my back. Between the two of us, we're covered on both sides. Personally, I'd either go with the top of the slide or the monkey bars."

"Yeah, because that's low profile. I'll climb the ladder on that shack of a building that looks like a shop."

"The food shack? Go for it," Skye said. She ran off from the car toward the tallest, sturdiest looking tree that had plenty of thick branches. Reaching up, she grabbed the nearest low branch while the other arm wrapped around the trunk. She wrapped her legs around the tree and used the friction to push herself up using the power of her legs. She climbed on top of the branch she gripped and looked up. "How's it going over there?"

"There's nobody outside this late. I see a local baseball field way off, but it's empty."

Skye continued her ascent. She was nearly twenty feet up at this point. "How about you two inside?"

"They're working," Jim said. "He seems to be doing as we ask. You two are armed, yes?"

"I'm always armed when we go out," Ashley said, "with both ranged and melee options."

"I'm fine," Skye said. "Hold on. Did they just do something?" She reached into her hoodie's pocket, pulled out a pair of binoculars, and looked over at the warehouse. Willard exited the building, along with a group of men.

"He showed me a backdoor into their camera system," Jason said. "Why?"

"Old MacDonald is not happy tonight," Skye said in a singing tone. "He looks pissed."

She could hear Milo over Jason's earpiece. "It wouldn't

be from me," he said. "The dude is a savant with security, but he's a regular Luddite with technology. The only way he'd know is if we tripped a safeguard I implemented. My apprentices aren't advanced enough to set up any defenses without telling me."

"To your knowledge," Ashley said. "Maybe someone wants to move up the food chain. What better method than to outperform your boss and brag to the brass?"

"If I'd set the system off, I'd know." Milo's voice was angry at this point. "Stop distracting me already, or I really might fuck up. Then we're all screwed, being this close to them."

The creak of the tree branch, the sound of distant engines, and the wind blowing in her ears was all Skye heard. The frosty night air enveloped her in its icy embrace. "He's yelling angrily at a bunch of regular guys."

"He's probably trying to make sure another attack doesn't catch them off guard," Jim said, his voice remaining cool and collected.

"Addendum," Skye said. "The sizeable group is splitting into smaller groups and leaving the warehouse property. They're in groups of three. It looks like five total groups are going out and searching. Ah shit," she said. "An armed group or two is headed closer. Let's think on our feet and deal with them."

"No firearms," Jim said. "We'd attract more attention than we want."

"Shall I move to a better position to welcome our curious interlopers?" Ashley asked. "Two versus six is a lot better than one."

"This needn't get bloody," Milo said.

"In about four more minutes, it will," Skye said. "They're

going slow but methodically. They'll be here within five minutes."

"A distraction will fit the bill," Milo said. "I'm working on it now."

"What are you doing now?" Jason asked. "That looks like their database. What kind of distraction are you planning?"

"A cyber attack of sorts. This is all coming from your laptop. If my assistants notice, then they'll call an alarm and trace it back to this hardware. That will stunt any damned physical search they're conducting right now. They're trained to respond in less than five minutes. If they have a breach, every security personnel returns to base and secures the building against all threats."

"Attacking your own group's network? Nice," Ashley said.

"Don't compliment me yet," Milo said. "There, it's done. Let's see how long they take to notice. You all better hope I'm an excellent teacher, because it's all riding on how well I taught them."

"Three security groups are turning. It did not deter, however, our two additional groups of friends."

"With nine men, they could secure the warehouse. Well, shit," Milo said. "It's up to you all now."

"Can you take them out quietly?"

"That many? I wouldn't want to push my luck. All it would take is a quick trigger finger that can aim, and I'm toast," Skye said. "Even with Blind at my side, it'd be iffy."

"Fine," Jim said. "I guess I'm making another appearance. Three should make this easier. Everybody set up around the tree line."

Skye heard a car door slam and spotted Jim jogging over toward her. He met with Ashley halfway over. Ashley was behind the nearest tree to his right. "What's the plan, boss?"

"I don't fancy swords against that many guns," Ashley said. "It's not like we can shoot them either. We're in the middle of a giant city. Someone would hear and call it in."

"The name of the game is divide and conquer. We don't want all six guards at once. Three would work a lot better. We watch where they're going and set up ambushes that are silent. It's our only play here. Luckily, we have a perfect cover for the first group. They'll come through the tree line. We'll be ready. The second group will be harder since it looks like they're swinging wide around the park."

"The technical front is done," Jason said. "Nothing says we have to engage if we can get out of here quick."

"Too late," Jim said, watching the two groups of guards approaching. "We're going to have to at least clear out this group."

"That would get their panties ruffled," Jason said. "A pile of dead bodies right outside their base of operations would put them in the hot seat."

"It wouldn't quite work like that. I can guarantee it," Milo said.

"Enough on that. Blind, you stand behind that tree." He pointed to one a few feet to his right. "I'll stand behind this one." He moved toward a few trees to his left, leaving Skye's tree in the middle. "Silent. I hope you're quick on the draw tonight. After this fight, I need you to climb down immediately and accompany us to the car."

"You have approximately one and a half minutes until they arrive," Jason said.

"How could you know that?" Ashley asked.

"They have cameras pinned to their chest. The transmission's feeding to the warehouse."

"That's how they'd know to send a team to control the bodies if something goes wrong," Skye said.

"Seems risky to have cameras recording footage," Ashley said.

"Not if they can control where that footage goes and keep it under wraps," Jason said. "They have those files under lock and key, and according to Milo, they delete them every week."

"If worse comes to worst, firearms are an option," Jim saw the encroaching group pull within a hundred and fifty feet. He could make out the faint sound of them talking. "Radio silence until it's done from here on out."

The speech was becoming clearer from the men approaching the group. The one in the middle spoke, clear as day, as the group took a brief pause twenty feet from the tree line. "Why the fuck are we even patrolling here, anyway? No one's dumb enough to sit on our turf this time of night."

"Someone was recently," the one who was leading said. "Don't bitch. This is a simple job. All we're doing is walking around the park. Appreciate your good fortune, new guy, and stop complaining like a bitch. It's unsightly. You work for Patterson now. Conduct yourself accordingly."

The one who was following from the rear adjusted his glasses with an uproarious laugh. "If you're not careful, you'll end up like that one guy. What was his name again?" He snapped his fingers, trying to figure out the name that was on the tip of his tongue.

"Wilkins?" The other veteran asked.

"Wilkins," he said. "That's the one. The last I heard, he was on dead body clean up. Now that's a nasty detail I wouldn't wish on the biggest bastard I know."

"Ah shit." The apparent leader reached up into his ear with a wince. "Sorry, sir. We were about to resume our search now." He removed his finger from his ear and cleared his throat. "I want us to spread into this tree line, side by side. Do not have your firearms visible. There may be mothers with children present. Have them at the ready, though."

"Pay-dirt," Jason said over the call into everyone's ears. "Who'd have thought a group of gangsters being considerate would be their downfall?"

"It's not consideration," Milo could be heard speaking. "They don't want any attention nearby after whatever you and that Specter guy did, I imagine."

Skye got to her feet, placing a hand on the nearby solid trunk to steady herself, then turned around, careful to not lose her balance. Looking down at the group of gangsters passing through the trees, she pulled an arrow from her shoulder slung quiver and nocked the arrow on the bowstring. She angled her aim downward toward the one in the middle, almost directly below her. She waited until he was at a decent angle and let loose the shot.

A sickening squelch and a loud cry of pain erupted as her target fell to the ground on his back. The shot had hit him in the chest. The shaft of the arrow was visible as it stuck out from him. He squirmed on the ground, screaming, as he grasped the foreign obstruction resting in his torso.

"Jesus Christ!" another voice called out. "Ambush. Where are they?" The voice was silenced immediately after speaking. Skye saw Ashley deliver a swift slice of the blade across the man's throat. Spurts of blood escaped the fatal wound until he slapped a hand across his throat, trying to stifle the blood loss.

She looked over to see Jim's encounter being more difficult. He rolled on the ground with his opponent, obviously struggling. Jim held his short sword in his right hand. She saw the aggressor was clutching a large knife. "Blind, help

Masked Justice. I can't get a clear shot from here. Damn it."
She climbed down the tree after securing her bow over her
shoulder. Thankfully, sliding down was much quicker than
climbing.

By the time she reached the grass, she noticed the pair
still trying to keep the other from stabbing them. Only now,
Ashley grabbed the assailant's knife hand and sawed at the
wrist with her own sharpened blade.

Skye quickly readied her bow and nocked an arrow in
one smooth motion and finished off her initial target,
keeping him from ever moving again on the night grass.

"Drop the damned thing already," Ashley growled.
"You're not stabbing him, end of story here."

"Fuck, I'll do it myself," Jim said. He got his right hand
free and thrust the steel forward into his opponent's side.

The knife dropped. Ashley quickly snapped it up. The
man rolled off Jim and covered the fresh puncture site. He
held out a hand. "Don't kill me, man. Please."

Jim didn't answer. He got off the ground and dusted
himself off.

Ashley, meanwhile, had thrust the blade again into the
man's chest cavity. She withdrew the blade and sheathed it
at her side in the scabbard hanging on her hip. "Let's get out
of here already. They've had to have seen us on those
cameras by now."

The group quickly ran over to the car and got inside.

"Cameras weren't a problem," Jason said.

"You guys said he had cameras on his personnel," Ashley
turned and said as Jim backed out of the parking space. Her
head lightly bounced off the window. "Ow," she reached a
hand up to cradle her head.

"Sorry about that. We're just in a bit of a hurry," Jim said.

The sound of glass shattering interrupted the argument

about to take place. Jim hit the gas and lowered his head as best he could while still seeing where he was driving. "Get your heads down!" Horns blared outside of the vehicle.

A van that was riding past them on the two-lane road veered right and crashed into a nearby tree. Its horn was blaring incessantly, signaling the driver was dead or at least knocked out.

"Christ." Milo had his head as near between his legs as he could manage. "I told you the guy was crazy, but we just had to approach. I nearly got my head blown off, you fools." His tone was one of anger, bordering on hysterical fear.

"Quiet." Jim turned as quickly as was safe, breaking the line of sight of the aggressors who were shooting.

"We'd better get off the road quickly," Jason said. "Not to mention, I don't know how you're planning to explain this one to the mechanics, boss."

"He's right," Skye said. She looked back at the webbed glass. "The cops will pull us over for this if they see shattered glass, and then we're fucked."

"He'll tell them we kidnapped him," Ashley said. "That can't happen."

"I know all of this." Jim's voice was abrasive and firm. "No shit. Getting off the road is a priority. I got it already. It's not like I can teleport us back to Milo's house and then somewhere else."

"We better think quick. It's only a matter of time before a cop car notices," Skye said. "I have an idea."

"Why do I feel I will not approve of this idea?" Ashley asked, bringing a hand upward to rest her head upon.

"Pull into a secluded alley, or at least what passes for it. This is our only chance," Skye said.

Jim slowed down and pulled into an alleyway between two business buildings. The lights inside were all turned off, judging from the dark windows. Only light from nearby staircases leading into the alley from between the office buildings illuminated the dumpsters.

"What's the plan?" Ashley asked.

"Give me your sword." Skye extended her palm.

"Be careful with it," Ashley said.

"Boss, give yours to Guardian. We're going to remove the glass. It's smarter to miss a back window than to look like we've visited a war zone. At least if a police cruiser drives past us, it won't look like anything's wrong at first glance."

"They'd still notice if they're behind us," Jim said. "It'd be pretty obvious."

"One problem at a time," Skye said. "This is our best play." She kept the weapon sheathed and used the handle to slam against the webbed glass. "Give it all your strength, Guardian. It's already cracked, so it shouldn't take too much effort."

"It'd be easier outside to get the torque needed," Ashley said.

"The glass would rain inside," Skye said in a deadpan voice. "That's not an option." She reared back and slammed the handle into the webbed glass with a grunt of exertion.

Jason followed suit. "Hit it near the sides," he said with a smack near where he said. "If we're lucky, we might get it out in one piece. Then we could just dump it in the nearby dumpster so some homeless dude doesn't accidentally kill himself."

"Who the fuck cares about the homeless?" Milo asked. "We were all nearly killed. Do you even get that? Patterson and MacDonald already know someone's after them. I wouldn't be surprised if they sent a van full of men to chase us. We need to keep moving right now." His voice cracked at the end of his last sentence.

"Less bitching, more helping," Skye said with another strike to the glass. She was rewarded with a loud cracking noise coming from the glass. "It's almost out. Then we can move and get you home."

Jason reared back as far as he could manage and slammed the handle forward with his gloved hand. His efforts resulted in his side of the window dislodging itself. "My side's done." He handed Jim back his blade. "All that's left is yours."

"I'm almost done," Skye said. She gave her next hit all her might, and the glass popped out of place in one complete, albeit webbed, piece. She opened her door and got out. "Let's get this done."

She and Jason hurried outside and gripped their respective side of the window. They slowly lifted it up and moved toward the nearest dumpster, which had one side already open. The pair lifted the piece of glass up over their heads and dropped it inside. They rushed back into the car and entered.

"Let me make sure any spare pieces are gone." She ran her glove clad hand over the bottom and pushed any glass straight back, off the trunk area. "Now we can go. Guardian, put the blindfold back on him. We'll swap cars before driving him home. Let's try to limit driving around in this thing for safety's sake."

"Again?" Milo asked. "I can't take this right now."

"Tough for you then, isn't it?" Jason asked, tying the cloth around his eyes and head while Skye handled Milo's hands.

Jim got the engine started and resumed their journey back to the warehouse.

"Who's paying for this shit?" Jim asked. No one in the cabin dared answer him. "It's going to be me, of course..."

14

"What do you want?" Cynthia answered the door, already fully dressed in her business attire. "I'm surprised you're up this early." She stepped to the side and let Jim inside. "Word on the news is they found bodies near some warehouse and park area. I assumed you were involved. Not to mention a car crash near there with one civilian dead."

"They're dead?" Jim asked. "We were in the car leaving, they were driving past us toward where we were, and they got clipped in the crossfire. I couldn't believe they'd fire in public like that at a moving car. That brings me to why I'm here."

"I don't relish where this conversation is going," Cynthia said, pulling her hair into a ponytail.

"It's not what you're thinking," Jim said, putting both palms up in front of him. "You said one of your first clients here ran a chop shop?"

"Allegedly," Cynthia said. "Why? Do you need a mechanic who keeps a secret?" She paused, staring ahead past Jim. "Your back window was hit. That's it, isn't it? If that civilian got hit in the front window, your back window's busted up. How'd you even return without the police stopping you?"

"Long story. I'll tell you later. Can you give me the location of the guy's business? It'd be a huge favor."

"You are not to mention my name. If I were you, I'd go in with a mask." She walked over to the nearest table and picked up a notepad. She scribbled as she spoke. "This client wasn't exactly on the up and up. I just gave her a court obligated defense." She tore the paper out and handed it to Jim.

"Don't tell me you got a guilty man free?"

"I gave her an American right to a defense," Cynthia said. "It's not my fault I'm so good at my job. Besides, the kid's upbringing isn't what you'd call the American dream."

"Oh, I'm sure that's what he told you," Jim said. He looked down at the address. "Thanks for this. I'll have to bring a lot of scratch to cover it and the privacy tax."

"I would," Cynthia said. "Money talks in those circles. Now, before you head off, there is one thing you should learn before you arrive," she said. "It's not a guy."

"Does that matter?" Jim asked.

"It could," she said. She reached up and playfully tapped Jim's cheek and spoke in a condescending tone. "Do you remember a ways back when you and Skye saved those people in the shipping crates from Eric Webb?"

"I remember one crate of women getting offed because of their draconian defense measures is what I remember. Freeing them and getting them set up for another chance at life was the goal. What about it?"

"I didn't mention anything at the time since it was none of your business, but she was one survivor. The news tracked her, and she gave an interview. Her name was Amelia Chavez."

"You're shitting me," Jim said with his eyes wide. "We saved this woman?"

"If you remember any tomboy looking woman, that was probably her. She's a legal migrant from Mexico. They tried to get her for some bullshit with her documents, but I kept that from happening."

"How's this information going to help me?"

"Dumbass," Cynthia rolled her eyes. "She knows who Masked Justice is, and she loves him for setting her free and giving her another chance at life. You should scope the property to make sure she's alone. If you go in with the mask, odds are she'll jump at the chance to help you. If not, the worst-case scenario is you didn't get your face on camera. I don't know if she has cameras on her business property. It never came up."

"Anything else I should know about her?"

"She was proud that her service was the best in the city, according to her. I'd imagine that means her cost is to match. I'd go in with plenty of cash. Be respectful, don't act creepy, and be ready for her to say no. Few would serve a wanted criminal, even if they owed said criminal a massive favor weeks ago."

"I'm always nice. You know me."

"Ignoring the lie, how is your little group doing, aside from the getting shot at part? What's your plans now?"

"Are you sure you want to know? It'd be easier to deny if you don't know."

"It won't make any difference. I can't unlearn you're Masked Justice or that I don't know who Blind, Silent, or Guardian of Justice is. Tell me you're not going to keep lighting up the evening and morning news. Are you keeping the girls in line? If you give them an inch, they'll take a mile. Trust me on that. It's admirable trying to leave the outlaw life, but Ashley, Jason, and Skye need to be ready."

"If I didn't know better, I'd think you're excited about me getting out of it. Whatever could be the reason?" He winked at her with a devilish grin. "It couldn't be because you love me, now could it?"

"Who knows?" Cynthia looked away with a visible blush. "It wouldn't be the weirdest occurrence worldwide. Speaking of which, you are coming tonight for our scheduled dinner, yes?"

"I wouldn't miss it for the world. Do I need to pick up steaks?"

"Optimistic of you to assume she'd have it ready by then. I'll pick some up on the way back from my case today. You just be sure you're here by six. If you're going to be late, call me and let me know. Otherwise, I'll expect you then. Got it?"

"Loud and clear," Jim said. "I'll visit your client, get the car fixed, and come home to work before heading over. Tonight will be busy though, so no drinking for me."

"I didn't assume so," she said with a smile. She led them back toward the door. "My wine's for me anyway. That stuff's expensive."

"Only because you waste your money on the expensive stuff."

"It tastes the best." Cynthia rested her hand on the doorknob leading outside. "What can I say? I like to treat myself. It helps with the stress of knowing what I do."

"You'd best watch that, and make sure it doesn't become a problem." Jim watched her open the door and followed her out into the empty hallway.

"Like you're one to talk." She locked the door and walked with Jim toward the stairwell leading down. "I remember a certain someone's twenty-first birthday. I also remember how plastered he got."

"Right," Jim said as they walked down the stairs. "I suppose I'm not the guy to point out other's flaws. I'm simply looking out for you is all."

"It's noted," Cynthia said at Jim's side. "Appreciated, but pointless. It's a drink to calm down after a long day of lawyering. That's all. Surely you can understand living a high stress lifestyle?"

"I deal with stress in my unique way," Jim said with a smile and shrug as they reached the ground level and headed for the nearby door. The glass of the double door revealed they were headed toward the apartment's parking lot. "There's nothing wrong with working out."

"Far be it from me to condemn different coping methods. Speaking of which, Ashley's got me in better shape. No wonder she got hired in that hoity-toity gym." She stressed her point by trying to pinch imaginary fat on her hip. She pushed the door open with her other hand.

"Ashley had an excellent teacher," Jim said with a smug grin.

"Her trainer must have been humble, too."

"You trained her before I did, if you'll remember," Jim said.

The pair reached Cynthia's car. She stood by the driver's door. "Sure, that's what you meant. Now remember what I said. Are you heading over there now?"

"A guy can't desire to spend more time with you, sweetie?" Jim asked with a genuine smile.

"Your flirting isn't half as effective as you think it is," she said. She opened the door. "Get up there and do some work. God knows you probably haven't done enough of that lately with all that's happening."

"Yes, dear," Jim said.

"While you're at it, watch some tv and drink a tea. Coffee all the time will ruin your blood pressure."

"It's like we're married already, and I love every minute."

"Get out of here already." She shook her head and got into the driver's seat.

Jim waved as he watched her pull out of the parking lot and into traffic. "Guess it's time to go have the world's most awkward conversation, isn't it?" He sighed and turned around to head inside the apartment complex. "I forgot my fucking keys. Damn."

Across town, at the address Cynthia gave Jim...

"Jesus, I'll be lucky if the woman doesn't blow me away before she realizes who I am," he said. He eyed the garage as he turned onto the correct street. He reached down with one hand and raised the neck gaiter over his nose. "No one's there. I guess that's to be expected. No time to think of an approach. I'm winging it, apparently. It's not like there's a subtle method of pulling your car inside with a mask donned, is there?"

He pulled the vehicle onto the property and turned the engine off. No one came out to greet him. He spotted a sign that read. "Head into the garage for service." He followed the simple directions and jogged over to the open garage. He heard loud rock music playing as he approached and quickly turned the corner. A young woman with headphones donned, sitting at a nearby computer, could be seen through a window leading to the office area of the building.

He spotted several piles of magazines ranging from automobile to news, and even some newspapers could be seen.

He cleared his throat loudly, his mask still covering his identity.

She didn't hear him or chose not to acknowledge him - it was difficult to tell. He walked a little closer and knocked on the desk she was sitting at with decent force, causing her to jump. She spun the reclinable chair a hundred and eighty degrees and looked up at Jim's covered face. "Oh shit," he heard her say.

"Easy," Jim said, trying to keep her calm. He lifted a hand out, palm toward her. "I'm not here to hurt or rob you, despite the mask." He used the other hand to point toward the neck gaiter obscuring his facial features.

"What the fuck are you doing wearing a mask if you're not here to rob or hurt me?" Her gaze moved to her left, down to the desk before returning to him.

"Do not make any sudden moves toward any weapons. I realize this is not a normal occurrence, but does the name Masked Justice mean anything to you?"

"No way." Her focus moved from the presumably concealed weapon in the drawer to studying Jim's masked face with intense focus. She stood up and took a few cautious steps toward him. "What about Masked Justice?"

"He needs help with his car on the down low, and my sources say you're the best and can keep a secret."

"You saw my trial, or at least heard it." What she said wasn't a question. She crossed her arms and eyed him from head to toe. "That's how you heard of me. You know, for the record, they cleared me of those charges. Besides, you can't possibly expect me to believe you're Masked Justice."

"You were at Webb's warehouse when Silent and I released two crates full. I remember you." He pointed at her. "I also remember you going on the news and singing my praises, even if I don't deserve such words. What upset me more was losing the one crate because of the booby trap they had set up on the last one."

"You really are Masked Justice. I never informed the news crews about the crate of victims who didn't survive that tragedy. I didn't want the media getting hold of me again, and I figured dead bodies wouldn't be conducive to that."

"Look, I need help. I'm on a big job right now, Amelia."

"How do you know my name? Oh right. I don't know if you've noticed," she pointed out the window toward the open garage door, "but business isn't exactly flooding in ever since my trial a month ago. I'd love to offer my services free, but it's not in the cards."

"Wasn't expecting a free job," Jim said. "I came ready to pay."

"Oh," she said. "At least there's that. Fine. What do you need done?"

"Come walk with me," Jim said with a nod of his head toward the door of the garage. "You'll understand once you see it." He led her out of the building and showed her his car. "This." He walked to the rear of the car and extended an arm toward the broken window. "This is the problem right here."

"I'm surprised the police didn't pull you over on the way here."

"I'm very careful," he said, looking over his shoulder at the sparse traffic passing by on the road behind them, amid the sounds of engines and the occasional honking.

"Goodness gracious," she said, leaning forward and inspecting the damage. "What happened to the glass?"

"I'll explain it after we get this inside, yeah?" Jim asked.

"Hand me the keys," she said, holding out her hands, signaling him to toss them to her.

He tossed them underhanded to her and watched her get in and bring the car inside before following her. She kept the keys and placed them in a pouch in the uniform she had on. She walked over to the garage and closed the large door. "Now spill it. How does a vigilante who operates quietly just lose their back window?"

"I don't think that's pertinent. Just bullets were involved, and we were lucky to escape alive. Not all involved were so lucky, if you get my meaning. These villains kidnap, blackmail, and do all manner of heinous things. Anyway, we took all the glass out because we figured it'd be safer driving without it than with webbed glass."

"That was probably the best call. Alright, looking at the damage, I see opportunities for upgrades too."

"You really are in sales, I see."

"I'm not doing the usual schtick where I try to upsell and change their oil or check their tire pressure, etc. I mean, I see potential for some less than street legal modifications, if you catch my meaning. A replaced back window will be the smallest aspect."

"Explain further. I'm intrigued. You're not talking anything too extreme?"

"Define too extreme. In your line of work, I'd imagine they'd be useful." She lifted a hand, a finger extended for each of the upgrades. "I'm talking about reinforcing your car against gunfire. I can install bullet resistant windows and tires. They're not bulletproof, but they're still functional with one in them. I can also install a wireless modem and router combo if you utilize such things. I'll throw in the maximum legally allowed tinted windows on the house if you order all these, as well as checking all your fluids and the regular checkup stuff."

"How much would you want?" Jim asked.

"Normally, if some random Joe walked in and wanted all that, I'd charge them over fifteen thousand. For you, I'd give a discount of only ten thousand dollars, plus my fee for labor."

Jim looked at his relatively new car. It wasn't a sports car by any means, but it wasn't a jalopy. He looked back at Amelia. "Alright. I don't guess you take catcoins?"

"Normally I don't," she said. "Why? Is crypto the only method you can pay?"

"No, it would simply be the most private and secure if we process the payment locally. Paper wallets are a thing of beauty. Privacy is paramount in this line of work, as you can no doubt imagine." He reached into his jean's pocket and pulled out a small USB device and displayed it to her.

"Ordinarily I'd tell you to fuck off, but given who you are and the work you do, I'll accept it. It'll just be a pain to cash out."

"I find spreading out the withdrawals and going to different towns works wonders, but it's a pain, true. Now, shall we head to your office?" He pointed toward the computer room. "I can pay now, assuming you can deliver sometime soon. This is a sensitive matter, and I need my means of transportation."

"Hot on the trail of some scumbags?" Amelia asked. "You're lucky I keep a stock of every service I offer. Few want to reinforce their car or pimp it out, so I have everything in stock. It's just a matter of installing it. How soon do you need it?"

"The sooner the better," Jim said. "I have a social engagement I have to be at tonight."

"Is that an actual social visit, or are you trying to talk in code?"

"It's an actual social event. Now when's the soonest you can be done?"

She looked at a nearby clock hanging above a line of shelves holding various tools and parts. She saw it display that it was nine in the morning. "If I worked all day, I could have it done by ten tonight, maybe. That's iffy right there. It all depends on how finicky your car is. I guarantee it'll be in better shape than before."

"I trust you're available for any other problems that happen in the future?" Jim asked.

"So long as you can pay a discounted price, I'll fix anything that you throw at me. I can help with bullet holes, broken windows, jacked up suspension, and anything else your fast living lifestyle can inflict on your vehicle. Can I just ask a few odd questions that I've had ever since you got me out?"

"Go for it," Jim said. "Depending on the contents, I may not tell you for your safety, though."

"I thought you were supposed to be in Oklahoma? Wasn't that where Masked Justice started? I did all kinds of research on the internet after I got home. It was tough sifting through all the fan sites and hate click farming trash media. As varied as all of them were, one constant was among them. You came from Oklahoma. Why are you here in Denver now?"

"I pissed off a former employer of mine. It turns out an organization that has assassins that hunt pedophiles are not the most empathetic to adopting a victimized girl I saved from a monster."

"Bold move. Was it the PHR?"

"Possibly," he said, keeping his answer short and curt.

"That was my other question. People say they're just an urban legend. Are they?"

"Not at all. They are zealots. They're also infested at every level of government, if you can believe it. Questions? Do you wish to see how deep the rabbit hole goes? I know this sounds insane. Then again, you don't ask someone like me something expecting a normal answer."

"I won't ask too much for now," Amelia said. "That's good enough for me. I assume who you're hunting now deserves it?"

"They're kidnapping women to sell to someone overseas involving a massive sexual slavery business. Does that answer your question?"

"I hope you fucking kill them. This will be done by ten. I'll make sure of it. We can't have Masked Justice having to take the bus, can we?"

"I'd appreciate that. I'll leave you to your work then. You have a lot."

"You have a way home?" she asked. "It's not like you can walk home with that mask and hoodie up. You look like you're about to rob a liquor store."

"I can call a ride. Speaking of privacy, does this business have cameras inside or outside? I know the street doesn't. Does this interior possess a CCTV feed or anything?"

"As soon as you leave, I'm deleting the feed while you were here. You realize I know your license plate number now, though?"

"You know the set of plates I have on there," he said. "The ones right now, anyway."

"I should have known you wouldn't have anything I could try to identify you with. The glove box doesn't have any documents? I'm just checking so you don't have any surprises if I find them. This place is rumored to be a chop shop after all." Her subject was odd, but her smile betrayed the joke she attempted.

"I didn't get away by being stupid, Amelia. You don't want to know my secret identity. If anyone ever asks, I threatened you to do this, alright? Otherwise, you're an accomplice and your little former allegations will be chicken feed compared. Do you understand?"

"I don't know if you knew, but this business is famous locally for its privacy. We value customer privacy above all else, especially our preferred clients."

"Is that what I am?"

"Anyone who saves my ass and pays for a couple months' rent is my preferred customer," she said with a wink. "One last thing before you go, is there a Mrs. Masked Justice? Also, can I meet Silent Justice?"

"As of now, no, and possibly. We'll see." With that, he backed up. "I'm heading out. You have fun today."

She watched him lift the door enough to leave her establishment before it shut again behind him. "Who'd have imagined this is how my morning would start? They say never meet your heroes. What do they know?"

15

"You seriously left your car with some mechanic?" Skye asked. She looked at Jim in the passenger seat as she drove. "Not that I don't appreciate the business."

"You've met her before, you know."

"I have?"

"You did - from that job at Webb's warehouse."

"Oh, right." Her voice lost any form of joy. "I've tried to forget that night. It never works."

"Just stay quiet and be cool. She's friendly and trustworthy. In fact, I brought you along so you'd have this connection if you ever decide to do a job on your own or with Ashley and Jason. You never know when a skilled mechanic might help after an operation gone wrong."

"We need assurances she won't talk to anyone," Skye said, turning onto the now familiar road. "This neighborhood's kind of a dive. I suppose that's a good sign since we need privacy. No one comes near this kind of place."

"It has its merits," Jim said. He raised his neck gaiter over his nose. "Mask up and get ready to meet her."

She used a hand to do as he said before pulling into the

garage's front parking lot. "How did you find this sympathetic mechanic?"

"Cynthia. Now be nice."

Skye didn't answer, but got out of the car and followed Jim to the closed vertical garage door. He knocked on it and stepped back.

A few moments later, the sound of a sliding chain and moving metal rang as the door rose. There stood a happy, but obviously tired, Amelia. Her attire was stained with all manner of dirt and grime. She had a satisfied smile adorning her youthful face as she closed the door behind them. "Hello again," she said.

"The job is done, I trust?" Jim asked, stepping inside the garage with Skye.

"Done and tested. She's perfect now. If anything's wrong, the repair's on the house. I stand by my work." She puffed out her flat chest.

"I told you she was skilled." Jim walked to the car and inspected the new looking back window. "This is Silent Justice. She's here to inspect your work and make your acquaintance."

"Hello," Skye said. She kept her hands firmly embedded in the hoodie's pockets in the front.

"That's the same voice and mask. I'd recognize it anywhere." Amelia said.

"You remember my voice?" Skye asked.

"Getting rescued from a life of servitude is a lifelong memory of mine, miss." Amelia gushed, stepping to within a few feet of Skye. "I owe you two my life."

"Turns out to not matter," Jim said. "The confirmations went through just fine for your crypto."

"A girl's got to eat," Amelia said with a sheepish grin and shrug. "I installed all the upgrades I mentioned earlier."

"Recount them for me if you would," Skye said. She walked around the car and listened to Amelia.

"I upgraded the chassis to be reinforced against small arms fire." Amelia stepped up and patted the orange exterior of Jim's car. "I upgraded the tires to the best bullet resistant model I have access to. As for the router and modem combo, it was the least amount of effort, comparatively speaking. It's rock solid. As for the tinting, see for yourself. It's not quite the darkest you're allowed, but I figured you'd want to avoid any overzealous cops from talking to you. I also checked all the basics. She's as ready for action as she ever will be."

"You must have charged an arm and leg for this." Skye placed her hands on her knees and bent forward, inspecting the windows. She kept walking until she reached the back tire and kicked it. "These are premium brands. How much were they?"

"We paid ten thousand," Jim said.

"Repairs included at a discounted price," Amelia said. "Sorry, but I don't have a lot of clients yet, and I need the business to stay afloat."

"It's not like we can't afford it," Jim said.

"Can I ask you something, Ms. Silent Justice?" Amelia asked. She clasped her gloved hands in front of her.

"Go ahead," Skye kept inspecting the newly improved vehicle.

"Why do this?"

"Wouldn't you like to know?" Skye asked. "I'm not telling you that for security reasons. I had a good reason, alright?"

"Oh, I didn't mean to pry. I wanted to learn about the bloody infamous hero who saved my bacon, and why you were there naturally sprang to mind. If you can't answer that, then how can I help?"

"What?" Both Jim and Skye asked.

"I don't mind being the Justice mechanic if needed."

"You already are," Skye said. "At least judging by this. I'll have to get you to modify mine before long. It's a nice investment with this level of skill."

"Really?" Amelia jumped in place. She hurried over and gave her a tight hug, surprising Skye. "Oh, thank you both so much," she said. She released Skye, leaving her to catch her breath from the bear hug.

She enveloped Jim in her grip and squeezed. "I thought I was going to be homeless if business kept tanking. You saved me again."

"We appreciate the enthusiasm, but you know if you're ever connected to us, you're going to prison for a long time," Jim said, removing himself from the embrace. "Just deny knowing anything about us. It's for your own good."

"Sure, for appearances," Amelia said. "We all know the truth though."

Skye pulled out her phone and spotted a sign inside the window of the office. She pointed to it. "Is that this place's number?"

"Yes, it is."

Skye input the number into her phone's memory. "I'll call ahead and ask before I drop mine off. I imagine the boss dropped in unannounced. He's not the most subtle man, you see."

"No one has ever accused me of subtlety. Just know her rates match her craftsmanship, so be prepared to pay up. Now if you'd excuse us, we have things to do. You deserve some rest after a job well done, Amelia."

"Sure thing." Amelia dug into one of her many pockets and fished out Jim's keys. She tossed them over to the masked vigilante. "Don't go getting yourselves killed, you hear? There are tons more victims out there that require help."

"We're doing what we can," Jim said. He gripped the keys in his hand. "Now keep your head down and stay legit. Your reputation will come back before you know it. I bet you anything."

"I wish I had your confidence," Amelia said. She raised the garage door and watched Jim get in and back the car out beside Skye's. As she and Skye exited the building, she spotted Skye's vehicle. "Is that your car?"

"It is. You need to delete your CCTV tapes if you have any. I can't have you knowing my license plate number. Where is it?"

"I was going to do it as soon as you leave. It's a nice car," Amelia said.

"It's a piece of shit," Skye snorted in laughter. "Thank you for being polite, though. I'll catch you later."

"Good night. It's time for me to close shop then." Amelia disappeared inside and shut the door, leaving the pair outside with their cars.

"Why do you think her reputation is going to improve, anyway? It was such a thinly veiled fake compliment. It was a little cringy," Skye said.

"Well, excuse the hell out of me for trying to be nice," Jim said.

Back at Jim's apartment twenty minutes later...

"I'm glad you sent me a message earlier. I would have been pissed if you'd been this late," Cynthia said. She crossed her pajama clad legs under the table. She took another sip from the wineglass sitting near her. "When did you get these mood candles? Are these scented?" She closed her eyes and took a deep inhale. "Oh my God, you got my favorite. Is that cinnamon?"

"I had to pick up my newly improved car," Jim said. He took a bite of the cut steak in front of him. "Thank you for recommending Amelia. She's a joy - maybe a little expensive for her upgrades, but damned good."

"I can't believe you went with the full action hero package. Bullet resistant windows and tires along with armor for it? Talk about a splurge purchase," she said. "Most folks buy too much weed, alcohol, or a cake. Not you. You're one of a kind."

"Stop," Jim said. "You're going to make me blush with all these compliments."

"Where are the kids, anyway?" Cynthia asked over the kitchen table. "Are they working out or something?"

"No," Jim said. "That's earlier in the day. They have some free time. What do teenagers do in their free time nowadays?"

"Who knows?" Cynthia asked. "Not me with running my firm. I barely have time to schedule dates. As long as the kids aren't appearing on the evening or morning news show, who cares?"

"They're fine," Jim said, leaning forward, staring at Cynthia across the table. His voice was suave and smooth. "You're exhausted, and don't even think of denying it. I can see the cute little way your eyes twitch when the phone rings. You're always at work. I can't just let you run yourself ragged as your best friend, can I?"

"It'll only last a couple of years," Cynthia said. "For right now, it's job to job living. When I'm not working hand over foot for my clients, I wait and see if I'll get another one. People wonder why we charge so much. It's called bills, people." She took another drink, emptying the wineglass for the second time already tonight. "Empty again? Where does it all go?"

"Into your liver soon enough," Jim said with a smile. "Shall I get you a glass of water?"

"I'm fine with this," Cynthia took the nearby bottle of wine and refilled her glass with the sloshing purple liquid. "My limit's three. Don't worry so much. I don't want a hangover tomorrow morning. This much is fine."

"Three? Good to hear," Jim said. "Then we'll stash the bottle for another time?"

"We may as well just finish the bottle, right?" Cynthia said between drinks. "It's not like you can save it for later. It tastes worse after it's opened. I take it you're not going to drink any since you have a job later tonight, yeah?"

"I wasn't planning on it." Jim reached across the table and grabbed the wine bottle.

"Did you change your mind?" Cynthia took a swig and watched Jim get up from the dining table and head toward the glass cabinet.

"Not quite." Jim stopped in front of the sink.

"Wait a minute," Cynthia finished the drink and placed the glass down on the table before getting up. "You're not going to waste that? At least put it in the refrigerator."

"How do you propose we do that?" Jim held up the bottle and pointed toward the opening. "It came with a cork. How do you propose we close it?"

"Open the fridge," Cynthia said. "My container's in there. Just pour it in there."

Jim looked at the refrigerator and toward the bottle in his hand. "I'm a little concerned you have a dedicated wine storage container, if I'm honest." He moved to the appliance and opened the door, spotting an empty container. He reached inside and grabbed it before shutting the door. "Is this it?"

"That's the one. Be a dear and pour the rest inside, would you?"

Jim unscrewed the cap and transferred the alcohol between containers. "I'll just take this home with me for after my job tonight, if you don't mind," Jim said. "I'll need a nice little nightcap."

"Fine by me," Cynthia said, slurring her words a slight bit. "I've had enough tonight. I can tell already. My head's all woozy. Enjoy that stuff. It's stronger than I thought."

"Hold on." Jim finished transferring the alcohol and placed it down on the bar before rushing over. He helped her up.

"I'm dizzy," Cynthia said. "Help me over to the couch."

Jim wrapped his arm around Cynthia and held her close. He led them over to the living room's couch.

She fell onto the couch with as much grace as a sack of potatoes, falling with a giggle, and reached up to the arm of the couch and grabbed the remote control. She pulled herself up into a sitting position and patted right beside her. "Come sit beside me."

"You won't find me arguing with that command," Jim said with a smile. He took a seat a few inches from her. Almost immediately he felt Cynthia leaning into his side and snuggling into his torso. "Is something wrong?"

"Just work business," Cynthia said, staring at the television screen. "Nothing to be done but to relax and wait until tomorrow." She closed her eyes and relaxed into Jim.

He looked down at her, a warm smile on his face. "It's been a while since I've seen you so relaxed."

"So says the source of my biggest worry," Cynthia said. "I'm going to have white hair sooner because of you and your little team. That's if Charlie doesn't make our lives hell first. You know he got elected, right?"

"I figured he would," Jim said. "He had the media at his beck and call, always getting sweetheart interviews. He stoked the fires against us vigilantes and still is to my knowledge."

"Now he's trying to empower police to take additional steps against your kind." Her hand fell to his lap and rested on his thigh. "What he's suggesting is awfully dangerous territory, though. He wants to spy on the general population with more cyber surveillance and 'reasonable search laws'."

"Do I want to know what they consider reasonable?"

"It's all very vague right now," she said. "He's been blustering on the house floor about needing to take measures to curb violent crime and dangerous serial killers. He suggested if you're suspected, that the police wouldn't need a warrant to enter your house and search. It's getting some push back, but not nearly enough to make me secure." She used her other hand to reach around Jim and pull herself closer.

"You said that it's not law?"

"It's not even a bill yet." Her voice came out, sounding tired. "Why are you so interested in Charlie now, of all times, anyway?"

"He has a score to settle with me," Jim said, keeping his face stoic. "He has unbelievable power now, or at least he could wield it to harm me. It only makes sense to keep in mind what he's doing to shape this nation."

"He also blasts Masked Justice on national television as often as he can. That scar really pissed him off." Cynthia looked up at Jim. "I think he's due to debate some internet pundit about Masked Justice and the rise of vigilante crime soon enough in some publicity stunt - no doubt to win over voters."

"You knowing all this must mean you've kept up with what he was doing," Jim said. He covered her hand with one of his.

"I enjoy knowing when the potential axe will fall on my neck. All clear on that front," Cynthia said. She looked at the commercial playing on the television.

"Just rest your weary head." Jim raised an arm and wrapped it over Cynthia. She took his hand and rested it on her shoulder. "You have nothing incriminating in here, anyway. I'd be the one screwed, or one of the others."

He looked down at Cynthia. She didn't retort or rebuke his claim. Her back was rising and falling rhythmically.

Jim felt the phone in his back pocket buzzing, along with the sound. "Perfect timing," he whispered to himself with a roll of his eyes. The buzzing was unrelenting until the incessant noise ceased. He fished it out without waking Cynthia up and turned it on to check. "What's so damned important now?"

He had received an encrypted email judging from his notifications. "Why now of all times?" He looked down at Cynthia and over toward where her bedroom was. "You want to head to bed?" he asked loud enough for her to hear. He received no answer. "Okay, fine then. If you don't wake, you're going to miss the single fantasy every young woman had when they were growing up." He got off the couch and gently lowered Cynthia into a laying position on the sofa.

"Fine then," he said, bending over. "See if I care if you remember this." He picked her up and carried her bridal style over to her room. He lifted a foot and, with great concentration and coordination, kicked the door open.

She grunted in his arms and shifted, burying her head

into the crook of his neck with a high-pitched whining at the noise of the door opening. "Tired," was the only word he could make out among the incoherent but entirely adorable sounds she was emitting.

He carried her over to her bed. "I should've planned this," Jim said in a quiet voice. "Cyn?"

"Mm?"

"Wake up. It's bedtime. You need to get under the covers."

"Already?"

He placed her down on the bed and watched as she turned down the sheets and crawled inside.

"Let's get you tucked in, and then I'll lock up before I leave tonight. Alright?" he asked in as soothing a voice as he could muster.

"Stay," she said. She was lying on her side, facing Jim. She had a hand reached out toward him. "Get in here. I'm cold."

"I was leaving soon." Jim looked at the open doorframe and back at Cynthia. "Alright, but just for a little while."

She was obviously feeling the effects of alcohol intoxication by this point. "Good," she slurred. She let Jim crawl under the covers beside her and laid her head on his chest.

"Who knew getting you drunk would persuade you to invite me to sleep with you?" Jim asked. "A less reputable red-blooded male would take advantage of such a revelation."

She swung a leg over Jim's and rested a hand over his shirt clad chest. "Mm, I'm just cold is all."

"Whatever you say." Jim took out his phone and tapped at the screen.

"What are you doing?"

"Setting an alarm so I don't overstay."

"Right, with your job." Her tone conveyed she clearly didn't approve of his hobby. "Can't be late to playing God on the streets."

"I'm going to attribute that to the drinks. Now just relax and fall away into a peaceful slumber for me, alright?"

"You're lucky I'm tired, or I'd give you an earful. Just stay quiet and still." Those were the last words she spoke. Before long, he heard soft snores coming from Cynthia. He sneaked out of the bed, covering her with the blankets. He snuck out of the room, taking great care not to wake her. Jim left her apartment...

Jim's apartment a bit earlier...

"Ashley's late," Jason said.

"She had a date with some guy from her gym."

"Did she?"

"Found out at lunch today, apparently," Skye said. She looked over at Jason sitting on the opposite end of the couch. "She said she'd be back before the job tonight. How much homework do you have left?"

"It's all done. I always get it done before I leave campus," Jason said. "It leaves more time for me to plan for the job."

"If you're not careful, you'll end up alone with that approach to life," Skye said. "All work and no play makes Jason a dull boy."

"Like you can talk," Jason laughed. "You drive people, workout, and do the same workaholic lifestyle I do."

"You're not supposed to point that out," Skye said with genuine laughter, looking over at her partner in crime. "Didn't Jim ever teach you how to be a gentleman?"

Both shared a mutual laugh in the dim interior. The

nearby lamp and muted television were the only lights in the living room of Jim's apartment.

Jason cleared his throat. "I don't think we've had a chance to learn about each other. Besides this whole vigilante thing, what do you do for fun?"

"Of all the questions, that's the one you pick?" Skye asked. "Fair enough. I play games and flock to social media."

"Nah, you're not the type," Jason said with a shake of his head. "The people I see in classes, they're the social media addicts. They always have their phones out and are typing some message. I believe the video game part though."

"Why is that? Has Ashley informed you how skilled I am or something?"

"That, and I noticed you had consoles in your room when we helped you move in. I swear it wasn't in some creepy way. I noticed your choice of platforms, and I approve. Having a PC besides your console of choice gives a lot of versatility to play in bed."

"Add me, and we can play if we ever have off nights in the future." She pulled out her phone and set to typing.

Jason's phone rumbled in his pocket before she put hers away.

"That is, unless you're chicken of losing to a girl?"

"That's how you want to play it, huh?"

"Got a problem with it?" Skye reached out her sock clad foot and poked Jason in the thigh with it, sticking her tongue out. "I'll even give you the first pick in games."

"Ignoring your impending defeat, you are in a good mood tonight."

"I enjoy having a purpose. I get antsy when I'm idle. We know our targets, we know the goal, and we're implementing our plan. Slap my ass and call me sunshine if it's not going well so far."

"I will not follow that command," Jason said, shaking his head. "Not unless you're into that kink."

"Shut up. It's a figure of speech, you pervert." She kicked him again with little force. "How do you think Jim's doing over at Cynthia's place?"

"It depends," Jason said. "If they've got alcohol, it's either going well or in the dumpster. I don't know if she's an angry or clingy drunk though."

"I take it you've heard her rat theory?"

"Rat theory?" Jason placed his laptop down. "What does that even mean?"

"That if one of us gets caught, we'll all rat on each other for lighter sentences. She went on a huge spiel right after we freed her from the PHR when they kidnapped her."

"She knows law," Jason said. "I would never betray the team."

"Let's hope she's wrong. We all know what we signed up for when we joined this team."

"I'll keep my eye on her digital footprint," Jason said. He leaned forward, typing on his laptop. "That is not a healthy mindset."

"She's just paranoid," Skye said. "What do you even mean, watch her? She's Jim's friend. We can't spy on one of our own, man."

"Don't think of it as spying," Jason said. "Think of it as making sure she's loyal."

"I don't think you really understand how bad that sounds, but I get the point. You need to work on wording. You're not going to spy on her personal or business dealings, right?"

"I would only check her computer files. If she was planning on ratting, it'd be clear. There'd be files containing damning evidence."

"Something tells me you're breaking tons of digital privacy laws right now."

"Possibly," he said. The typing was sporadic. He occasionally stopped to click through the next prompt on the app.

"You have trust issues, clearly." Skye sat up straight and looked at his screen. "You know this kind of shit isn't normal, right?"

"What is normal?" Jason asked. "I'm not trying to be a deep fourteen-year-old here. I just mean nobody is normal when we get down to it."

"Right, but I think there's a special exception when we break laws to investigate people close to us." She reached for the laptop and closed it on him.

"She had nothing on her desktop anyway."

"There is no way you checked that fast." Skye met his gaze. "You're bluffing."

"Am I? Wouldn't you like to know of impending betrayal? Or do you trust her enough to trust that I'm not lying?"

She removed her hand and raised the screen back up. "Shut up. This does not mean I'm as bad as you."

"Whatever you say," Jason said.

They both leaned in to inspect the findings on the screen.

"What are we even looking for? It's not like she'd have a folder labeled 'Masked Justice evidence'," Skye said. "All I'm seeing is a bunch of cat GIFS and what looks like work related files."

"Exactly," Jason said. "You didn't trust me. Who was it that has trust issues?" Jason reached forward and closed the laptop. He stood and walked into the kitchen.

"I see why she thinks he's annoying now," Skye said

under her breath. "We all have issues, boy wonder," Skye said. She stood and moved toward Jim's room. "You want to spar while we wait for everyone to arrive or at least work-out? Extra time and effort in the gym's never wasted."

"I'll do whatever." Jason came back with two bottles of water and tossed one of them toward her.

She opened a door as they walked and pulled two towels free before handing one to Jason. "Good. Let's get you combat ready in case the worst comes to pass one day."

"That works for me..."

16

"Are you two okay?" Ashley looked over at Skye and Jason. Each had a towel wrapped around their neck and were leaning against the table in the kitchen.

"How was the date?" Skye asked, not answering Ashley's question.

"The guy was nice enough."

"Going for a date two?" Skye asked.

"Not planning on it," Ashley said. "What about you, boss?" She looked at the nearby seat to see Jim sitting and inspecting a bunch of papers.

"My date went great. In fact, the only reason I'm here now is the text I received from Jason. I assume it was for a good reason and not that you were bored waiting?" Jim looked at the wall mounted clock to see it had just struck ten.

"It was a reminder, boss," Jason said. "It wasn't my intention to be a cock block."

"Let's assume I trust that. What was so important that you had to message me during my date?"

"You haven't decrypted it yet?"

"I am as we speak, but I figured why not speed it up and ask you directly."

"It was mostly with an idea of where we head tonight. We know their network inside and out and where they're taking the women from. We know their client and where she's staying. I'd suggest we go to the local bars that Milo mentioned."

"That's a lot of ground to cover, even in one zip code," Skye said.

"I'd suggest Jim, Ashley, and you all take different bars. I'd be inside the car watching for anything."

"They'd probably bring at least two big men to kidnap anyone," Jim said. "Even with college girls, they won't want it to be a hassle. We'd need more than one at each site. It'd be like trying to catch a needle in a haystack."

"Then use a magnet," Jason said. "By that, I mean we set a perfect trap."

"There's no way of knowing that they'd see said trap," Jim said. "That's unless we know where they are tonight."

"Milo sent an encrypted email to the tertiary email address I gave him. He gave the block they're prowling tonight. We can set up both Skye and Ashley as bait. They're both that age, and you and I could be ready to pounce. That's if the girls hadn't already taken care of them."

"It'd work, but it'd entail dangerous work for you two," Jim said, looking at the two younger women. "Would you two be willing to act as bait? Before you say yes, you'd have to act the part."

"The part of what?" Ashley asked. "A couple of drunk young women? That'd be easy."

"Easy, but you'd have to get their attention," Jim said.

"Think you can do that? There will be a dozen college-aged women inside. You'd have to be sure they want you. You'd also have to delay them enough outside. Once you get in their car, you'd be on your own until we could mount a rescue attempt."

"With significant risk comes substantial reward," Skye said. "I'm in. What about you, Ashley?"

"It wouldn't be my first time fighting someone while I was drunk, and I won that one too," she said. "Yeah, I'm in."

"Alright then," Jim said.

"You two will need to wear these." Jason reached down to the floor near the couch and pulled up a white plastic shopping bag drooping from the items inside.

Ashley reached inside the container and pulled out a package. "What is this?"

"You're not going to wear your earpiece inside and not stick out," Jason said. "This will enable me to hear and see everything you do. It's a tiny camera with a microphone. The quality won't be great, but it'll get the job done. If they saw you with an earpiece in, they'd skip right over you, seeing as it'd be too big of a problem."

"Talk about a pain in the ass." Ashley ripped open the package and pulled out the device. "You call this small? Where in the hell do you expect us to hide this without anyone seeing it? It's the size of a fingernail."

"I already thought of that," Jason said with a knowing smile. "I hope you liked arts and crafts in school, because this is brilliant if I say so myself."

"You've got to be kidding. I fucking hated that part of art class," Ashley muttered to herself and watched as he kept digging into the shopping bag. She watched him pull out two barrette clips. "I know you don't expect me to wear that in my hair."

"Why?" Jim asked. "Is it too girlie for your taste?"

"Why did you get the flowery themed ones?" Ashley whined, taking one of them and inspecting it. "I'd rather have had something a little less girly. It doesn't suit me."

"You are playing an innocent frat college girl," Jason said. "You need to play into some stereotypes. Many women like flowers, ergo you're wearing that."

"I'm going to let the generalization slide there," Skye said, looking at hers. "You're not thinking we can simply glue these to them and nobody will notice?"

"They may well see it, but no one will inspect you close enough to see they're cameras. Even if some drunk notices, play it off. It's our best shot at having eyes and ears inside with no one noticing. Boss, how many times have you looked at Miss Cynthia's hair accessories?"

Jim paused before answering. "I don't think I ever noticed, now that you mention it. I know sometimes she wears them, but I never paid that close of attention."

"See? You'll be fine. Horny drunk college frat boys aren't going to be more observant than Boss. As far as Patterson's men, they won't get close enough to notice, and if they do, then they won't be paying attention to your hair. Now take this heavy-duty glue and align it properly before attaching it. We can't have it misaligned. That would draw attention. We need you to blend in."

"At least you're old enough to drink," Jim said. "That should help you blend in. Just don't drink too much. We need you in control of your faculties for your own safety."

"Drinking is not the top of my priority list," Skye said. "I'll do just enough to not draw attention."

"Good. Now we need to designate where we're waiting," Jim said. "I assume we're going to the district Milo said they scout from?" He stood and left the group, heading into his room, and returned with his opened laptop. He held it with one arm and typed with the other as he walked. "According to this map, the area has three bars on the street. We can park in one of the nearby alleys and wait there." He sat down in the middle of the couch between Skye and Ashley.

"Are you kidding?" Ashley asked. "People will notice men sitting inside a car in an alley in that neighborhood."

"That's the least of our problems," Jim said.

"We'd be able to monitor nearby traffic while we sit there, so we could see if Patterson's men show up anywhere with a camera. If they're in an alley, we'll see them enter and can intercept."

"Just kill them in the middle of the city with cameras everywhere?" Skye asked, shaking her head. "Not a good idea."

"What's your idea then?" Jason asked. "Just let them snatch some victims and try to catch up after it's done?"

"Even if you use your blades, people will hear the struggle. Not even Hyde Fisher could manage that level of stealth."

"Who the hell is that?" Jim asked.

"It's a video game protagonist that specializes in silent killing and infiltration," Jason said. "The only other idea I have is to cause a huge public scene. They'll leave if we draw enough attention to them."

"I vote that plan," Skye said. "We're not there to kill them. We're there to upset their immediate plans."

"That's neat, but we need a concrete plan of action to finish this whole mess for good. Once we get them to leave, I say we do some recon at their hotel."

"To what end?" Jason asked. "If we're worried about cameras, then a hotel isn't the location to hang and surveil."

"Our other option is to camp outside the hotel and follow Miss Henderson around until they get to a deserted location. Good luck with that," Ashley said. "She never leaves the place without her entourage of armed guards."

"I planted a camera there after classes today," Jason said. "I should be able to pull up the feed. Give me a minute." He reached down beside the recliner and picked up his laptop. "Let's hope rubber cement is as durable as they say."

"I trust you had your gloves on," Skye said. "If not, that's evidence."

"I was careful," Jason said. "With this, we'll see when they leave."

"You're going to sit monitoring that all morning and evening?" Ashley asked with a snort. "Talk about boring."

"Don't need to. I can fast forward the thing and it's easy to notice the limo leaving. At least when I'm in class. Otherwise, yeah, it's unmonitored. The limo is there now. See?"

"It means the women aren't in Patterson's possession yet," Skye said. "Or they'd be scrambling to get out and export them out of the country. Now we need to hurry. Frat types are out drinking this late, and the kidnappings could be happening now."

"True," Jim said, standing up. "Everybody get your gear. Ladies, go put on your best college girl outfit and conceal any weapons you can. We're heading out to stop some kidnappings tonight."

Across town soon after...

Skye took a drink from the glass filled with red liquid. She studied the inside of the bar. Hole In the Wall would be a generous description of this establishment. It was dim, rowdy, and there were many drunk college students causing a ruckus in the cramped interior. The bartender had his work cut out for him as patrons were giving no quarter, swamping him with orders.

"I don't think I've seen you around here before." A man sat down on the stool beside her.

"It's my first time coming here. My bestie claimed it had the best prices. It seems she was right," she said. She looked up and saw that he was a young man her age. The only defining trait was his bald head. "Nice cue ball," she said.

"Eh," the young man smiled and shrugged. "Some of us receive all the positive genes, while others get shafted. What are you drinking there?"

"A bloody Mary."

"Surprised it's not some cocktail filled with sugar," the young man said. "I'm Kyle. Nice to meet you."

"I prefer something a bit more savory." Skye looked down and made a show of checking Kyle's body, "if you get my meaning. I'm playing around, but I always liked this. You?"

"Just a domestic beer," Kyle held up the open bottle he'd been drinking. "I'm surprised I was the first to approach and talk to you. You have a distinct air about you. Maybe they're scared of you."

"Or they already have their chosen dates for the night." Skye looked over at the number of couples sitting and enjoying their drinks. "I'm the odd one out, which fits me just fine."

"Aww," Kyle said, "such a pretty girl like you? Tell me it isn't so."

"Afraid it is," Skye said. "Why? Don't tell me you're interested."

"Any straight man would be," Kyle said. "Don't get me wrong. If you're not interested, I'll leave you be. I just thought I should try. You miss every shot you don't take, right?"

"Admirable courage you're showing. If it was any other evening, I'd take you up on that offer."

"Really?"

"Sure," Skye said. "I like suitors who take risks and aren't afraid to lay it on the line." She spotted a couple of men in suits enter the establishment. Her eyes trailed down the nearest and spotted a suspicious bulge.

Kyle turned and looked at where her attention stayed. "Geez, talk about being overdressed. Am I right? Some fellas need to make a splash wherever they visit."

"I guess so." Skye watched as they took a seat at a table.

One of them walked to the bar and said something she couldn't quite hear to the bartender.

"Don't tell me they're your type," Kyle said.

"Not quite. They're out of place."

"Let's ignore them for the moment and continue our previous conversation." He kept talking afterward, but Skye wasn't listening.

She kept her gaze on Kyle with the occasional glance over at the group. She nodded and gave meaningless platitudes when she heard his voice inflection go up in pitch.

"Then I decided I'd take another trip to the moon and talk to the president. I was also the leader of a shrimping company. Can you believe that?"

"You don't say?" Skye watched the group when she heard a door behind her open and close.

"You know, if you're not going to even pay attention, I'll talk to someone else. Have a good night." Kyle took his drink and moved further down the bar to converse with the other patrons.

"Real smooth, Skye." She took another drink from the half full glass. She looked around at the other patrons. "I wonder how it's going with Ashley right now..."

17

"What was that?" Ashley asked the man now sitting at her table. "I don't remember inviting you to sit down." She took another drink, upending her shot glass, and looked at the disheveled man.

"Don't be uptight," he said. "There's nowhere else to sit, lady. Give me a break." He gestured toward the packed bar. All the stools and seats at every table were filled, except hers. "Frankly, I'm surprised it was even open, considering how lovely you are."

"You think so?" She flexed her bare arm. Her tank top showed just how in shape she was. "A lot of guys don't like the toned physique."

"Let the insecure ones be that way. A lot of us appreciate a woman who takes care of herself, which you obviously do. Are you a student?"

"Yes. You know how it is," Ashley lied with a straight face. "I had a paper due, and I wanted to unwind after getting it done early. Nothing quite like a relaxing night cap."

"Is this seat taken?" another male voice asked.

Ashley looked up to see two men. One was behind the man sitting beside her at the table. The other stood over her shoulder, looking not at her, but at everyone else populating the crowded bar.

"I arrived here first, buddy. There's a seat here, but only for one."

"We ordered you a free drink. All it costs is this seat." The man's eyes were hidden behind tinted glasses. His mouth contorted into a smile. His smug voice came out again. "Do you get my meaning?" He moved his suit coat to the side, flashing the firearm at his side.

"Real subtle," Ashley said under her breath.

"I'll leave. I don't want trouble."

"What's this supposed to be, exactly?" Ashley asked once the man was gone.

"It's just a friendly chat is all, miss," the talkative one said as they both took the remaining seats. "We overheard your previous conversation and would like to help."

"Help, huh?" Ashley looked between the two men. "How are you planning on doing that? Tutoring me before my next paper is due?"

"Nothing so pedestrian." The man snapped his fingers. "Show her what we mean, J."

"J? Is that a nickname or something?" Ashley looked at his partner.

His associate placed a briefcase on the table between them, angled it toward Ashley, and opened it, revealing cash piled in neat stacks. He quickly closed it.

"Interested now?"

"I'm going to guess that your help has some strings attached," Ashley said. "Men with money don't keep it by giving cash to random women in bars. What do you want?"

"Nothing so nefarious," he said.

"I didn't catch your name. What was it again?"

"Call me Kyle," he said.

Ashley turned to the other man. "What about you? What's your name, big guy?"

The man did not answer except with a low, almost imperceptible, growling noise from his throat.

"He's not a people person. Let's stay focused here. He's just here for my protection."

"Surely you don't fear a girl like little old me?"

"Not from you. Drunken frat boys are rowdy, shall we say?"

"Right," Ashley said.

"Let's get some fresh air just outside," Kyle said. "It's awfully stuffy in here." He pulled at the collar of his suit. "We can discuss the terms of our help there."

Ashley kept her eye on Kyle's partner as he got up. "If I say no?"

"Surely you wouldn't be so wasteful with this opportunity. It's not every day you get thousands of dollars offered to you to simply walk outside and talk."

"See, I have a different theory," Ashley said with a fake sweet smile and tone of voice. She raised her hand, signaling that she wanted another round. "I know why you're here. You're not as slick as you imagine. Tell Patterson a girl outsmarted you, why don't you?"

"Come on. Let's leave this idiot to her drink. She doesn't want our offer. We can make it to other students who will appreciate our generosity."

"I think you're here to kidnap young, drunk, and vulnerable women for your boss." She paid the bartender after he placed the drink down in front of her. She waited until he left before she kept talking. "I think you can't let me leave now. What if I called the police? I've seen your face and all."

"What?"

Ashley quickly lashed out, knocking the glasses of Kyle and his associate to the table below, revealing their eyes and the rest of their faces for all to see. "Oh, would you look at that?" She giggled. "I've seen your faces now. Kyle, was it? I doubt that's your real name, but I have footage of you anyway. A girl's got to protect herself when she's out drinking. Right?" She reached up and tapped the hair accessory.

Kyle squinted his brown eyes, trying to inspect it when his eyes widened. "A camera?"

"Bingo," Ashley smirked.

Kyle's associate grabbed Ashley by the arm.

"Easy there, big guy," Ashley said. She raised her voice. "Get off of me, creep!"

The rowdy bar settled as patrons turned to see why the commotion started.

Ashley got out of her seat and used her free hand to slap the man grabbing her. "Let me go. I said no."

"Hey, buddy, let the girl go, huh?" the bartender asked from behind the bar.

"That hurts," Ashley whined, trying to pull away.

"Let her go," Kyle said under his breath.

"Let go!" Ashley stomped on his foot and tackled him to the ground.

With that, the bar fight started. Crashing from thrown furniture, yelling from the bartender, the bouncer, and the various patrons all intermixed together into a chaotic mess of noise inside the small building.

Ashley scurried to her feet and delivered a withering kick to the bodyguard's privates, causing him to roll on the floor. She turned to see Jim and Kyle already locked into a power struggle only feet away. "What are you doing here? I had it all under control."

"My ass you did." Jim delivered an uppercut to Kyle's jaw, knocking him to the floor beside his bodyguard.

A gunshot rang out in the cramped space. Jim rushed over to Ashley and forced her to lower herself to a knee. "Get down."

"Everybody calm the fuck down. Right now!" The bartender had a handgun pointed at the ceiling of the establishment. Pieces of said ceiling rained down nearby from the freshly produced bullet holes in the establishment's roof. "This shit's done now. Any arguments?"

Most of the college age patrons shook their heads and muttered incoherent platitudes. The horde pushed each other, clearing their path, desperately attempting to leave the premises. Some uttered words of shock, others of gunfire and police.

"Good, now get out, everybody." He turned toward Ashley, Jim, and the two men who started the brawl. "As for you. Stay for a minute."

"The guy's ballsy," Jim said, quietly enough to not be heard by the approaching bouncer and bartender.

"Are you alright, ma'am?" the bartender asked.

"I'm not hurt," Ashley said.

"Excellent." He turned to Jim. "Who are you? Her boyfriend and knight in shining armor?"

"Not quite," Jim said.

"He's just nervous, is all." Ashley clung to Jim's arm with a smile plastered on her face. "He's just shy. Did you see how he stepped in and kept them from having their way with me? You two as well." She disentangled herself from Jim long enough to walk to the two men and gave them momentary hugs. "Thank you so much. Who knows what would have happened if you two hadn't helped us."

"We're just glad you're alright. You two should probably

head on home. We're closing early tonight." He looked around the now wrecked room. "We'll keep these two here until the police arrive. One of our patrons has to be calling them as we speak."

"Thank you," Jim said, reaching out a hand and shaking the bartender's hand. "If she'd been hurt, I don't know what I'd have done." He wrapped an arm around Ashley's shoulder and pulled her close, moving to exit the building.

The pair exited the building out into the night air. Ashley pushed off Jim once they broke the line of sight with the bar. "What's happening with Skye?"

"She's got her own leads. It shows they're casting their net wide, so to speak. Last I saw, she had a bead on a suspicious group, and she was just talking to a guy called Kyle, I believe."

"Kyle? The same as my guy?"

"Yes, that's why I mentioned it. I believe they're scouting her, albeit not quite as forwardly as yours did." The pair turned a corner, seeing their vehicle further down the urban landscape. They saw the back door open, and Jason bolting in the other direction.

"That's not a good sign," Jim said, jogging ahead.

"Wait for me." Ashley tried to keep pace. She nearly ran into him as he stopped in front of the car. "You get inside and keep watch. I'm going to see what's happening."

She reached forward and grabbed his arm. "One guy rushing into a bar is fine, two in coordinated timing is as suspicious as fuck. You can't risk raising any alarms." Her voice was quieter as she opened the car door and guided him inside. "You're not wearing your mask, nor am I. We'll have to trust that he's as smooth as you. That's not a high bar. He can probably do it."

"Thanks," Jim said. "You're lucky the bartender and his

bouncer got Patterson's men; otherwise, you'd be the one explaining all that at the police station. You know that, right?"

"I hadn't really thought of that." Ashley's tanned skin seemed to pale at the realization. "What would I have even said?"

"No idea," Jim said, peering at the already open laptop in the front passenger seat. He reached forward and picked it up, leaning back into the seat. "I see why he rushed."

"Let me see..."

Just earlier...

"What'd you say to me?" One young gentleman in a backward baseball hat poked the other with his finger and got in his face. "Say that to my face, bitch."

"You are a pussy," the other said and laughed, obviously intoxicated - if not by his behavior, then by the near empty glass in his hand. "There, I said it again. What are you going to do?"

"Come on," a young woman grabbed the bare headed drunk. "Let's not do this."

Skye watched the entire exchange and finished her drink. "Shit's about to go down." She eyed the rest of the interior, knowing the chaos that was about to ensue. The group she spotted earlier had entered the washroom a few minutes ago and had yet to return. Before she knew it, the arguing had escalated until crashing sounds accompanied grunts and yells from different patrons.

She watched the bartender shake his head and leave into the kitchen area with other employees. *They're fucking off. Not that I blame them. It's not their fight.*

She got up and placed her back against the wall,

watching for any potential oncoming threat. She saw a chair getting thrown in her direction, so she jumped to the left, dodging it. "Christ," she said to herself. People backed off, trying in vain to create distance from the rowdy drunken patrons beating the snot out of each other nearby.

"Ow," a young woman's voice rang out. "They hit me with a glass."

"You son of a bitch," another male's voice, presumably the woman's friend, said.

"Idiots," Skye said. She saw the front door fling open and Jason run in. "What the hell's he doing here?" She saw him get in the crossfire as one man in the fight fell backwards and punched him before continuing his previous fight. She tried to approach him, only to feel a wave of dizziness. Skye felt someone wrap their arms around her stomach, entrapping her arms against her sides.

Jason recovered from the blow, holding his soon to be swelling eye. He spotted a group of three men surrounding where he knew Skye was.

Skye stomped on the aggressor's feet behind her with as much strength as she could. Her limbs felt heavy. She couldn't summon her usual strength, and her brain felt foggy. The grip on her didn't lessen. Instead, the man in front of her picked up her feet and held them together as they hauled her away.

Jason grabbed a bottle sitting long forgotten on a nearby table and swung as hard as he could on the nearest man's head, knocking him down to the floor below.

"What?" The others turned and noticed Jason recovering from the aggressive motion. "A hero, huh?" The man delivered a right punch to Jason's jaw.

He fell backwards and soon found a knee embedded in his face, knocking him to the floor proper. "You couldn't mind your own business, huh?" He climbed on top of Jason's chest, throwing punch after punch down at Jason, landing most of the blows.

Jason tried to defend himself as best he could. While he rolled side to side, keeping his arms up, he noticed Skye being dragged away through the nearby door. His guard fell when an especially straight punch connected with his head. His skull bounced back onto the wood behind with a loud noise. He lost his senses, and was trying to simply stay alive. His body moved on pure instinct, trying to dodge any blow coming in. This was mostly successful except for letting in some shots to his ribs.

The blows did not relent. In fact, the man he'd sucker punched was now delivering kicks into his side, making it hard to even breathe amidst the onslaught. Eventually, the attacks ceased coming in. He looked up and saw his opponent spit on him. He felt the warm saliva spatter on his cheek.

The noise of the brawl died down. He rolled onto his stomach to find the front door opening. He saw Ashley come inside.

"Leave it to him to play hero," she said, trying to spot him.

He barely raised a hand, trying to signal to her.

"Oh no," Ashley spotted his body amid the broken chairs, bottles, and assorted debris left in the room. "Hey." She got to a knee in front of him. "Be glad you're not that guy. I think he's still alive, but he's in even worse shape than you. He must have really pissed him off. You look like shit. Did he break anything?"

Jason tried to articulate his concerns, but all that came out was, "What happened? Where am I?"

"He must have beat you good," Ashley said. "Come on,

we're escorting you outside. Someone had to have called the police. We can't be here when they arrive. Help me get you up, yeah?"

"Uh huh," was all he could manage in his dizzy, confused state.

She got him to his feet. "We're in a bit of a pickle, but don't worry," she said. "Jim's chasing after the rat fuckers who got Skye. We're on our own currently." She used her spare hand to fish out her phone. "Now, to signal a taxi and get us home."

"I feel like death," Jason said.

"Don't say stuff like that, you fool," Ashley said. "Oh, and stay awake. I see those eyelids drooping. I heard somewhere you're not supposed to fall asleep after a concussion, and I'm suspecting you have just that."

"Is that why I'm so tired?"

"What did I just say?" Ashley asked, her voice sharp, jarring his eyes back wide open. "Now stay awake while I call us our ride, will you?"

Jason gave his best affirmation, closely resembling a grunt. He zoned out as she started talking. The scene he'd just been a part of replayed in his mind. He saw Skye's eyes closing and being carried off by Patterson's men. "The bartender," he said.

"Goodbye." Ashley hung up and pocketed the phone. "What about him?"

"He was in on it."

"What? Why do you think that?"

"They drugged her. They didn't hit her, but she was out cold."

"She'd never let someone drug her drink."

Jason shook his head. "The guy ran into the kitchen as

soon as the brawl started, and they moved at the perfect time. He's in on it. I know it."

"Maybe you're right," Ashley said. "Just try to stay calm. We can talk about this later at the apartment."

"I can't believe they got away." Jason hung his head, his arm still looped over Ashley's shoulder. "If only I'd have been better."

"It was two versus one, dude," Ashley said. Her voice was brittle and sad. "None of us could have managed getting her out without killing them and getting our faces on camera. At least if you're right, you don't have to worry about the police calling. The bartender would just delete the footage." She spotted a telltale yellow taxi turning onto their road. She raised her free arm, signaling the cab over. "Please succeed," she said to herself as it approached. "We can't lose her…"

18

Jim stood beside his car in the mechanic's parking lot facing the garage doors with his neck gaiter and eyewear already donned. Peering into the back seat, he spotted Jason. He knocked on the window, jolting him back awake. He opened the back door. "Get out, stand up, and don your mask. We can't have you falling asleep." The light had not yet dawned since Skye had been taken. Jason had dark bags under his eyes as he tried in vain to stifle a yawn, following Jim's command. A car pulled in beside his. He watched Amelia exit and slam her door as she approached.

As he watched Amelia approach, Jason spoke up. "Skye's camera is dead, for the record. It's a black screen. I checked earlier."

Amelia walked up to Jim and asked, "What was so important that you were forced to wake me at this ungodly hour? Also, who is this?" Amelia rubbed her eyes. "Your text said nothing."

Jim kicked off his car, and his eyes snapped to attention. "It's Guardian of Justice. We can't chance sensitive intel getting leaked. I'm just lucky you know how encrypting and decrypting works. You'd be surprised how long it takes some people to learn it. Moving on, we're in a real bind. Silent Justice has been abducted, and we need help to get her back."

"What do you need?" Amelia's previous whining tone was replaced with steely determination. Her jaw clenched into place and her eyes were locked on Jim's.

"I need to stop a moving vehicle that can be activated remotely. Is there anything that could do that?"

"Sure, but it's anything but cheap. It's also a little unreliable, seeing as it's such a new tech. Honestly, it's a legal gray area. That's why they're so expensive. It also takes knowledge to even plant the thing. If you're off, it's as useless as a one-legged man in an ass kicking contest, so to speak."

"I get the picture," Jim said. He showed no hint of amusement at the attempted quip. "Can you teach me how to install it?"

"Not quite. It's quite pricy to even install it because of its difficulty. I'd have to do it. Why? Is it the smuggler's car or something?"

"It's exactly that," Jim said. "It's dangerous, I won't lie. We need an ace up our sleeve for later. Will you help with this or at least try to teach me? I'd rather you not get physically involved in this, anyway. It's risky, but the cameras in the parking lot won't be a problem. So long as nobody sees your face, you're a ghost."

"If it's to help Silent get out of the shit, I'll help," Amelia said. "Is that why you need my help, so you can find Silent?"

"I know where she is. I need a plan to kill the one who ordered it. You sure you still want to help, knowing that?"

"Obviously I'm not backing out now," she said.

"Good. Get your equipment, and get in. I'll pay when we get back. This is time sensitive."

"Alright, give me a few minutes. I need to gather the device along with the tools I'll need to install it." She rushed over to her establishment's door and fumbled with her keys before dropping them. "Damn," she said. She reached down and grabbed them, unlocked the door, and disappeared inside.

Jim looked at the street as Jason climbed into the back while Amelia gathered her tools inside. His thoughts wandered back to earlier that night when he pulled into a familiar hotel's parking lot. He remembered a group of young women coming out and dragging an obviously drugged Skye into the lobby and presumably up into a room.

"Why a hotel, though?" Jim asked himself. "It's not secure enough to hold prisoners, and it has cameras everywhere. I'm missing a piece of the puzzle here, and I hate that feeling."

"I don't know." Amelia reappeared in the opening door. "It's not the ideal place I'd expect people being kidnapped to be housed. Are you sure of the location?"

"I followed them myself. I'm sure. Are you ready? Time is of the essence."

"I've collected everything." She had a bag in her hand along with her tool belt secured around her waist. "Let's get this rolling."

Jim opened the driver's door and climbed inside before unlocking the passenger door so Amelia could enter. As soon as she was inside, the engine started and they were in motion. "We'll be there before you know it."

"If she's inside the hotel, you never really explained why you needed me to plant this."

"I'm pretty sure I did. This will help me kill the head boss behind this kidnapping shit. Without her, the underlings have no financial incentive to kidnap anyone else. I know for a fact the limo you're planting that on is hers. She leaves routinely and meets her criminal cohorts. Ergo, if I can control when her engines go out, we can control where they are before our ambush. Make sense yet?"

"Seems like when they leave would be the perfect time to bust her out. There are cameras everywhere in there. It's not like leftover security can fight you if she opens the door to her room."

"I have a plan for that. You and me this morning are a minor cog in the wheel that is our plan involving this entire operation."

"What would you have done if I said I had nothing to stop the car? Also, why is your other partner here? Is he acting as a distraction?"

"He's the one helping with the cameras in the hotel parking lot. We've had to improvise, and it always gets dirty when that's the plan I've found. Even when we have one, it still goes sideways sometimes. You see why we're so happy you helped."

"One might wonder why you do it then."

"Because I've set free hundreds who, if I hadn't, would have been forced into lives of indentured servitude. How many lives can the average person say they've impacted at that level?"

"I don't argue with the crusade's inherent merits, but the innocents caught in the crossfire need to be factored in."

"Indeed," Jim said, turning onto a busier street. "It happens. It's always a tragedy and usually the result of a mistake. My counter argument to that is, if we save fifty and one accidentally gets screwed - would it be preferable if we didn't attempt rescue in the first place? I say no."

"Quite the utilitarian line of thinking. Why do you really do it? Don't give me the whole spiel."

"Aren't you curious this morning?" Jim asked.

"Call it payment on waking my ass up so early."

Jim rolled his eyes and stopped in the gridlocked lanes a few blocks from the hotel. "Because I have to try, and I see problems slip between the cracks only to harm others. I will not allow the scum who fall through the cracks to harm any more innocents."

"That's all I'm getting?"

"Are you writing a book?"

"Fine," Amelia said. "I get it. You don't want to talk. It's been a long night."

"To put it mildly. Have you ever seen someone you loved taken away and you couldn't do anything to stop it? How about having to jump through hoops afterwards and then playing twenty questions about how I feel?"

"Point taken. I'm sorry. I just wanted to learn more about all this."

"The less you know, the less they can charge you with."

"I think that's a moot point right now."

"We're here." He pulled into the parking lot of the hotel and parked near the limousine. "Get the cameras taken care of, Guardian. You better not be asleep back there."

"I'm awake, damn you," Jason's voice was strained, obviously tired. "I'm on it already."

"Forgive him. He's not normally this ill-tempered, nor am I." Jim leaned forward, keeping his hands gripped on the wheel.

Amelia turned around in the car. "Did you get the shit kicked out of you, Guardian? That's quite the shiner Guardian's got."

"Remember what I said about questions? Shit went

down, and we're fixing it. Leave it at that."

"The feeds are repeating." Jason shook his head and rapidly blinked.

"Let me double check." Jim looked as Jason flipped the laptop so he could see it. "Okay. Don't fall asleep in here."

"Concussion? You should visit the doctor and get that checked. Tell him you hit your head doing whatever you do," Amelia said. "Which is the car we're installing this on?"

Jim looked ahead. "You see the limousine parked around the hotel's side?"

"I do."

"That's the one. How do you want to approach this?"

"I should go alone over there. The less attention, the better. Why don't you run interference? Oh, right," she said. "You having that mask on in broad daylight wouldn't be the best spectacle for people passing by to notice, huh?"

"I won't have the mask on, but you won't see my face. I'll come up with something to keep their attention on me and draw their eyes away if anyone comes out or pulls in."

"Aren't you worried about me possibly seeing your face?" Amelia asked.

"You're an accomplice now. If we cross that bridge, you'll be briefed. Let's hope it doesn't come to that. I'll keep an eye out for you. How long does it normally take to install properly? It's so I have a window of reference."

"Give me a good five minutes, and it'll be good."

"Got it. Make sure you have everything and make your approach. I'll follow behind a minute after. Prepare accordingly."

Amelia took a deep breath and gripped the bag in her lap tightly.

"Nervous?" Jim asked. "You'll do fine. You're the best in the business. No one's out there. The valet guy isn't present, so now's the time, Amelia." He nodded his head toward the windshield with the traffic passing by in front of them before it stopped when the nearby traffic light turned red. "Now's your chance, while that traffic's stopped. We'll pick you up around there." He pointed to the right. "We'll be around that corner in the gas station parking lot. Remember that."

"Alright." She opened the door and exited.

Jim watched her cross the street at the nearest crosswalk and approach the target. He pulled the car into the opposite side of the parking lot. "Keep watch on the feeds and don't pass out. You're not sleeping until this evening."

"I'll be fine," Jason said, rubbing his eyes with a yawn. "I promise I'll be vigilant."

"Good." Jim lowered his mask, exited the car, and took a deep breath. He looked at the towering building and then scanned the parking garage connected for supplementary parking. He spotted Amelia moving down to the ground next to the limousine. Walking in that direction, he was still a distance off. Before he could get anywhere near, the hotel's front doors opened to have a man in a suit stand behind the nearby podium.

Of course, he comes back right now, Jim thought.

"Excuse me," Jim said, drawing his attention toward him, away from Amelia and her work.

"Yes, how may I help you, sir?" his Caribbean accent-soaked voice asked.

"I was wondering if you were familiar with this area? I hate to be that guy," Jim pointed over to the road, "but I'm new to the city. See, I need to find the local baseball stadium. The problem is, I don't know my way around. Of course I accidentally left my smart phone at home charging this morning as I rushed out the door."

"I believe I can help you with that issue, sir," the valet said. He pushed the glasses further up his nose before continuing. "There is only one problem I believe. I don't think they have a home game today."

"I'm not here to watch the game," Jim said, looking over the valet's shoulders. Amelia was still nowhere to be seen. "I have a job interview there today for working in the concession stands, and I need that job to cover the apartment cost. You see where I'm coming from? It's either this or being a delivery app driver. I'd rather get the guaranteed job if I can manage it. You get me?"

"Perfectly, sir. In that case, I will do what I can to assist you. If you'll wait, I'll head inside and get you directions from this hotel. It may take a few minutes to hand write them. Is that alright?"

"One hundred percent, man." Jim exhaled. "You're really saving my bacon, dude."

"One moment, sir." The valet disappeared inside the hotel doors again. Jim looked at the limousine, half expecting to see Amelia pop up and retreat. He looked away from her direction and waited with his arms crossed, pacing back and forth in front of the hotel's doors. While he paced, he stared at the ground. He noticed a lone barrette laying on the concrete below. He remembered Skye wearing this exact barrette last night.

The doors opening stopped his musing. He stopped beside the valet's podium and waited.

The valet cleared his throat and handed Jim a small notepad paper. "Here you are, sir," he said. "I asked the resident sports nut, known as our manager, how to get to the stadium for you. You can trust these directions. The man goes to their every home game, to my knowledge."

Finally, Jim saw Amelia pop up in the corner of his eye.

He saw her scurry off away from the car in question. He took the folded up paper and stuffed it in his pants pocket. "You are a lifesaver, my man. Thank you so much. If you'll excuse me, I have an interview to get to."

"Good luck, sir," the valet said after the retreating Jim.

Jim got back inside the car and slammed the door shut. "Hope I'm not waking you," he said before turning on the engine and getting it in gear.

"It was as boring as expected," Jason said. "The cameras saw neither you nor Amelia. The only order of business remaining is if she completed the job."

"She did," Jim said. He crossed traffic and headed to the meetup point. He turned and pulled into the nearby gas station before pulling his mask up.

Amelia hopped in once they came to a halt. They were parked in the far corner of the gas station's lot. "It's done," she said. "Let's get out of here."

Jim stepped on the gas pedal and moved onto the road.

"You know, you're cute for a vigilante."

"Oh fuck," Jim said.

"You saw his face, did you?" Jason asked.

"Only when I was on my walk. I couldn't help but glance over and make sure no one saw me. Imagine my shock when I see such a handsome man distracting the valet, keeping him looking the other direction.

"Fine, then know now that you're officially on the hook. If you try to rat us out to get a plea deal in the future, we'll be displeased."

"Are you threatening me?"

"I would like to imagine not, since that's only if you rat. If you keep your mouth shut, there's no need for such conversations. Look, you're an accomplice to Masked Justice. For everybody's sake, it's best if we don't get too close or get all buddy-buddy. Which one do you prefer? Very close or very far? Those are your choices."

"Of course I'll keep it professional. I just wanted you to know you're handsome."

"I'm getting sloppy, letting you see my face." He grit his teeth and kept driving. "Lack of sleep does that. We don't have a choice. Silent's in danger."

"Just make sure you guys rest before the rescue operation for Silent, please."

"We will not fail. It's not an option." Jim's tone was one of absolute determination and left no room for doubt or questioning.

Earlier that morning...

Skye could hear assorted female voices talking in her immediate area. She blinked her eyes open. Her movements were sluggish. She could not remember last night beyond entering the bar and ordering a bloody Mary cocktail. After that, nothing else remained. She rolled to her side and groaned.

"I think she's finally awake," one voice said.

"Don't crowd her," one of the younger sounding ones said. "She's probably feeling like crap after last night."

Skye sat up in the spacious bed and held her head, which throbbed in pain when she opened her eyes to the brightly lit hotel room. She saw a crowd of three women surrounding the bed she sat on. "Where am I? Who are you?"

"I guess that's a sensible question," the one in the center said. Her black hair was pulled into a bun. She pressed a hand on her red lipstick clad lips. "You were wasted last night after all. I'm Leslie. What do you remember?"

"I remember going to a bar, and the next thing I know, I'm waking here."

"Talk about a lucky drunk," the younger one to her right said. "I'm Sarah." Her blonde hair bounced as she chuckled and bounced on the bed's side. "If you're here, then you caught the eye of one of Miss Angela's scouts." She blew a pink bubble and popped it before continuing. "You were probably sweet-talked while you were hammered. Wonder if you signed the contract already? You must've."

"Contract?" Skye brought a hand up to her head. She closed her eyes and turned away from the open window leading out onto a balcony. She shielded her eyes from the piercing beams of the morning sun. "What are you talking about? The last thing I remember was drinking my bloody Mary and then waking here. It makes no sense."

"It sounds like you just can't hold your drink," the third one said from her left, speaking up for the first time and eliciting laughs from the surrounding young women. "My name is Michelle. Nice to meet you. It was quite the entrance you made last night." Her brown hair was short but styled. "They had to get a group of us to drag you upstairs. You were slurring your words and were totally out of it."

"Why are you all here?" Skye dared finally to open her eyes more than a few centimeters. She saw a pair of guards standing near the hallway leading to the door exiting outside into the hotel.

"We're just hopeful models like you," Leslie said.

"Model? What the hell are you on about?"

"You signed the contract last night. Don't you remember?" The youngest girl swiped a blonde strand of hair out of her face. "To get here, you had to have signed a contract to make it official and join Miss Angela's talent agency. You joined at just the right time."

"Yeah," Michelle said, sitting on the bed. "Miss Angela said we're leaving tomorrow night for Paris. We'll be on a catwalk by next weekend, modeling for the elite of Europe."

"Don't tell me you believe that?" Skye asked.

"I know," the young blonde one said. "It's hard to believe we finally got our break, but it's legitimate. Miss Angela has her own private jet, yacht, and everything."

"It is nice to see you awake." One guard stepped out from the hallway. "Miss Angela would like to speak with you to finalize your joining us. Come with me."

The girls all around her grabbed her by her hands and dragged her into a standing position near the bed. "Get it over with," Leslie said. "It's just paperwork. You'll be fine. Smile. You need the practice, from what I see."

"Paperwork?" Skye was pushed toward the guard, who took her by the arm and led her outside. Before they left, the guard looked over his shoulder at the group. "We'll be right back."

The other guard opened the door, and they entered the hallway.

"I think I'll just go on home now, boys, if it's all the same to you," Skye tried to jerk her arm loose from the men at her sides, only to find their grips holding fast. "Look, let me go."

"There's no need for cold feet, miss. If you don't wish to sign, then you can explain why to Miss Angela. It's above our paygrade, and you don't want to involve us in trouble, do you?"

"You are terrible at acting," Skye said. "Fine, I'll talk to her already."

"I am security, not customer service. Show Miss Angela

more deference than you have us if you know what's good for you."

"Piss off," Skye said. She watched as the talking guard stopped in front and turned before knocking.

A few moments later, the door popped open to reveal another guard. He stepped to the side, gesturing inside.

Skye stepped forward, leaving the guards that escorted her outside. Once she'd entered the room proper, she spotted a familiar face she'd seen many times from their research. Martha Henderson's long, dyed, platinum blonde hair was tied into a long ponytail behind her. She sat at a table near the window drinking a hot beverage while she stared out over the city below. "Welcome, Skye," she said between sips.

"I see someone went through my purse while I was drugged."

Martha laughed. "That, or you informed my employees while you enjoyed the time of your life. A fun tip from girl to girl. Taking complimentary drinks is not always the proper call. Take a seat over here, darling." She waved her over toward the vacant seat across the table.

Skye took the seat offered and noticed only one guard in the room accompanying them.

"Don't be intimidated by Duke. He's my personal body-guard. Where I go, he goes. Whom I talk to, he watches for anything untoward. We don't have to worry about such matters with you, do we?"

"Me? No," Skye said, turning her gaze away from the visibly armed Duke and back to Martha. "I presume you're Ms. Angela?"

"I see you pick things up quickly." Martha placed the cup down on the nearby cup holder and pushed the stack of papers along with a pen over toward Skye. "You sign that, and your new life awaits. You'll be flying in private jets, attending yacht parties with influential figures in Hollywood, politics - you name it, and you'll be there. Well, that's between shows anyway."

"I'm going to be honest. I remember nothing involving last night."

"That hardly surprises me. My associates told me you were quite inebriated last night. Read it over, just don't dawdle. Fortune favors the bold, and something tells me you are a bold one."

"What happens if I refuse?"

"If you refuse?" Martha simply smirked. "You'd be turning down a lifetime of leisure, money, and fame. For what? What plausible reason could you have?"

Skye pushed the end of the pen, extending the writing end, and gripped it in her right hand. "My mother always taught me to exercise caution when signing contracts. The fine print will kill you, she said."

"Your mother sounds like a wise woman." Martha showed a warm smile and turned to look at Skye. She looked Skye over from head to toe. "She wouldn't want you to miss your chance at a lavish lifestyle though, would she? You could provide for her if that's your prerogative."

"Is it true you guys are leaving soon? Am I pressed for time to decide?"

"This lifestyle is fast and enriching. If you are slow, you're left behind. You don't want that, trust me. Living with the regret of not being a fashion star would be life's biggest regret, especially for a lovely young girl like you. Don't think I haven't noticed that physique. That's not just eating right. You're putting a load of work into your appearance. Why not benefit from it beyond the health perks? I'm sure men approve of the gothic appearance you're shooting for, but there's untapped potential lying in wait. Trust me, dear. I'm a professional."

"Surely you admit it's a life-changing decision? Asking for time is not unreasonable, Miss Angela."

"Dawdle all you like, dear. If you don't take me up on my offer, there are always replacement girls who fit the mold just like you." Her casual demeanor was still polite, but the edge was clear in her voice. "Do not think you're special because you exercise and possess a cute face. Don't waste this once in a lifetime opportunity because of foolish reticence."

"I'll take your words under advisement. I'm going home now." She pushed the seat away from the table and stood up. She dusted her lap off. "When I have my answer I can come here, I trust?"

"Go home if you like," Martha waved her away. "Just know once you leave, you're no longer welcome, and the offer is off the table. We'll just have another prospect take your place. Think well before you leave, young woman. That will be all."

Skye backed up, careful not to back into Duke. She turned and walked to the exit, speaking over her shoulder. "We'll see." She opened the door and stepped out into the hotel's hallway. No guards were present. She spotted an elevator further down the hall and looked toward the room where she had woken. Her mind wandered to the young women entangled in this whole mess. Henderson's words replayed, fresh in her mind. "There's always replacement girls who fit the mold, just like you." She bit her lip. Another quote played in her mind. "We'll have another prospect take your place."

She walked away from Henderson's door and stopped between the girl's hotel room and Henderson's. She held a hand up to her mouth, trying desperately to reach a decision. *Can I really leave these girls to their fate now that I've met them? Could I live with myself?* She thought to herself. *Maybe I could screw with their operations if I stayed? Is the team planning a rescue operation as I think to myself? Would it help if I'm here or with Jim?*

A door nearby opened to reveal one girl from earlier. She saw Skye and approached. "Did you get the paperwork all done?"

"Not quite," Skye said. "Did you sign a contract yet?"

"We all did. Didn't you?"

"Not yet."

"Why are you here then?" The blonde girl asked. "We all signed before they even took us here. We assumed you signed a contract wherever you were. You're positive you didn't sign anything last night, given the condition you were in?"

"I signed nothing that I remember."

"That is odd. You still haven't?"

"No," Skye said. "She said I can head home, but then the offer's gone." Skye kept her voice quiet. "Don't you find that odd? That's what con-men do to rush their marks. They rush their target into thinking they have no time, so they make a rash decision."

"I think you're reading too much into this."

"Look," Skye said. "What was your name? Sorry. I forgot it."

"It's Sarah," the blonde girl around Skye's age said. "Sarah Richards."

"Look, Sarah, join me a moment. Where were you going, anyway?"

"I was heading down to lobby level to get a table at the restaurant. Want to join me? It's on Miss Angela."

"Seriously?"

"Sure. You go downstairs and inform them of who you're with. They won't charge you."

Skye nodded and walked along with Sarah. "Let's go. I could use something to eat."

"Excellent. Maybe then you'll realize that joining the agency would be smart."

"I'm just cautious is all." Skye reached forward and pressed the down arrow on the buttons by the elevators. "There's no such thing as a free lunch is all I'm saying."

They entered the elevator. Sarah reached forward and pressed the lobby button. The doors closed, and the elevator whirred to life. The dulcet tones of hotel elevator music met their ears.

"Has anyone ever told you that you're a paranoid person?" Sarah snickered behind a hand she brought before her mouth.

"Better paranoid than surprised I've found," Skye said with an amiable smile. "Are those girls up there your friends?"

"How did you know?" Sarah asked. "We were out drinking after work."

"Call it a hunch," Skye said before the elevator doors opened. They exited, and Skye followed Sarah.

"We all had a crap day. We work different jobs, but we all have demanding bosses. I won't bore you with the inane drama and pointless details, but their offer seemed like a deal too good to be true. So we jumped on it for fear it'd dissipate into the night sky."

"Quite the linguist, aren't you?" Skye asked, pushing the glass door open to the dining facility.

"I write in my spare time," Sarah blushed.

"Come on, writer lady. Let's get some food and a table..."

19

"Yeah, I'm at the same hotel," Skye talked into the cell phone. She made sure the door to her toilet stall was closed. Her voice was hushed. "I'm okay, really."

Jim's voice responded. "You're still there? Why on earth are they keeping their prisoners there?"

"They don't even realize they're prisoners. They all came voluntarily under false pretenses of being models in some bull shit fashion agency Henderson supposedly has. Only now she has everyone call her Miss Angela or some crap."

"Makes sense, from what happened with Ashley. Where are you now? You're not taking any risks by calling, are you?"

"She said I'm free to go; but if I do, she gets another girl to replace me."

"You cannot stay. There's no telling what they'll do once they move the girls. If we can't get them out, we can't have you getting shipped off to God knows where."

"I can be a wrench in their plans. We can coordinate your rescue attempt and strike from both inside and out. Besides, if worse comes to worst, I can defend myself."

"From multiple armed men without a weapon?" Jim

asked. "Don't be foolish. Besides, who knows when they'll take your phone? The safe play is to leave, and we can go back inside with the full group."

"We both know we can't assault this hotel. There are way too many cameras. I can create an opening while we're on the road, for example. I can cause us to pull over for a solid few minutes. It'd give you the perfect opportunity to wipe them all out in one fell swoop."

Jason's voice spoke up. "You're very confident, but we can already stop the vehicle."

"Jason?" Skye asked. She stopped when she heard the bathroom door open. She went quiet, not talking while the other occupant went about her business.

"It's been taken care of already," Jason continued. "Get out. It's far too risky."

"There you go," Jim said. "Don't worry the boy. We're stronger as a united group."

Skye heard a nearby toilet flush, followed by the sound of running water, ripping paper, and finally the sound of the door opening and swinging closed. "We're sure we can stop the car? You're sure it's the right car? You're sure that's the one they're going to transport us in? I don't see how you could be."

"What?" Jim asked. His voice wasn't there, sounding distant. "No, hold on."

There were sounds of shuffling and struggle until a new voice entered her ears.

"Do not tell me you are actually fucking thinking of staying there," Ashley said. "That's insane."

"It's the best way to guarantee none of these girls get sold overseas," Skye said. "Trust me on this one."

"I don't trust any plan where my friend sits in the clutches of human smugglers."

Judging from the sounds of the sudden noise on the other end, Jim snagged the phone from Ashley as his voice returned.

"You two can talk until they take her phone away. Call her after this. Now then, you're dead set on staying there against everyone's advisement?" he asked.

"I am. I know where the girls are staying, and I know what floor. There are too many bodies to transport via a limousine. According to the girls, they have almost thirty victims. Did your little plan account for that kind of transportation?"

"We had it on the limo," Jim said.

"That won't cut it. You'll need to watch this hotel all day tomorrow. We're leaving then. That's the best time to strike. They're taking us to a private airport outside the city. I'll get them to stop whatever we're in then."

"Odds are they'll take the limousine with them wherever they're going," Jason said. "They've been taking it everywhere. Maybe we can still use it. You could keep the girls inside calm. We don't need them stampeding over us when we get them out."

"If we're lucky, I can turn the tides in our favor from within. When it's lights out tonight, I aim to create an improvised weapon I can hide."

"You can't hide a weapon on your person that would be effective," Jason scoffed over the line.

"Clearly you don't know women's secrets," Jim said. "Look, don't out yourself in there. From what you told me, they want you to sign this little fake contract. Yeah? If you must go ahead with this plan, you're forced to sign. We'll get you out, come hell or high water. Otherwise, you'd better learn French."

"Thanks for the vote of confidence. I'll send texts throughout the night. Keep watch on those."

"I'll make sure of it," Jason said.

"I have to go. The girl I escorted downstairs might think I died if I take longer."

"If you don't keep sending messages, I'm assuming the worst," Jason said. "Keep in touch."

"You know it," Skye said. She hung up and jammed the device in her pants pocket. She pushed open the door, walked to the sink, and washed her hands before exiting into the restaurant.

Approaching the table they had chosen, she saw a few more familiar faces. "Hey, girls."

"Welcome back," Sarah said.

"Decide?" Leslie asked.

"Is that your business?" Sarah asked.

"I suppose not," Leslie laughed. "I've always been too nosy. You know why better than anyone, though." She reached over and pinched Sarah's cheek. "Someone had to watch out for gullible, impressionable maidens. Without me, you'd have been taken advantage of throughout high school if I recall."

"Don't remind me." Sarah freed herself from Leslie's grip

The larger woman reached up and pulled out the hair accessory, causing her brown hair to fall down over her shoulders. "You know I don't mean any harm. Sorry about that, Skye. I forget not everyone knows me all that well. I didn't mean to pry. It's the one thing we all have in common here anyway."

"Don't worry about it," Skye said. "I'm leaning toward signing it for what it's worth."

"I thought you might," the brunette said.

"Did you size me up that quickly?" Skye asked. She

reached down and picked up the fork before cutting off a piece of the remaining cheesecake on her plate. "What made you think so?"

"Mainly that you hadn't left yet. That tells me you had misgivings about giving up this chance." Leslie lifted her coffee mug and took a long drink of the hot liquid.

"You don't know how correct you are..."

Later that night...

"I'm glad you came around, my dear." Martha watched as Skye signed the paper between them in the luxurious room.

"Had to weigh my options," Skye said. She looked over her shoulder when she was done and saw Duke standing there. She could see his eyes hadn't left her since she entered the room. If she didn't know better, she could have sworn he hadn't blinked either. "Like I said before, assessing my options was all I wanted."

"You chose wisely." Martha picked up the paper and stuffed it into a nearby file she had on the table. "Now, I must inform you of our travel plans. Don't worry about packing anything. We'll get you a whole new wardrobe once we're in Paris. All we ask is that you are ready by ten p.m. tomorrow night. That's when our jet is scheduled to leave."

"Don't I need my passport or something?" Skye asked, raising an eyebrow. "I need to head home and grab that at least. Correct?"

"How silly of me," Martha said. She tried to hide her gritting teeth. "Of course. I thought you already had it, since the others already do. You are consistently the last to complete our preflight protocols it seems. Forgive me. After living this life for so long, the insignificant details escape my view. You may leave and return to your house to pack a briefcase, but I advise you to keep it light. You'll need all the space you can for your new wardrobe. I'd get a large suitcase. Take your daily skincare regimen too. If you don't, you'll be using what we provide, which, while luxurious, is not negotiable."

"I'll keep that in mind."

"Yes, very good," Martha's voice morphed from fake concern to one of boredom. "Now hurry on home. One of my men can drive you there if you'd like, or you can call someone to give you a ride. Either way, so long as you have your passport and report back here no later than six tomorrow evening, it doesn't matter. If you're late, do not expect us to hold our jet. Is that clear?"

Skye got out of the seat. "I got it," she said. "I'll be here on time. Punctuality is a virtue as far as I'm concerned."

"Good. Only selfish slobs make others wait while they wallow in their mediocrity. We've had a record of girls going to parties and not showing up to shows they were contractually obligated to attend. Remember that when you're attending those parties in the next few weeks, huh? I do so hate having to run interference when one of you girls gets it in your head to live like hedonists and it gets leaked to paparazzi."

"I got it," Skye said as she turned and walked past Duke, heading to the door. Opening it, she exited into the hallway. She pressed the nearby elevator button down and entered once it opened. She pulled out her cell phone and checked its signal. "No signal. Of course there's none. It's a fucking elevator." She stepped through the doors once they opened and entered the lobby area where she tried the phone again, this time finding success.

"It's been too long," Jason's voice greeted her. "Why didn't you call earlier?"

"I was taking care of phase one of my plan." She walked through the busy lobby and exited through the hotel's doors. "Can you give me a ride?"

"I can help with that," Jason said. "I finally got some sleep, and I'm wide awake. The others are napping as we speak to prepare for tonight. Wait, did I hear a door?"

"I have to head home and retrieve my passport," Skye said. "It seems I'm going overseas. I had to remind my hostess I needed one to even leave the country." She left the hotel property and got onto the sidewalk, which was demonstrably emptier than the hotel lobby. "She has to look legitimate, or she's worried I might get cold feet. It's less work for her employees and less money she'd have to pay. She probably pays for each head that walks through those doors. She may be evil, but she knows how to save money and time on labor."

"Don't tell me you like her?"

"No," Skye said. "I've talked with her a couple times, and she gives me a slimy feeling. It's almost like I can sense anger beneath the surface, but she keeps it under control. It's an odd feeling. She's some kind of psychopath or sociopath. I'd put my money on it. I see how she and her minions convinced those girls this is legitimate."

The sound of an opening door followed by one closing and the jingling of keys met her ears, along with Jason's voice. "When charismatic people have a lot of money and prioritize it over everything, including human life and decency, they can be a dangerous force. They are the single most evil form of life on earth. At least with a fool, you know what they're up to."

"Personal experiences talking?" Skye asked. She was

walking down the street when she heard a honking to her right. Looking over, she saw one driver flipping off a nearby car. She shook her head and looked away. "Just get here quick. I need to make sure I'm ready for tonight."

"I'm on my way," Jason said amid the sound of a car door closing and the engine starting faintly.

"Don't drive and talk, jackass. Be careful."

"Aww, you do care."

"Shut up."

20

_____

"How nice of you to arrive," Ashley said, looking at Skye across Jim's kitchen table. "You scared the shit out of us."

"I'm here now, aren't I?" Skye asked. "I'm here to help all of you take her down. Jason, do they leave the hotel every night?"

"They've exited every evening that I've kept eyes on them," he said. "Logic follows tonight will be no different. She's always been with a bunch of bodyguards. It won't be easy, but this is our best shot at cutting the head off this snake. The car they use is under our control, for lack of a better term. We can calculate where their car will stop. If they visit Patterson's, then I know just the place to stop them."

"Look at the big brain on Jason," Jim said, an approving smile adorning his face. "However, let's not assume to know their route. We will adjust on the fly. We are ending this tonight. When she and her men die, we get those girls out of that hotel. That's where Skye comes in. You've built a rapport with them?"

"I know a few of them. The others I only had conversations in passing. They will eventually have to leave the hotel if there is no one to escort them out. Still, I can try to let them down easy that they were duped."

"Let's double check our plan works, so that's the only reason to go back to that damned hotel," Ashley said. "How are we planning on killing her? Guns, blades, vehicular assault?"

"Straight to the point, I see," Jim said. He leaned forward and placed his palms on the table. "We're going with old faithful." He reached into the shoulder holsters he wore and pulled out a pistol, then planted it on the table. "I hope you all have been practicing at the range like I advised, because accuracy will be king tonight."

"If it's the same to you," Skye said, pointing at her bow and arrow nearby in the adjoining room, "I'll use my setup. I'm more comfortable with it than a gun."

"So long as you're accurate, I don't care," Jim said.

"Jason, you're staying in the car for this one. You're still recovering, and the cabin in my car is protected from bullets. You'll be fine. Skye, you and Ashley will be with me. Jason, you'll also take care of any nearby cameras." Jim held up a single finger as Jason responded. "Do not argue with me. You have the hardest job of all of us. You're the one stopping their car. Our choice of battlefield is in your hands. Don't screw us over by stopping them in the wrong place."

"Speaking of which..." Ashley's voice softened. "Is your head alright? You've still got those bruises. You're not woozy anymore, are you?"

"That dissipated after I slept. You remember that long torturous day when you both kept me awake after I got the shit beat out of me trying and failing to keep Skye here from getting kidnapped? We see how the hell that went. Total failure."

"Don't be so hard on yourself," Skye said. "I don't remember specifics about that night, but I know you did everything in your power. Look at me. I got myself drugged, and I prided myself on watching my drink."

"Jason here thinks it was the bartender, for the record," Ashley said. "According to him, the bartender booked it to the back immediately after. He said they'd deleted their footage after accessing their system remotely. It makes sense that he was bribed, or in on it by my reckoning."

"Focus on the present, not the past," Jim said. "We can deal with the bartender after. I don't relish the thought of a bartender helping Patterson kidnap. Jason, do you know where you're going to try to stop them?"

"I'm assuming they're going to see Patterson again. Most likely it's to either pay them tonight, or they're getting one last round of girls. Either way, assuming that's where they're going again and that's their likely route, I have a good idea. It's a little close to their destination, and by extension, Patterson's men. But it's also our best shot at firing off guns without civilian casualties or a fast police response. It is the warehouse district, after all. This will have to be fast. They don't leave the city. This is our best shot."

"It'll be over in a matter of seconds," Jim said. "We're going to arrive early and post up outside of the car behind cover. Maintain a low profile. Jason, you'll be nearby in the car. When they get close, you'll stop them. Now this is important," Jim said. "We do not open fire until the doors open. If we don't get her, then we retreat. We cannot have an elongated affair."

"If they get away?" Ashley asked. "What do we do then?

We can't send Skye back in there knowing what's in store for her."

"We'll cross that bridge when we come to it," Skye said, ignoring the question. "With any luck, I won't have to decide that. How are we getting out? Surely we're not all going to run across the open into a car? The retreat is as important as the ambush itself. Assuming we're in a prolonged firefight, we need an escape plan that doesn't leave our collective asses hanging in the wind."

"You said your car's bullet resistant, right boss?" Jason asked.

"Yeah, why? You're not saying what I think you are?"

"It would be the simplest method of getting you all out safely, assuming you weren't spread too far."

"Care to share with the class?" Ashley asked.

"I can drive it to you all, providing cover as you get in. It's simple, but it would be effective. Not everything needs to be high tech."

"I suppose the new plating needs to be tested," Jim said. "Though I hoped that would come later rather than sooner. Are you sure you want to drive through a combat zone? Bullets flying and hitting your vehicle will still be mortifying, even if it is armored."

"I'm prepared for whatever happens. You can count on me doing what I have to," Jason said.

"He has guts," Ashley said. "If we didn't already know that, he proved it before. He'll get us out or die trying."

"It's the die trying part I'm more concerned about," Jim said. "Not that I don't trust you. It's a dangerous job for anyone to undertake. I trust you can do it, provided you are feeling better. We don't need someone with vertigo or amnesia in charge of our escape."

"Give me any cognitive tests you wish," Jason said. "I'm ready for this."

"You don't need to prove anything to us," Jim said. "If you say you're ready, that's good enough for me. Now then, make sure you have plenty of ammunition for your chosen weapons. Ashley, do you still have all those boxes of ammo I got for you?"

"Of course," she said.

"Good. Go get them from your two's apartment. I assume Skye has to fetch her arrows and bow, anyway. You two go get prepared. I need to talk to Jason before we leave. Do not dawdle."

"I'll be glad when she's finally dead," Ashley said. "Maybe kidnappings will finally subside in this city. Come on. I want to talk to you while the boys are busy talking."

The men watched the two girls exit the apartment.

Jason immediately turned to Jim once the door shut. "Sir, I'm alright. I know you're worried, but I can do this. I know I failed in saving Silent Justice, I mean Skye, last time, but give me another chance."

"Easy there," Jim said. He placed a hand on Jason's shoulder. "I don't doubt your willingness to be there for us and the team. I'm worried you're not showing enough concern for you." He used his other hand to poke Jason in the chest. "You can't guard us, Guardian, if you're not taking care of yourself properly. Now, you got some sleep today, didn't you?"

"As soon as you and Ashley said I could, I did. I had to go pick up Skye after I woke up, but I'm not sleep deprived, sir. I'm in full control of my faculties. The bruises hurt, but that has no bearing on my ability. I'm not dizzy."

"Chill out already," Jim said. He removed his hands from Jason and walked into the living room. He picked up a bag sitting beside the sofa before walking back to Jason. "You're not being replaced or kicked off the job. I wanted to ask a few questions before we departed."

"Go for it."

"It's more of a hypothetical question that's not pertinent to our current case of sorts. It's about Charles Baskins. Do you know who that is?"

"I've heard Ashley and Skye talk about him in passing before, but I never pressed further. I believe he's in the government. What was it - the House, maybe?"

"You have an excellent memory," Jim said. "Yes, he's a member of the House. I wanted to know if there's any way you could help get information on Charlie's doings. It's not urgent. Think of it as a pet project of mine. I suspect that, sooner rather than later, he's going to be a pain in our asses once again. This time he'll be more dangerous than a guy wielding a sword. He's a politician with influence. I want to be two steps ahead of him. You're my way of making that happen if you would. At least teach me how to gather intel safely if you can't."

"That's all?" Jason asked.

"Buddy, I believe he's going to have access to all kinds of secrets. I doubt you can just hack and get any of it."

"No, and I wouldn't be dumb enough to try anything rudimentary. I've heard tale of it happening, but I wouldn't risk it. There are safer alternatives. Odds are I'll find an old email and start there in tracing. I can't guarantee anything, but I can keep watch."

"That'd mean the world, partner," Jim said. He playfully slapped Jason's shoulder with a wide smile. "Let's get ready. We don't want the girls to beat us in getting ready. We'd lose our pride as men."

"Sir?" Jason asked.

"Come on, dude. You know how women can be." He looked at the apartment door, ensuring it was closed and they were alone. His voice lowered so low that only he and Jason could conceivably hear, even if Skye and Ashley returned. "You go to their house to pick them up for some date, and they're always still getting ready. Surely you've had that happen? It's a common occurrence. I mean, maybe it's just Cynthia, but I know I've heard guys make jokes about it before."

"I'm not the guy to look to in getting dates, sir."

"I'll help you with that when this is done. We can't have Guardian of Justice remaining celibate his whole life. There'd truly be no justice in this cruel, unforgiving world should you never experience the touch of an attractive female."

"Uh, okay."

"I'm joking, man," Jim said. "You need to lighten up. Women like it when you have a sense of humor."

In Skye's Apartment...

"Where's my mask?" Ashley asked across the apartment. "I can't find it anywhere."

"I put it in the wash. Look in the dryer basket. You need to wash that regularly." Her voice lowered so Ashley couldn't hear. "How she can stand not washing it regularly is beyond me."

Ashley entered Skye's room and leaned on the side of the door frame. Her mask was firmly clutched in her hand. "When did you have time?"

"Cleanliness is next to Godliness, as mother used to say. I saw it on your floor, so I put it in the laundry basket. I assumed you were done wearing it until next wash, since it was there. This isn't about your mask," Skye said.

"No, it's not,"

Skye felt two hands wrap around her stomach. "I knew it."

"I thought you were gone, at least until we got you out." She felt the momentary embrace end.

Skye turned around after making sure the arrows inside the quiver were stocked as she liked. "Don't get all mushy on me yet," she said. "I appreciate the concern and apologize for the worry, but risk is part of this job."

"I get that," Ashley said. "It just doesn't help when I had to drag Jason out after seeing you get taken off."

"Close calls are going to happen," Skye said. "God knows I learned my lesson about drinking anything a stranger makes now. Don't worry. That won't happen again."

"If you ever make me worry that much again, I'll slap you."

"Gee, thanks," Skye said. The nearby television in Skye's room showed a news feed. "What's going on now?"

Ashley picked up the remote from on top of the tv stand and unmuted it.

"The vigilante known as the Soaring Specter has struck again, folks," the news anchorwoman said. She shuffled the stack of papers in front of her and looked over at her dashing male co-host. "Do you think they'll catch him soon?"

"I sure hope so. Crime has been rising in Denver, and we the people need to feel safe. Not that we're going to be gutted by some random freak in a mask who feels he's worthy to dish out death and destruction. For all the children watching," he said, "do not make a mistake. These people are monstrous criminals. Stay in school."

"Turn that drivel off," Skye said.

Ashley hit the red button on it and placed it back atop the stand the television sat on. "You know he's right."

"Not quite. We know our victims are guilty. There is no guessing. We are removing evil. It's all a matter of math. Without us, how many monsters would linger wandering the earth? Never forget why we do this. It gives us purpose and strength when we need it most."

"You have quite the knack for inspiring speeches. I entered the room nervous, and now I feel we can conquer the world. You still require work as a potential leader."

"Do I now?"

"Leaders do not get taken by surprise," Ashley said. "I couldn't have done anything else myself in that position. I'm not a leader though."

"That was literally out of my control. We both know that was the exception. You know what? I'm not sitting here trying to convince you of my leadership abilities. Let's go. We don't want to keep the guys waiting while we're sitting in here jabbering about inane topics."

"Inane?" Ashley asked, watching Skye walk past her and out of the room. She turned and followed her. "I don't know what that word means, but it annoys the hell out of me. Hey wait a second..."

21

"How much longer are we waiting?" Ashley asked over the call. She leaned around the nearby dumpster by the street. "Even with this mask and getup, I'm getting a chill. It's like forty degrees, and we've been here for over an hour. Not to mention the damned smell. Why am I always the one near the trash?"

"Henderson's entourage left the hotel about fifteen minutes ago. They should be here soon. Get ready, and keep alert."

"If you're not quick, you get the remaining spots," Skye said. "Besides, I have the grappling gun. You're near the car, so don't complain. You're in probably the safest spot for this party. Maybe this will cause you to do laundry more often anyway."

"I knew there was an ulterior motive!" Ashley's voice raised in volume.

"Simmer down, kids," Jim said. "I'm the one with flimsy cover here. If anyone should bitch, it's me. Cynthia's going to be pissed until we finish this operation, so focus and get it done safely. Everyone has made sure their safety's disengaged, yes? Also, make sure it's loaded. I know not everyone is very experienced with firearms. Just point and shoot. Never have your finger on the trigger unless you mean to kill whatever or whoever it is."

"I find it's a good rule for weapons," Skye said. "Quiet. I hear an engine coming. It might be them. Guardian, can you see them on your computer?"

"Negative," he said. "It's probably someone cutting through this warehouse district on their way home after a long day. Still, keep watch, Silent. You're the one with the best vantage point. Boss, you sure sitting on that bench is the best place?"

"I look like a hobo, don't I?"

"I guess, maybe?"

"It'll be fine. If worse comes to worst, I can duck behind this car." He looked up from his phone at the lone car sitting in front of him, the only cover he saw on the barren street. "Sorry, whoever's car this is, but you left it here. It's not all my fault."

"They have insurance," Ashley said. "Who cares so long as they're not hurt?"

"I see another car coming. Get battle ready." Skye paused. "It's a limousine. I have eyes on our target headed this way. They'll turn onto the street in approximately twenty seconds. They'll be coming from Masked Justice's right, so adjust accordingly. I want us all firing volleys into that damned car and at anyone who gets out."

"She gets kidnapped once, and she's bloodthirsty," Jim said. "She's not wrong." The sound of a handgun readying up echoed over the call. "God be with us," he said. "Stay down and keep behind cover when you're not firing. I don't want anyone getting shot."

Nobody had time to speak before a pair of headlights turned onto the nearby street Jim sat on.

"I'm hitting it now," Jason said. "Watch your eyes. This could be bright."

Skye saw a flash of light and averted her eyes quickly. She slowly opened her eyes and saw the limousine slowing down, rolling until it was across the street from Jim. She nocked an arrow and watched the proceedings below. "On your call, boss."

"Wait for it," Jim's voice was low and even.

The car finally came to a dead stop a little past Jim. Its door opened, and two men stepped out of the car's front seats. The car's hood popped open as the men exited. One guard held a gun, and the other had empty hands. The empty-handed guard stopped in front of the now exposed engine. "Of all the fucking nights." Jim could hear the would-be mechanic speak. "I can't find shit. What are we going to do? Call for a tow truck?"

"Open fire," Jim said.

Skye saw Jim stand up from the bench below. She readied an arrow, aiming at the man keeping watch below. She let loose an arrow. Before the arrow had even landed, the sound of gunfire erupted. It was a good thing she aimed for the chest as her target ducked straight down. The arrow that would have punctured his abdomen instead punctured his throat.

His hand instinctively reached up to the foreign obstruction. He felt the arrow piercing through but left it alone, instead laying in front of their limousine.

The car's doors slammed shut. A shadowy figure inside could be seen crawling up from the back seat into the front driver's seat.

Two guards emerged from the limo. They fired over the

top of the limousine, causing Jim to duck behind the nearby civilian car.

The man up front ducked and returned fire in Jim's direction, but otherwise did not move.

More gunfire rang out, presumably from Ashley, as Skye readied another shot. She fired off another arrow, aiming at one of the two peeking their head. Her shot missed the mark, hitting the top of the vehicle as the target's head ducked out of sight. "Shit," she cursed to herself.

"We need to leave soon," Jason said. "We have around five minutes before we're in dangerous territory."

"Just a minute," Jim yelled over the line. "Get the engine started. We'll leave momentarily."

Jason could barely hear Jim over the deafening gunfire over the earpiece. He placed his laptop to the side in the back seat and climbed forward into the front seat. He started the engine. "We're ready anytime."

Jim chanced a peek over his cover and fired at where the enemy's head had peeked up a few times prior. Just before he squeezed the trigger, the target's head appeared again. The shot exited the back of his victim's skull and onto the pavement below.

The sound of an engine starting roared out as the street went silent. Henderson's limousine roared to life and plowed over the top of the bodyguard that was in front. His crushed body was left lying on the street. The car accelerated down the road, leaving a bloody trail from the body and one more bodyguard sitting now without cover.

"Take him down and we're leaving."

The man ran down the street, trying to reach the nearby alleyway to find cover, desperately pumping his arms and breathing rapidly.

One last shot rang out, and the target fell to the ground.

Jim got to his feet and rushed over to the fallen man. He double tapped him in the back of the head, finishing the job. "Get out here. We're leaving now."

No verbal answer was given, but the sound of a rapidly approaching car met his ears. The car stopped a few feet away from Jim.

Ashley emerged from a nearby alleyway and jumped into the back seat.

Skye slid down a ladder connected to a nearby building and rushed inside after chucking the grappling hook into the rear compartment.

Jim made sure everyone was inside before climbing into the front passenger side. "Get us out of here. Now!"

Jason didn't waste time. The car was moving before Jim's sentence even finished. "It looked like we got a lot of them."

"We didn't get the target, though," Jim said. "It was only some bodyguards. One of which she killed herself. Those are expendable. How'd they restart their engine?"

"Our mechanic's gift must've run out of juice, allowing the engine to restart."

"I didn't see Duke," Skye said.

"Who the hell's Duke?" Jim asked. "Oh right," he said. "You told me earlier. That's her personal bodyguard, yeah? It makes sense he'd send all the others out to be the first line of defense so he could stay alive."

"She's got to be shitting bricks now," Ashley said. "I don't care who you are. That'd rattle anyone. Is that a good thing or bad?"

"It means she'll run," Skye said, her voice even. "She's not the type to battle it out to the death. More likely she'll run and cut her losses, or she'll send more men to their death to keep her safe. She's arrogant and thinks she's better than everyone else. It doesn't surprise me that she'd be fine with killing and sacrificing her own men."

"Hopefully they had life insurance plans for their families, but they knew the bed they were climbing in when they took the job from her," Jim said. "Now this is important - did everyone use the rounds I gave you? Please tell me you did."

"You think I carry a bunch of rounds from anyone else?" Ashley asked.

"Good," Jim breathed a sigh of relief. He gathered himself and looked over his shoulder at Skye and Ashley. "I predict you'll get a phone call tomorrow morning from Miss Henderson. I bet she'll be mad or sound angry from what you've said."

"No doubt she will," Skye said. "She'll want to get out and deliver her cargo to her client. She'll probably never come back to Denver again after this job, now that she knows we're onto her. This is our last chance, if you ask me."

"You're not returning to that hotel now?" Ashley asked.

"Give me a reason not to. Tell me it's easier with me here outside with you and not a stealth force on the inside."

"I doubt you'd make much difference on the inside," Jason said. "They're on notice now and will take no chances. They'll stop for no one after tonight. If you go in there, you're going to Paris unless we on the outside stop them. The point is, you're better off with us."

"Don't make the boy worry," Jim said with a smirk. "He's right," he said. "Another pair of practiced hands is ideal for what's probably going to happen. You wouldn't be armed back inside."

"I know the airport they're taking the girls to," Skye said after a momentary pause. She picked up the recently abandoned laptop and navigated to the open internet browser. She found the map browser Jason routinely used and moved the cursor to the airport she recognized on the map outside of town. "It's about an hour outside town. My bet is they like the privacy of departing out there. Everything would look like business as usual. The girls think they're going to Paris to be runway models."

"We'd have our pick of the battlefield." Ashley leaned over and looked at the screen Skye had in her lap. "We could scout out a fitting area and kill her."

"Take them out, how?" Jim asked. He placed an arm on the headrest and half turned around in his seat. "We already used the gadget from Amelia. It worked, but now that we've used it, we have to assume it's compromised and it wouldn't work again. That's assuming we could even install another, which I doubt. They'll have men outside all night watching whatever vehicle they're going to use, if they have sense."

"Just shoot their tires out," Ashley said. "It works in the movies."

"You're suggesting we casually lean out the side of our car windows and try to aim at a moving car's tires at over sixty miles an hour, and just hope that no civilians are injured as a result?" Jason asked. "Our best option is something I've heard tell of that I've never tried before. I would need help from one of you."

"What's the idea?" Skye asked.

"As we all know, cars nowadays have onboard computers. Hell, some like this pimped out car, possess their own router and modems for the internet."

"What's your point?" Ashley asked. "You're not talking of trying to hack in and try to control their car?"

"Precisely, but it would be more complicated than how you're making it sound."

"How can we help?" Jim asked. "You're the most technologically gifted. If you're unsure, how could we assist?"

"I don't need your expertise," he said. "I need one of your cars to test it out."

"Use your own," Ashley said. "You're not messing with my car's system."

"I would if I could," Jason said. "My parents, bless them, gave me a car. The catch is it's as old as the fossil fuel in its tank. It doesn't have an onboard computer, nor an air conditioning or heating system, I might add."

"I'll help you out," Skye said.

"What?" Ashley asked. "You have work tomorrow. How can you give your car to science when you need it?"

"I assumed we'd be taking tomorrow off work, Chucklehead," Skye said. "My job's more of a work your own hours thing anyway. All I do is log in and accept jobs. If I don't log in, I'm not working."

"Not all of us possess that luxury," Ashley said. "I can call in sick, but then I'm screwed if I get sick. Elite fitness doesn't play around with their employees showing up."

"When does your shift end tomorrow?" Jim asked.

"My last client is at two p.m. tomorrow. It's an early day. Everybody signed up for morning and early afternoon sessions."

"Let's hope that's early enough. If not, you'll have to call off early and let chips fall where they may," Jim said. "Do you understand me? We're finishing this tomorrow, and I won't take any excuses. Everybody shows up tomorrow. I'll aid how I can, buddy. My apartment is your home until you figure out the process."

"It's all a matter of actually doing it and figuring it out myself. It may take hours, and you may need to take your car to a mechanic afterward."

"Luckily, I know one who's very good," Skye said. "It'll be fine."

22

"You've been busy lately." Cynthia poured herself a cup of coffee. She looked at Skye and Jason sitting on the couch before turning back to the nearby Jim, keeping her voice low. She whispered into his ear. "What are they doing? Don't they have class or a job?"

"It's a special day, sweetie," Jim said, flashing a smile. "Let the kids have their fun. Our job is ending today."

"Well, there's good news," Cynthia said. She leaned into his side and wrapped an arm around him. "You keep that up, and I may just be in a good mood tonight."

"Good mood, you say?"

"In so many words," Cynthia said. "Assuming all goes well, would you have spare time tonight?"

"We'd want a party. Doesn't that sound grand?" he asked. "We hadn't quite decided on the food, but it'll probably be pizza."

"Who doesn't love a pizza party?" Cynthia asked. "Now, what are they working on?"

"You're positive you want to know?" Jim asked.

"I asked, didn't I?"

"They're working on how to stop a car remotely. You know how cars have computers on them nowadays. He seems to think it's possible."

"It's possible alright. It was crucial in the Mantle versus Sexton ruling."

"What is that again? Some of us didn't go to law school."

"That was the first ruling that dealt with homicide via what you're talking about precisely. It was cited in legislation that those who're found guilty should suffer over thirty years inside a federal penitentiary. Does he know that?" She reached into the nearby freezer and grabbed a small, sealed package of ice cream. She retrieved a spoon from the nearby drawer and opened it.

"I doubt very much that he would care," Jim said. He watched her eat the frozen dairy treat. "You want to hear the funniest part?"

"Go on." Cynthia licked the spoon, purposely being suggestive.

"She is letting him experiment on her car to see if he's got it down. Imagine taking off work and not knowing if it'll work afterward. We'd have to tow it ourselves to Amelia's if that happened. Not to mention rework the admittedly shaky plan we're running with."

Cynthia devoured another spoonful. "You really think the kid can manage it? It was notoriously difficult unless you had a program that automated it to a degree. He's trying to free ball it? You know how difficult learning that networking miracle alone would be?"

"Let's see if that works." Jason pushed himself off the couch. He looked at Skye nearby. "Shall we go to the parking lot?"

"Let's hope you've got it right. I could finish some work if you're correct."

Jim and Cynthia watched the pair wander out of the apartment.

"If I were you," Cynthia said, "I'd get a backup plan to this. I like Jason and all. He's got a good work ethic. It's just a tall ask. Those bruises over his face tell me he's got something to prove. That could be inspirational, or it might push him over the edge."

"I owe it to him to give him another chance. This time it'd be on his own home turf. He doesn't know how to fight, but with computers he's at home. It would also raise his confidence, and maybe he'd actually find a girlfriend."

"Lord help anyone that gets involved with another one of you." Cynthia tossed the spent ice cream container into the nearby trash can. "Won't take long for you anyway."

"Huh?" Jim followed Cynthia into the living room. She walked toward the hallway leading to the bedrooms. "Where are we going?"

"I did not wake early only to be left hanging because of your using your apartment as a staging point for your little assault. Come on. I need a shower."

"A shower, you say?" Jim asked.

"I need you to show me how to turn on your shower. Duh." Cynthia stopped at the entrance to Jim's bathroom. She turned around. "What did you think I meant? We aren't even official yet."

"Seriously?"

"You never asked me officially. What kind of girl do you take me for?"

"My apologies." Jim reached down and grabbed her hands, enveloping hers. He stepped closer and whispered huskily, "Will you go out with me?"

"Yes. Now was that so hard? We're officially an item now. Grab my bag I brought. I put it behind the couch there." She pointed past him.

Jim did the task and returned it to her.

"Good, now come inside. We can't allow the kids to see us enter together."

"Coming out of the bathroom together is totally fine, though?" Jim asked.

"Are you trying to talk me out of this, Mr. Benning?"

"I'd never dream of it." He opened the door and let Cynthia enter the tiled room first. "If I can help your pre-day routine, then what kind of boyfriend would I be if I denied you?" He stepped in after her and shut the door. The sound of running water was heard. Mischievous female giggles and moans were drowned out by the rushing water.

In the parking lot…

"I will not pretend I understand anything on that screen," Skye said. "Is that flashing a good sign?"

"Bad unfortunately," Jason said. The corners of his mouth curved downward. "I thought that was it for sure. Maybe if I try another avenue of attacking this problem." He leaned back in Skye's passenger seat. He looked over at her in the driver's seat. The heating was on, blowing air in their faces all the while.

"It's early in the morning yet. We have time to try new avenues," Skye said. "It's what, six in the morning? If you can figure something out by noon, we'll be set. You still have a good six hours, I bet." She was interrupted by her cell phone buzzing in her pocket. "That's me," she said. She pulled out the device and checked what caused the notification. "We have our new timetable it seems."

"What time did she set for you to return?" Jason asked.

"She says they're leaving at three and that I'm to arrive by two. Last night spooked Ms. Henderson - originally it was six."

"That cuts my available time," Jason said. "That's seven hours, give or take," he said. "I have an idea." He leaned forward and got back to work on the laptop perched above the glove compartment.

"I have faith that you'll pull through for us," Skye said.

"Funny that you're encouraging me," Jason said while working. His fingers were busy, and the sound of keystrokes filled the air between his words. "I was the one who couldn't stop you from getting dragged off. Everyone's been supportive and all, but I know the truth of the matter. I was useless when the meat hit the metal, so to speak."

"Seriously?" Skye asked. "You're an idiot."

"Is that right?"

"You showed more bravery inside that bar than almost any other grown ass adult. I bet if you placed any other male, except for Jim, in that position, he'd look out only for himself."

"Courage doesn't mean much if you cannot capitalize. I think they call those inept fools in modern times."

"Stop getting so down on yourself. Do you think that helps? All you're doing is putting extra pressure on yourself."

"Did you hear Cynthia before we left the apartment?" Jason asked. "I did. She doesn't think I can do this, no doubt inspired by that failure."

"She said that because this technological mountain is rough to climb. Not because of you or your abilities. Jim put you in charge because he trusts your abilities, and so do I.

You think I'm an idiot for my confidence? What does it mean for you?"

"That I'm more realistic?"

"You're in your own way," Skye said. "Focus, and think about the past later. You can't change it. Deal with it and move on to be a richer individual. Which, mind you, I don't believe you should be ashamed of your attempt to rescue me. You showed courage by taking on three guys to hear Jim and Ashley tell the story."

Jason looked up from the screen. His bruised face was covered in purple, and his eye was half swollen. "Maybe I should convince Jim to train me in fighting, not simply staying in shape. At least then I'd be useful in the field."

"You act like fieldwork is all that matters. It's not. Having someone watching your back and working behind the scenes to support the soldiers is basic warfare. We're in a war of sorts. You are playing your part. It's sweet that you think you have to contribute the way we do, but you're already more than doing your part. Let's switch off the pity party and find our answer before our newest deadline."

"I guess you're right," Jason said. "Let's head back inside. I don't fancy wasting all your gas keeping the heat on in here all day, or your battery."

The pair got out of Skye's car and headed back inside the apartment complex. They stopped at the ground floor elevator. Jason reached forward and pushed the up button. "The only option I see," Jason said, "is if I bypass the security of the onboard motherboard."

"Great," Skye said. "You have a plan."

The door dinged and opened. The pair entered and watched the doors shut.

"It's a proprietary antivirus and firewall software combination," Jason said, "which is much easier said than done. It's not like I have a USB stick that has some program. If only I was so lucky."

The elevator door opened. The pair got out and brushed past a couple entering the confined space. They turned and headed for Jim's apartment. "Is that something they'd have on the local black market?"

"Hell no," Jason said. "If it's anywhere, it'd be online on the black market - which is our perfect answer." He turned to look at Skye. His eyes were wide, his voice hitched in excitement. "The delivery would be digital, so it'd be near instantaneous. I'd just need some crypto that has been mixed already to maintain anonymity."

"I didn't understand half that last sentence, but you know what you're doing it sounds like." Skye reached for the doorknob, only for it to open outwards. She quickly stepped back, avoiding getting smacked in the face.

Cynthia emerged and shut the door behind her. "Any luck with your project, you two?" Cynthia had her purse draped over her shoulder and her hair was wet. She stepped to the side, allowing them access.

"He has an idea," Skye said. "That's better than he had five minutes ago." Skye noticed Cynthia's hair. "Is your hair wet? It wasn't when you came here."

"So what if it is?" Cynthia asked. "I need to be going. You two keep working on that, and Jim said tonight we're having a party. Don't be late for your own party. I trust you all will get it done."

"We appreciate the vote of confidence." Skye watched Cynthia turn and walk off down the hall toward the elevator they'd just left.

"She showered here," Skye said, quietly enough so only Jason could hear.

"So?" Jason asked with a shrug.

"I'm willing to bet the boss was in there with her," Skye said. "Let's see. Don't make a big deal of it if I'm right. It's cute they're finally getting together. It's about time."

Skye opened the door, and they both stepped inside.

"Any luck?" Jim sat on the couch.

"I assume you two had fun while he was working?" Skye asked, a knowing smile finding its way to her face. "Cynthia's hair was wet. So is yours I see."

"Saving water has always been one of my most important values. Had it drilled into my head from years of my parents complaining to me. Now let's ignore my relationship and get back on track. How close are we?"

"I got a message from Henderson." Skye fished the device out and handed it to Jim.

"I have an idea," Jason said while Jim was reading the message.

"Lay it on us," Jim said.

"I need some already mixed catcoins," Jason said.

"What do you need crypto for?" Jim asked, handing the phone back to Skye. "Anything you order will take multiple days to arrive."

"Not if I find a digital seller. What I need isn't physical," Jason said. He raised his laptop lid and navigated to a new browser specially designed for browsing the underside of the internet. "If I find the right seller, one that's not bullshitting, then I can use their software as a sort of shortcut."

"You think there's someone looking to sell such dangerous technology over the internet?" Jim asked. "That'd be risky."

"No more than selling weed online, which is a modern thing - not that I recommend buying it that way with cannabis turning legal slowly."

"Back on point." Skye elbowed Jason in the ribs with gentle care.

"Right," Jason said. He typed in the username and password he'd created for the marketplace before. "I need to decrypt this key, and I'll be logged in. Then I can peruse their electronic section."

"Electronic?" Jim asked.

"It's not like these are big name brand companies. Their categorization leaves a lot to be desired. I know that's where they sell DDoS attacks on whoever you want, along with people's personal information. I assume it'd be next to those."

"Won't they need somewhere to send this mythical program? How are you going to get it?"

"Private emails are a thing. I set these up with special care in case something like this ever happened. There's no way they can trace it back, even if they tried. Most sellers on these illicit sites don't give a crap who you are so long as you pay promptly. It's nice since if you buy other merchandise, you need to give them an address. You really don't want to do that with random drug dealers online, hence why I didn't recommend it for that."

"I get it, professor," Jim said. "Any luck finding what you need?"

"I'm looking," Jason scrolled down the page and clicked on the next page number. "This is a rare program I'm searching for. The odds aren't fantastic they're listed in this marketplace. Only a few folks have access to such software, for safety's sake. Having said that," he said, "where there's money to be made, someone somewhere is always wanting to sell."

"Love of money is the root of evil," Skye said. "Not that it stops any of us."

"Least of all scumbags," Jim said. "How much do you figure it would cost if it's listed?"

"Who knows?" Jason asked. "If they have it, they have friends in dangerous places. The risk they'd be taking would reflect in the price."

"I ask because I only have so much crypto remaining," Jim said.

"What's this?" Jason asked. He clicked on one listing by a username of 'RemoteP'. "What have we here?" The screen dimmed black for a moment before finally loading. "Remote access tunneling program. Works on cars, phones, cameras. He lists twenty other things, but I'm wondering if he's not just trying to hype up his basic software."

Jim leaned over so he could peek at the screen. "Five thousand dollars? Good God. Wait a minute. Click on the images. It shows the interface."

"No, not on this browser. If I do that, anyone watching this could penetrate my network. I won't allow that. It's probably to fool unsuspecting normies into clicking. That's rule one. Never click on any videos, screenshots, or maximize your window. It tells anyone looking a lot of information."

"You're not serious?" Jim asked.

"There is only one safe method. It just takes a while."

"Do that," Jim said. "I'm not keen on blowing five thousand dollars without being sure of what we're getting."

"I'll do that while I'm sending him a message," Jason said.

"Why not just do that?" Skye asked. "That's simpler."

"Lying to make money springs to mind. If the screenshot checks out and he corroborates it, then I'd be reasonably confident in what we're getting. Nothing is a guarantee on the black market though."

"Of course it's not," Jim said. "It's only five thousand," he said to himself. "I can afford that, right?"

"I sure hope so," Skye said. "It looks like our best hope of getting this done."

"Looks like he's responded already," Jason said. He pulled up a page with a jumble of mismatched letters, numbers, and special characters.

"Let me decrypt this really quick."

"They take security seriously in these places, I see."

"One bad transaction is all it takes to go to prison for decades with these folks. Wouldn't you be careful too?"

Jason copied the encrypted message. His mouse curser went to the bottom right of the page and right clicked on the encryption program he used. He input the password for it and selected decrypt.

A new window popped up along with a progress bar that filled extraordinarily fast. He pasted onto a new blank document. "Let's see here." He read the message out loud, so the others didn't have to crowd him. "I understand your skepticism," he said. "The program on sale for this listing does indeed have the vehicular function. I have tested it myself and I guarantee on my honor that so long as you follow the included instructions, it will work for you. Do note," he said, "I do not condone any illegal acts you may or may not do. I do not wish to know about your plans. If you are interested, please place an order or reach out for further information. Have a great day."

"Quite the salesman, isn't he?" Skye asked. "His guarantee doesn't mean shit."

"It does in this case," Jason said. "Look." He pointed at the stars listed beside RemoteP. It showed a 4.8 out of 5 stars. "It's difficult to get much of a following on these sites. If he has that many review stars, he's either good, or he paid for a bunch of fake reviews and had no sales on his products. That is not just for this item. It's for his entire account. They take their reviewing system seriously. It is their livelihood after all."

"Who's going to enforce that?"

"On these kinds of places?" Jason asked. "They do themselves. Like I said, they have their clients' addresses. They can send it to police along with evidence that they bought illegal goods off a black market online, excluding any identifiable information on themselves if they're smart. If you enter a transaction on these sites, it's best to be nice and give an excellent review, or don't leave one period if you know what's good for you."

"You've done this before," Skye said. "What did you buy in the past?"

"Let's just say when I turned eighteen, I wasn't content with buying legal weed in dispensaries and wanted to branch out in my psychonaut adventures. Those were dark times in my life. As far as the story I just told you - it's a famous tale on the various marketplace forums that people tell the newbies so they don't abuse the review system. Whether it actually happens, I don't know."

"You think this is the real deal?" Jim asked. "I have about one hundred thousand left in this paper wallet."

"The PHR must have paid damned well." Skye whistled. "How much did they deign a human life worth?"

"Depended on who the target was. The harder the job, usually the higher the pay. On the low end, it was about ten thousand, and it soared higher from there. Are you planning to mix these coins again?"

"I figure I should," Jason said. He reached and held out his empty hand toward Jim.

Jim took his time before eventually dropping the USB

stick containing the crypto wallet into Jason's hand. "Fine. Buy it, and see if we're in business."

Jason took the USB stick and connected it to the side of his laptop. "Stick around. I'm going to need you to enter your password for this paper wallet to withdraw the funds. I appreciate the five-thousand-dollar investment. You must either be terrible with money or believe in my skills."

"What's five thousand dollars if we can save those girls' lives, right?" Jim asked. "The fact I know you can do it is icing on the cake. You're those girls' best chance right now, Jason. If this doesn't work, they might receive injuries."

"How do you mean?" Skye asked while Jason got to work mixing the already mixed catcoins. "How would they get hurt if we rescue them?"

"To get them out, we'd probably have to run them off the road - which could injure not just their cargo, aka the girls, but also us. This is the best option for everybody involved."

"I'm glad you didn't take your new girlfriend's advice," Jason said. He handed the laptop over to Jim. "Input the password to your wallet, please."

"Just a second." Jim left the computer on his lap. He leaned to the side and dug out his wallet from his back pocket. "God knows I'd never remember the password I set. I think it was the maximum limit on the password limit. I figured it'd be more secure, right?"

"It would also take forever to input if you're a slow typist too," Jason snickered. "Which I notice you can be, boss."

"I think I liked it better when you'd kiss my ass," Jim said, giving a momentary glance over at Jason before he continued inputting the characters into the text field. "I work on the computer, like you will soon. Don't forget that." He stressed his boast by speeding up his typing of the password before slamming enter with a triumphant flourish. He handed the laptop to Jason without even checking to make sure it accepted the password as correct. "There you are. How's that for typing?"

"You hate to lose, don't you, boss? Now we just wait while they mix, and I'll place the order."

"You heard her say that, huh?" Jim asked. "Look, don't take it personally. She's always been a pessimist while I'm more of a realist."

"I wasn't hurt," Jason said. "It made me motivated to hear someone say I couldn't achieve something. Especially when I know they're wrong deep down inside. I know computers, I know networks, and I damn well know I can figure out any problem if I put my mind to it."

"Don't get arrogant," Jim said. "It's as damaging as any bullet if it rears its ugly head at the wrong time."

"True, but I'd rather err on the side of arrogance than be a sniveling coward."

"Expertise is wonderful," Jim said. "It's why I recruited you, but exercise caution."

"You recruited me because I already knew your secret, but it was a good try, sir."

"He got you there," Skye said. She leaned over and looked at the laptop's screen. Her face hovered side by side with Jason's.

His face was tinted red when he noticed. He tried to ignore her encroaching on his personal space. "The coins are mixed again. Now to send them back to the paper wallet and send them to escrow."

"At least there's that," Jim said. He totally relaxed back into the sofa and covered his face with a hand. "It's not like I'm just handing five grand to a potential threat. I'm just handing them over to a dubious criminal site that then hands them over to the anonymous cyber expert who may or may not be sending you a program riddled with malware and viruses."

"That's much better," Skye's voice was riddled with sarcasm. "From the sounds of things, money won't become a problem for you soon. Don't worry about it. It's already done. You'll give yourself an ulcer like that."

"I always hate this part," Jason said. He winced as he clicked one last time. "The order's in. He advertises that if he's online, he fulfills orders within fifteen minutes. We're on the clock now. If it's true, then I should have some time to acclimate to whatever they're sending me and adapt it to work."

"They'll never expect their motor to shut down again. Jason said they've had a dude stationed outside ever since - I imagine to prevent it happening again. Imagine their horror when it happens again."

"I'm imagining how today's events unfurl," Jim said. He closed his eyes, fully sinking into the cushy couch. "We stop the car and what?"

"We kill the bodyguards and Martha," Skye said.

"Yes, how? If we shoot, we're endangering the women."

"We may not have a choice," Skye said. "It's still better than the life that's awaiting them. I assure you of that. If you'd given me or Ashley that choice, we'd have taken it. At least I would have."

"Christ," Jason said. "Here I thought I was an edgy teenager, but I never endured your tribulations. Here's to hoping we can prevent thirty more from ever doing so."

"When are we heading out?" Skye asked.

"She wanted you there by two p.m. They're leaving by

three, correct? Then I say we head out and be ready by one thirty. Hopefully Ashley's last client leaves early, or she'll be making up some bullshit excuse. She will be present; I assure both of you. We need all hands on deck."

"She'll be here," Skye said. She leaned away from Jim and over toward Jason. "Let me see that real quick, would you?"

Jason felt her chest pushing against his side and obliged without saying further words, trying his best to face away from her to hide the growing blush on his face.

"You've received a message in the marketplace," Skye said. She tapped Jason's knee. "Here, get working on your magic, mister tech wizard. A lot of lives depend on us, and we will not fail."

"Easy for you to say. I'm the one who's decrypting some anonymous readme file and trust this program they sent is what they claimed it is. If not, I look like a jackass who wasted five thousand dollars."

"I didn't buy it simply because you suggested it, you know," Jim said. "You gave me the option with all the different outcomes. I decided it was worth it," Jim said. "We're a team, remember?"

Jason took the laptop Skye was handing back to him. "Let's see here. Yeah, he says he sent me the email. The email contains a link to an online storage medium where I can download a copy, he says. Makes sense. There's no way you'd send such a sensitive program over an email provider. It'd get caught by the authorities in a heartbeat. Let me scope out the site and make sure its privacy policy is to my liking. I'm not touching it unless I'm satisfied. The last thing we need is a sting operation from a pissed off power-hungry alphabet agency."

"I'm glad he knows this shit," Skye said. "I'm lost right now with all this tech stuff. Give me a bad guy to turn into a pincushion or flying around rooftops. This stuff, though, is not for me. You must've been on the computer constantly growing up, huh?"

"What about it?" Jason asked. "You learn a few things when you're on it all your childhood. My parents didn't argue when I'd fix theirs when they got viruses on it. You learn by necessity."

"The video games had nothing to do with it?"

"Maybe, I won't lie..."

An hour later...

"Now let's see if my hypothesis is correct," Jason said. He clicked the button on the newfound app that was labeled 'Connect'. "Tell me this is the correct car. I'm tired of seeing their speedometers and seeing they're already moving. It panics me every time that I have access to their controls."

"That's the general idea of the app. So, it works?" Skye asked.

"It works, but the hard part is finding the correct system. We can thank the automobile industry for that advancement. There are nearly forty in range. It's going to be impossible to find our target unless I inject my code into this program."

"You can do that?"

"The dude gave me the file. It contained instructions for if you wanted to modify it. It came with a warning about not reimbursing us if it screwed the application."

"Tamper at your own risk. It's smart," Skye said. "Try it out."

"Right." Jason hit the button. The app showed a pop-up screen with graphics depicting a cord plugging into a wall socket. It changed to a picture of said cord plugged into a wall with a green checkmark along with success below it.

"It's not on already. Let's see whose car I'm inside," Jason said. He looked up at the empty parking lot outside town. He clicked on the button labeled ignition.

A nearby car engine roared to life and idled.

"That's my car alright!" Skye said, pointing at it nearby.

"So, it did work."

"What did your code thingy do, anyway? How did you know that was mine?"

"Do you remember when I had you put that action figure above your back seat? That was why," Jason said. "I figured out a way to utilize the camera built into every car nowadays."

"There's a camera in my damned car?" Skye asked, turning to Jason.

"Yes. It was put into law years ago. You need to stay informed about politics. I won't explain the whole affair, but yes. Now I can peek inside any car and view the occupants. "

"Let me test it out one more time. Here comes another signal. Let me see if it works again. Once to test the theory, twice to double check." Jason navigated his mouse up to the drop-down box. He clicked it and the two familiar IP numbers were listed. After hitting the refresh button, a new one appeared on the list. He hit the connect button.

Once connected, he clicked on the newfound, noticeably shabbier looking button labeled camera which he had created himself and placed in an empty portion of the program's UI. The program opened a video feed of albeit inferior quality. A female voice could be heard.

A young mother had two kids in the backseat. A young boy was visible behind the passenger seat. She rolled her eyes. "Carl, be nice to your sister. Just because your father isn't here doesn't mean you can act mean. You know I'll tell him when he gets home if you keep this up."

"She started it!" A young boy's voice could be heard. "She kicked my leg."

"I did not." The girl was out of frame behind the driver's seat.

"That's enough family drama." Jason disconnected from the feed. "That does it. Provided I can tell her bodyguards from civilians, we have our way into their network. If this hadn't worked, I was going to recommend we leverage their hacker."

"You're referring to Milo? If we got him involved any further, he'd probably be killed," Skye said.

"True, but he did knowingly join them. If I had to pick between getting him in trouble or those women getting taken to God knows where, I know what I'd have picked."

"True." Skye looked away. "It would have left a foul taste in my mouth. We don't have to worry ourselves. All we need is to complete this last part and the job's finished. You think we should call in any reinforcements?"

"Don't tell me you're talking about that Specter guy?" Jason said. "I don't think the boss likes him too much."

"He doesn't trust him. There's a difference. We'll stop by before we swing by the apartment and see if he's even open to the idea. If he is, we can ask Jim. An extra pair of hands or guns won't be amiss if it devolves into a gunfight."

"I suppose you're right. You know we're going to have to pay him back if he keeps helping us out on our jobs, though. That's the part I worry about."

"We did a job for him and then he did one with us. We're

even. What's wrong with helping another vigilante when we're chasing the same type of people, anyway? Better together than splintered."

"Easier said than done, but I agree. We can't become too trusting of him too quickly, either."

"There's Jim's line again. You can think for yourself you know," Skye laughed. "Don't worry. I won't tell anyone. It's kind of cute how you have this hero worship and all, but, I won't lie, it's a little odd too."

"Cute you say?" Jason turned to her, giving her his full attention. He ran a hand through his short hair and smiled. "That's not a phrase I've heard women say other than my mother."

"You're shitting me," Skye said.

"No. You want to hear a funny story?"

"We've got a few hours before this shit operation kicks off. I've got time if you're willing to tell it." Skye reached down and pulled the lever at her side. She pushed her back into the seat and it leaned back. She stared at the ceiling of her car. "Hit me. I'm good and relaxed."

"Did Ashley tell you of how we first met?"

"All she ever told me was how you joined the group. It involved stalking to hear her tell it. Is that true?"

"Partially," Jason said.

"I knew it," Skye said with a smirk.

"You didn't let me finish. I had been hunting for Masked Justice or any of the Justice family for a long time - ever since I heard of their exploits. I wasn't going to stalk if she was normal. You know that. That's not my point. The first time I met Ashley, she was piss drunk and attending a house party."

"Seriously?" Skye looked over. That caught her attention. She stared straight into Jason's eyes as he spoke. "Go on," she said.

"I saw her sitting in the room's corner, just holding a whiskey bottle and drinking it. I thought it weird, so I went over and struck up a conversation. This drunk frat member comes up, and well, you know how Ashley is."

"She started a fight?"

"She started a fight," Jason said. "I got my ass kicked then too," Jason laughed, devoid of any cheer. "Even drunk off her ass, she was ten times the fighter I am. Can you imagine that? Someone like me standing up to some college athlete?"

"I believe you said this was supposed to be a funny story, did you not?" Skye asked, her tone serious. "Try again, and give me a better one. I don't find a brave individual who's standing up for what's right getting beat up as funny."

"I thought it was funny," he said.

"No, you didn't."

"I actually do," Jason smiled. "It gave me the hunch that she was more than she appears. Had that never occurred, I'd never have met you. I choose to believe that things happen for a reason. Meaning even failures have worth in them. That's what I tell myself anyway."

"I see you've been thinking about this a lot," Skye said. "Everybody fails, man. What matters is how we grow and improve from it. From the sounds of it, you're doing exactly that. Keep your chin up, and you're good." She reached over and rested a hand on his shoulder. Her tone changed from one of heartfelt sincerity to one more suited to jokes. "Just don't let me catch you falling into the old habit of stalking one of us. I'll pop you one if I catch you doing that, like Ashley said you once did."

"That phase of my life is gone, thankfully," Jason said.

"Here I thought that was the hard part, and now we're about to go interrupt a prisoner transfer by utilizing top secret methods I got from an online black market. You never know where life will bring you."

Skye's phone rang. "Give me just a moment," she said. She answered the call, bringing the phone to her ear. "This is Skye," she said.

"I just received a call from a client. I get off work early," Ashley's excited voice said. "My client called and told me he had a stomach problem. He called off our session. He said we'd reschedule once he's feeling better."

"Uh huh." Skye glanced over at Jason and rolled her eyes. "Whatever you say. We've good news to share, but not over the phone."

"Someone's in a good mood," Ashley said. "I'll hurry back in time to not miss the pizza party. That's still on for tonight, right?"

"Assuming everything goes off without a hitch, it sure is. Alright. Well, I shouldn't keep you away from yet another client. Jason and I are heading home."

"Were you two on a date?" Ashley asked. "Did I interrupt?" Her voice changed to one full of sarcasm. "I'm so sorry. I didn't mean to ruin any moments you two might have been having."

"You are forgiven, and it was an excellent one."

Jason raised an eyebrow, only hearing half of the conversation.

"An excellent one?" Ashley's voice was taken aback. "What does that mean? Did you-?"

Skye cut her off. "Wouldn't you like to know? See you this afternoon. Don't be late." She hung up, preemptively cutting off any further questions Ashley might have been about to lob.

"A good one?" Jason asked.

"She asked about the plan we have," Skye said without missing a beat. "What did you imagine we were talking about? Something lewd?"

"Hell if I knew," Jason said. "We ready to head back?"

"No time like the present."

23

"A black market on the underside of the internet?" Ashley asked, her voice raising. "Are you fucking nuts? You paid some nutjob who may or not be a honey pot over five thousand dollars for a program?"

"That works," Jason said.

"That is not the point," she said.

"It kind of is, though," Skye said. "Don't worry about it. Jason took every security precaution."

"Where did you two even gain that amount of crypto currency bulk to purchase such an expensive program? I only know of one..." She paused and looked over at Jim's sheepish grin. "You." She pointed at the team leader. "You trusted them with five thousand dollars?"

"I trust you all with my life," Jim said in a suave voice. "You think five thousand dollars is any different?" Jim got up and walked over to Jason. He wrapped an arm around Jason's shoulders and pulled them together, shoulder to shoulder. "Besides, he proved my trust correct. He got it done with the purchase. We have our way of stopping

Henderson's convoy whenever we want, without endangering civilians. It's all thanks to Jason."

"It was a team effort," Jason said. "Skye helped by volunteering her car to experiment on, and she kept me focused the whole while or I'd have been wallowing in self-pity."

"That sounds like her," Ashley said. "Annoyingly so," she said with a side glance at Skye.

"You will never let me live it down that I have to constantly remind your ass when it's your turn to take out the trash, will you? Don't forget, and I won't have to keep reminding you. Not to mention, I'm the one trying to set you up on dates. Count your blessings, missy."

"Easy now," Jim said. "We're limited on time. Let's focus up and get ready. Now, Jason, I trust everything's ready on your end?"

"It's taken God knows how many hours and over five thousand bucks, but yeah," he said. "I'd say it's ready now, boss."

"Good man," Jim said with a nod. He turned to the girls. "Then the rest is on us. We have the hard job now that Jason's breezed through his with flying colors. Let's not let him down."

"Like hell I would," Ashley said. She pounded one of her fists into her other palm. "We know where she's going. Why not camp along an abandoned stretch of highway out of sight and ambush her ass?"

"It's not feasible to tell how fast the car will decelerate," Jason said. "I've never given this whole brake concept a road worthy test."

"Why not?"

"Did you want me to hijack a civilian's car and slam the brakes on the highway? I thought not. I didn't have the chance."

"We're going to be coming in hot on this one," Jim said. "Jason can stop the car, and then we'll drive past. We can use my car as cover should worse come to worst."

"Wait one moment," Skye said. "I have a suggestion and a question."

"Are they related?"

"Yes," she said. "Do we want another pair of hands?"

"Don't tell me you want Specter?" Jim asked. He rubbed his forehead with a shake of his head. "You're not serious?"

"We know he hates Patterson, and we know he is aware of Henderson. He's jumping at the bit to help us on this one," Skye said. She got up from the couch and walked over to Jim's nearby window. She opened the curtains and stared out at the city below. "We know he can take care of business, and he's proved dependable. Why not use the extra manpower for Henderson's final act? Don't act like we couldn't use help. I'm not saying invite him to the party afterward, but another combatant on our side would not be a bad idea. We've no clue about the number of bodyguards that'll pour outside."

"Hmm." Jim stopped rubbing his forehead. His hand lowered to his mouth and covered it for a long minute before removing it. He locked eyes with Skye. "Since you know he's interested, I assume you already asked him?"

"I asked if he would be. I did not invite him or make any promises since I knew it was your decision, not mine."

"Good," Jim said. He took a deep breath and stared at the floor. "Fine, we could use another vehicle helping on this. He knows we're going into an all-out war, yes?"

"I didn't go into specifics, but he knows the overall idea of the plan. He wanted me to send him a message if he was wanted, and said we could meet up before the last stretch."

"He'd have to meet us on the way," Jim said. "We don't

have time to visit his warehouse before heading out. We're already cutting this razor thin as it is. Henderson probably thinks you're MIA at this point."

"Let her," Skye said. "We'll see her soon enough, by my reckoning."

"Reckoning?" Ashley asked. "Who uses that word anymore?"

"You think a girl who hunted every fucking weekend of her life didn't pick up some of the rural mannerisms?"

"Someone's defensive," Ashley said. "Don't worry, cowgirl. I won't fling mud on your hootenanny."

"I knew I shouldn't have said that word. Now she'll never let me live it down."

"Let he who is without sin cast that first stone, Ashley," Jason said.

"Oh, who asked you anyway?"

"Children," Jim said with a shake of his head and a silent chuckle. "It amazes me how we're going to kill human beings, and you're here playing. I guess that's how we haven't gone insane from all the murders we've committed. Still, we can joke around tonight. I even drove the extra mile and collected party favors for tonight - but only if this job goes well. I will not reward shoddy work. Is that clear?"

"Party favors?" Ashley's ears seemed to perk up at the phrase. "What does that mean? Alcohol, weed, or maybe you mean a new video game?"

"It's not a video game," Jim said. "Why would I buy one of those? I don't even have a system."

"He didn't say no to drugs," Skye said.

"Alright, enough guessing." Jim clapped his hands. "Double check your gear and make sure that you have your masks. We're going to need them. After that, we move out and kick some ass."

"Agreed!" all three juniors said.

24

"Does Specter keep his costume on all day?" Jim asked. He looked at the truck across the street, between the hotel and its nearest building.

"It's cold out," Skye said. "Why do you think we're all sitting here with ski masks in our hoodies' pockets? No doubt that's why he has his on."

"He has his complete costume on. Still, we should focus. It's close to the time of their departure." Jim cleared his throat and moved his gaze to the hotel doors across the way.

"He's in an alley," Skye said. "No one will see him. If they do, he'll deal with it. It's his problem, not ours. As someone more experienced than I once said, 'Focus.'"

"Point taken," Jim said. He sat straight up as the doors of the hotel across the busy street opened. A large male bodyguard had sunglasses on. He led a large procession of young women out of the front glass doors. Beside the bodyguard was their primary target.

Martha watched left and right, as if paranoid from her recent near-death experience. She raised an arm and looked at her watch. She looked over and asked a question they couldn't hear.

The larger man shrugged before pulling out a phone. Within a minute, he shoved the phone in his pocket and pointed to the group's left.

They looked over and saw a large bus pulling into the hotel's parking lot. Martha pointed at it, signaling to the girls that their ride was here. The bus blocked the gang's view of the boarding, but they saw one important detail.

"She's not riding on the bus itself," Ashley said, leaning forward between the front seats. "She's too scared."

"Wouldn't you be?" Jim asked. "This is good news," he said. He couldn't hide the grin appearing. "We can stop her away from the girls. It's the perfect case scenario. We can stop the bus simultaneously and make sure to not lob rounds toward it." He twisted to look over his shoulder at Jason. "You can stop it too, right?"

"Of course I can," he said. "I'll get which hardware numbers are which so I can label them. One's the primary target and the other will be labeled hostages for easy, convenient access."

Skye leaned over, her head nearly resting on Jason's shoulder. "I'll never get over this technology stuff. To think it's feasible to stop a moving vehicle."

"It's just extending what I already know into another medium," Jason said. He didn't shy away from the slight contact, choosing instead to keep focusing on his work. A new window popped up, showing the front of a bus. Dozens of young women could be seen. Some already were seated, while others were filing in and taking their seats in an orderly fashion. "That's the hostage vehicle." He backed out of the live stream and returned to the app's UI. He right clicked and selected the label address before inputting the name.

"As far as actually doing the deed, have we decided on how?" Ashley asked. "I know it's late, but I don't remember us ever saying."

"We all have our weapons," Jim said. "If you're far away, use the gun. If you're close, use the blade. It's simple. Odds are you'll be at a distance, but use your own good judgement. I doubt they'll have tons of ammunition, so it may well devolve into a bloody melee."

"They're starting their engines. Get ready," Jason said. "Do you hear me?"

Specter's voice responded over the earpiece. "Acknowledged," he said. "I'll follow you."

"Roger that," Jason said. He reached up and pressed a button on the earpiece. "He's following us, so on your mark."

"Yeah." Jim watched the bus pull out ahead of the limousine. The longer vehicle followed close after. Jim waited until the traffic allowed him to exit into the busy, traffic filled mid-day streets. "Here we go," he said. He pulled out into traffic and started the chase.

A beat-up truck pulled out behind them and followed.

"Let's see what's on tv," Ashley said.

"You mean the feeds?" Jason asked.

"Yeah. Switch to Henderson's feed. I want to count how many bodyguards are packed inside."

"I doubt we'll see, but it's worth a shot," he said. He switched the feed to the other labeled vehicle. A video feed popped up. It showed two men in suits and sunglasses sitting in front of a pane of glass.

"It is a limo," Skye said. "What did you think you'd see? She doesn't strike me as the type of woman to leave the separating window down. My guess is the only person back there with her is Duke."

"The bodyguard?" Ashley asked. "You think they're together?"

"You're asking me to speculate whether she's having an inappropriate relationship with her bodyguard? I have no clue. They stay in the same room, from what I remember she said. Maybe?"

"How many beds were in there?"

"She's very interested in this," Jason said.

"Answer the question."

Skye closed her eyes and tried to remember the specifics of the room she had her chat with Henderson in. "I think maybe one."

"I knew it," Ashley said.

Jim spoke up from the front. "We're pulling out onto the highway. We'll be outside of town shortly. Get your irrelevant yammering out, because in a few minutes we'll be riding into battle, kids."

"You just can't let a girl have her fun, can you?" Ashley stuck her tongue out.

"This operation's many things," Jim said with a quick glare into the rear-view mirror. "Fun is not one of them," he said. He waited a minute. "It is kind of cool though, I'll admit."

"I know, right? We're chasing after crime lords that traffic young women while hacking their car's computers."

"Enough," Jim said. "We're nearly at the city's outskirts. Let's be ready. Guardian, how long until we're at the spot you've chosen?"

"I'd say about five minutes at our current speed. Though I was never terribly skilled at algebra questions that involved determining who'd reach where first."

"Check your weapons. Double check the safety's not engaged," he said. "Odds are you're going to need them. That's why I made sure we all carried extra rounds. Guardian, I never asked this, but can you steer these cars?"

"I sure can," he said. "I was planning on taking them off the road. It's less chance of any innocents getting caught in the crossfire. I can also lock them in their car until we get to our positions. Though they can still get out if they're quick thinkers."

"You hear that?" Jim said. "That means we need to get to our positions in a hurry."

"Speed is my middle name," Skye said. "There's a reason I'm not like muscles over here." She reached across Jason's lap and poked Ashley in the shoulder.

"It makes cutting easier if you have the raw strength. Excuse me."

"What did I say?" Jim's normally jovial voice turned full of ferocity. "Stop fucking around."

"Yes, sir," all three younger vigilantes immediately responded.

"Jason, on your mark." Jim took a hand off the wheel and reached for the gun in his shoulder holster. He removed it and deftly made sure the safety was off.

The two girls at Jason's side both mimicked Jim's action as best they could. "I'll do my best, sir."

"I know you will. I know you'll exceed my expectations, as you always do. If you don't, I know you'll do everything you can. That's why you're our guardian."

"We'll be there in a couple of minutes. I'm prepping the program so I can hit it on a dime. I've never tried to drive a car without a wheel, but uh..." he said. "We're treading new ground here today, so we'll see how it goes. You all won't mind if I accidentally crash Henderson's car, right?"

"Care?" Jim asked. "As far as I'm concerned you should purposely crash it once you're safely off the highway. The more of her guards that are concussed or unconscious, the bigger the advantage we'll possess."

"I understand. I'll get as much speed as I can manage after I get them off the main road."

"Call Specter and let him know it's going down soon. One of you two, not Guardian. He's busy, and I don't want him distracted."

"I got it," Skye said. She pulled out her phone and called him. "It's happening soon. Be prepared to follow us off-road. We're taking them off the highway."

"How on earth?" Specter's voice asked.

"We have our ways. Trust us. You're not the only one who has some technological marvels up their sleeves."

"I'm curious to see it in action. Duly noted," Specter said. The call ended as quickly as it began.

"Here we go," Jason said. "The dirt path is coming up. I'm turning off their engine. Get ready to slow down." He took a deep breath and clicked on Henderson's car's label. A list of instructions appeared alongside the car, accompanied by a few buttons on the sides of the screen. He clicked the button that said cut engine.

The car in front of them kept rolling, seeming to fall back closer to them with every passing second. "Let's see how this works. At least they used the WASD control scheme for driving, bless their hearts." Jason's left hand hovered over the infamous keys gamers around the world used.

The limousine behind the bus swerved slightly to the right before straightening itself.

"Be careful with that," Ashley said. "If you have to accidentally veer in a direction, pick right. Better to hit a tree than oncoming traffic."

"I was just getting a feel for how she handles," Jason said. His gaze was unwavering from the monitor. "The turn's coming." He slowed the car, causing Jim and Specter behind to slow down. Once the limousine had turned, they could see the bus still driving ahead.

"Nice one," Jim said. He turned to follow the bus. "Drive them a suitable distance inside. Let them have their engine back if need be."

"That's the plan," Jason said. He pressed the button to re-enable their engines and pressed the gas.

They followed them along the dirt covered road leading deeper into the local woods. The snow covered ground outside the windows stood in stark contrast to the black limousine they were following.

"Everybody exit on the driver's side," Jim said. "It'll give us all cover."

"That's assuming they break out of their locked doors before you all get out." He noticed a familiar notification bell in the bottom left reading 'A designated locked door has been overridden to be unlocked. Relock it? Hit shift to confirm.' He quickly hit the button. "It's going to be a game of whack a mole, so hurry,"

"At least he's honest," Ashley said. She looked down at her gloved right hand to see it shaking, then reached down and pulled the pistol out of her belt line. She gripped the weapon tight, trying in vain to stop the involuntary shaking of her hand.

"I'm going to need to move my bow, Jason," Skye said. She looked down at the bow resting on her and Jason's lap under his laptop. "I know this isn't the best time since you're driving and all, but it's kind of important."

"I'm driving a straight line," Jason said. "This isn't rocket science. You have around ten seconds before I need a stable platform to drive from. Make it quick."

Skye placed one hand toward the back of the laptop and lifted while using her other hand to slide the bow out from under the device. She slowly lowered it to Jason's lap, nearly getting her hand caught underneath. The bow pressed against the seats in front of her, but was otherwise free.

"I'm going to set them up in the middle of the upcoming clearing. Take us along the outer rim so you can all get to cover quickly."

"Oh, God. Once their car stops, how am I supposed to exit exactly?" Ashley asked beside Jason.

"Really?" Jim said. "Just crawl into his lap while moving over. I don't care. Just don't exit on your side." He watched the vehicle ahead pull off the dirt road and onto grass in the clearing ahead. He immediately pulled to his left. He stopped near the tree line and shut the engine off. "Everybody out, now."

Jason wedged his hand over the hotkey for relocking the doors. He felt the laptop lid pressing down hard on his hand as Ashley's butt was pressing down on the laptop, and by association, his lap. As soon as the pressure started, it ended as she hurried off his lap and out the nearby door.

Skye was already behind a nearby tree for cover. To her left, she saw Jim near the dirt path leading back toward the highway. To her right was Ashley rushing from tree to tree, trying to set up a crossfire as Jim had laid out earlier. She looked back in Jim's direction to see Specter park his truck sideways, blocking Henderson and her men's exit from the ambush.

Jason's voice met her ears. "They are becoming more insistent about leaving. Get in position, everybody.

They heard a door slam, along with more rapid footsteps. She saw Specter dash toward the clearing's opposite side, effectively completing the trap.

Skye ducked behind cover, nocked an arrow, and prepared for the inevitable battle. She turned and readied the arrow before sidestepping, bringing the car into sight again.

"Let them out," Skye said, steel in her voice.

"Do it," Jim said.

The limousine's doors did not instantly open as they were expecting. Indeed, the only movement they heard were distant engines going by on the highway they'd just exited. Sounds of birds, insects, and other sounds of nature were all they heard.

"What are they doing?" Skye asked. She tried to hold the form, keeping the arrow trained at the car. She eventually had to step back behind cover and return to her nocked and ready stance, resting her arms.

"Waiting, it seems," Jim said. "They're waiting for their reinforcements, if I had to guess. That bus may well be coming here. Guardian, I want you on it. Do not allow them to arrive come hell or high water."

"Understood, boss," Jason's voice said over the call.

Skye leaned her head around the tree and kept a watchful eye on the car. "What if they don't get out? We can't stay here all day and wait for their reinforcements."

"You have a better idea?" Jim asked. "It's not like I have explosives."

"You might not, but I possess my concoctions," Specter's voice said. "Would you like me to demonstrate?"

"Go for it," Jim said. "Everybody move behind cover, and don't peek until the blast is over."

"Wait a second, dammit," Jason said. "I can roll down their windows. Try to aim for that. Are you ready?"

"Ready."

The windows of the limousines dropped and paused temporarily before lowering fully. The doors flew open as a small projectile lofted its way toward the elongated vehicle. Men and woman alike poured out of the car and sprinted toward the tree line. An especially tall guard in a suit was at Henderson's side. He guided her away from the vigilantes' side and behind a tree. The others spread out wherever they could behind cover. One such guard was not so quick as his peers.

The homemade handheld explosive finally detonated. A man's scream could be heard. Skye waited for the initial wave of shrapnel to embed itself where it may before peeking around cover and looking at the carnage before them.

The slow bodyguard's right leg was nowhere to be seen. Exposed muscle tissue dangled from what was left of the limb. His screams pierced the veil over the ringing inside her ears. She fired off her arrow in the direction opposite them in the clearing. She aimed beside the tree.

A miss. She saw a guard poke his head around the tree before hurrying and ducking behind his cover.

All hell erupted as the battle began.

"God!" Jason's voice could be heard. "I know this car's bulletproof, but this scares the fuck out of me."

"Keep your damned head down," Jim said amid the cacophony. His voice was closer to a yell. "Specter, how many explosives do you have?"

"I have three and a few flashbangs." The older vigilante's voice was barely audible amid the chaos.

"Toss another one to your side. That's where they are. Shift around so you're not visible and open."

He didn't respond. The next thing that drew Skye's attention was another explosive going off across the clearing near the tree cover. The gunfire temporarily stopped as the deafening blast interrupted the struggle.

Once the dust cleared, it showed a few trees had taken visible damage. Chunks of wooden splinters were visible on the ground next to where they thought Henderson's men were. She fired off another shot. She couldn't spot her target and wasn't sure if it hit. The one-legged bodyguard was still visible, trying to crawl away from her and the others. His continued howling made it difficult to discern any other injuries or hits they had scored.

"We have to flank them," Jim said in the relative calm after the proverbial storm. "Any volunteers, or am I going?"

"I'll go," Skye said. "You'll need cover to draw their attention away from me. I'll circle around and shoot them from behind. It'll give you an opening if I'm successful."

"That's fucking risky," Ashley hissed to her over the call.

"Welcome to my life," Skye said. "On your mark. I'll run the other way from you, boss."

"Got it, get prepped. Here's your distraction. Blind, give covering fire on three. One, two, three." The last word was accompanied by more gunfire. Skye noted absentmindedly as she ran, that as her allies fired, there were no muzzle flashes across the way. *They're behind cover and cowering until they reload,* she thought.

She went deeper into the woods. The sounds of modern warfare were constant and hectic. The screams of the unfortunate casualties and already injured accompanied the chaos. She moved from tree to tree. Twigs snapped beneath her feet as the music of battle and mother nature's plants covered and obscured her movements.

She kept moving until she noticed ahead of her a guard with his back pressed against a tree. He was ejecting a magazine and sliding another in. Stopping her movement, she got out of his sight line. She readied an arrow and side stepped. She saw him peeking around his cover, facing to her side, completely oblivious to his imminent demise.

His recklessness and inability to keep aware of his surroundings led to the current predicament. He looked down and saw an arrow implanted firmly in his neck. He fell back behind cover to what he had to imagine was safety. Reaching up, he barely poked the shaft of the arrow before keeping his hands away. He tried to call out, but no understandable words were forthcoming other than garbled gurgles and wet noises.

Skye stepped a few more feet to her side and let loose another arrow. This one pinned his arm to the tree behind him. The pistol crashed to the forest floor below. She ran up to him and grabbed the arrow. "You picked the wrong client. I'm not sorry about this." She tried to pull the arrow out of his neck, but it got caught. The squelching, moaning, and gurgling from the guard before her accompanied the battle a short distance away. She brought her foot up and placed her foot somewhere quite sensitive on the young man before pushing her foot against him and pulling the arrow.

The arrow slipped out without further ado. She kicked the gun and looked down at the young guard, bleeding with every beat of his heart. "Nicked the artery, huh? Fantastic." She peeked around the tree to see more guards. "Back line, huh? Nice," she said.

She grasped the gun with her gloved left hand, still

holding the bow in her right. She sprinted and tossed the gun on the far side of her newest target.

The weapon landed at his side. He looked down at it before kneeling, picking it up, and ejecting the magazine. He smiled at his fortune of receiving a loaded magazine before giving a quick glance over in her direction. His eyes widened when he saw Skye standing so close, not more than a dozen yards away beside a tree, arrow already ready.

She held the string behind her and released the arrow. This one also found its target, but not his throat. This one punctured the man's arm. The shot still went off, but his arm inadvertently moved with the impact of the arrowhead plunging into his flesh.

The man looked at her. His next words were not stifled by seeing Skye lining up another shot. "Archer behind us!" he called out, his voice hoarse, trying to be heard over the noise of conflict. "They're flanking us!"

Skye quickly released her intended death blow, instead only hitting him in the chest. He fell back against the tree, his feet splayed out in front of him. He could see Skye in front of him. Wheezing, he tried to raise his right hand to fire, and did so.

Skye got behind the tree. She heard closer gunfire. She looked over her shoulder and saw the nearest trees behind her having their thinner branches snapped under more gunfire than was possible for one pistol. "They're focusing on me back here! Move in. Now's your chance. Hurry, before they overrun my position."

"We're on it," Jim said. "Blind, you're with me. Specter, cover our approach. Lay down suppressing fire on that tree line. Do not throw explosives."

Skye cowered behind the only thing between her and a death by bullet. She tried to make herself as small of a target as she could manage. *They're getting closer,* she thought. *My cover's getting shaky.* She looked up at the thick tree she hid behind. Chunks of bark were splintering off with every bullet that impacted it. She could feel the vibrations of the tree getting blasted with her chest. She was pressed up against it. It felt like dozens of ripples.

She looked to the side. *If they flank, I have nowhere to go. Shit. I should've thought of that possibility before approaching so close. Fuck, fuck, fuck,* she thought. *I'm going to die here today.* She shook her head. *No. If I'm going to die, I'm going to do it on my terms. Fuck dying like a coward. I lived for too long like that.* She gripped the bow so tightly that her knuckles turned white. She lowered herself behind cover, almost like she was a professional runner about to compete in the hundred-meter dash.

"Move now!" Jim yelled over the headset.

She needed no further commands. She burst off into as fast a run as she had ever run in her entire existence. Reaching into the quiver on her back, she removed an arrow as she ran. She spotted another guard in a suit further away. He either hadn't seen her, or had shifted his attention, as his focus was presumably on Jim and Ashley. She didn't stop. She continued hurdling toward the man. Her grip shifted on the arrow so she could stab him with the end.

By the time he noticed the footsteps, she was already within arm's reach. She reached up and jammed the arrowhead into his neck and dragged it across before cruelly yanking it free. Her assault wasn't over. Her clothes were splattered with his blood. She turned toward his weapon hand and looked down. She grabbed the hand containing the firearm and pointed it away from her.

His one hand was busy trying to staunch the blood flow exiting his sliced arteries and veins. His other was desperately attempting to point the business end of his weapon toward Skye.

She used her knee to slam into the firearm hand and pushed it away from her as the barrel erupted in orange light over and over. His finger squeezed the trigger, trying to end his attacker's life.

Skye could hear nothing other than a loud bell ringing in her ears. She saw her victim's eyes shift from a look of hatred to one of unmitigated pure fear. "Go to sleep," she tried to say. She wasn't sure if she did, but it didn't settle the dying guard.

She looked down and grabbed the pistol before prying it from his hand. He tried to fight her with his other hand now, having abandoned the hope of life. His hand snaked down to grab another magazine and used it to smack her with as much force as he could muster.

She felt the blow on her cheek, but it wasn't overly powerful. She finally grabbed the weapon and took the magazine, tossing her bow on the nearby ground, out of reach of the dying man. Looking down, she ejected the magazine before inserting the new one.

The newfound ringing in her ears abated. The sound of gunfire wasn't nearly as constant as it had been previously. She peeked around the tree and saw guards a dozen yards away toward the cars parked by the entrance.

"We can't get them," Ashley's voice said in annoyance. "I'm out over here. Shit."

"Hold your damned position," Jim said. "Do not approach further. Silent, what about you back there?"

"I'm fine," a chunk of the tree she was hiding behind was blown off, "for the moment anyway," she said.

"I've got something for them," Jason said.

"What?"

The smattering of gunfire slowed to a trickle and then stopped entirely.

"What the fuck did you do?" Skye asked, not daring to peek.

"Get away from that area now. Do not waste time asking. Get away from their position. That's an order."

"Fuck," Skye said. "Fine." She grabbed her bow in her left hand and kept the pistol in her right. She fired off a few rounds as she ran.

"They're about to get a delightful surprise. Sorry about your truck, though."

"What?" Specter asked. "You're not serious?"

A loud crash of metal slamming into metal met her ears. "Son of a bitch," she huffed as she continued to run. "Is that what I think it is?" Skye hopped over an especially big root when she turned to her side and confirmed her suspicions.

She saw a bus slam into Specter's parked truck, sealing off their little battlefield. The totaled truck flung sideways, spinning from the kinetic force of the impact. The bus, however, would not be dissuaded by an irrelevant obstacle. It kept pressing forward, getting closer to her. "Oh, no." Skye turned and ran deeper into the forest instead of sideways. She dared only look over her shoulder once she saw a suitably large tree. She peeked her head around and watched the destruction unfold.

The bus was still moving, despite plowing through the unmoving vehicle. She saw it slam into the tree line and stop with an abrupt halt.

"No!" a feminine voice could be heard. "Not the merchandise. I'll kill all of you!"

"You pissed her off pretty good," Ashley's voice said. Humor was clear. A moment passed. "Why are they not still firing?"

"Either they're out of ammunition, or they're too afraid to hit the bus," Jason said.

"How could you put those young women at risk?" Jim asked, distaste evident in his voice. "Never mind for now. Wait, hold. No one move. One's coming out with his hands up. He's a big one too."

"That's probably Duke," Skye said. "Watch out for him."

"He's not visibly armed," Specter said over the call. "I don't trust this still," he said.

"Parley," the man called out in his deep voice.

"Is he serious?" Jim asked.

"We have in our possession an explosive device powerful enough to incinerate this entire area and kill all of us. Don't shoot or she'll set it off," he said. "I am Duke, Miss Henderson's protector. Say something and show some good faith. We will take further silence as belligerence. Do not think about assassinating her. If she dies, the device goes off. Don't you get it? I'm keeping her safe for all our lives, not that you appreciate it."

"Bullshit," Ashley said over the call. "He's bluffing. Why would they possess explosives if they're heading to the airport?"

"They don't check the vehicles you ride in on," Skye said. "Not to mention everyone wants a good last line of defense. An explosive tied to your heartbeat is a good one."

"He could be telling the truth," Jason said.

"Fine," Jim said. He disconnected from the call. Skye watched Jim emerge from the other side of the clearing, still armed. He stayed beside the tree cover, never straying far from its safety as he spoke. He did not shoot, but kept his weapon trained on the lone bodyguard standing a few feet from his own cover in the open.

"You know what we desire," Jim could be heard. "Give up your employer, and the rest of you walk free."

"That's quite generous of you," Duke said. "Unfortunately, that's not part of the deal. We will die on our terms if it comes to it and take you out with us. It's better than dying alone."

"They're insane," Ashley said. "That, or they're bluffing."

"She's not so sure anymore," Jason said. "I cannot verify any signals that would indicate explosives, but that's not an assured no. I am not trained in detecting devices like that."

"We know you have an archer behind us. Call him off."

"Or what?" Jim asked. "You kill all of us anyway?"

"Now you're getting the hang of this exchange, finally." Duke laughed out loud. "Do it."

"Damn it." Jim scrambled to return to his wooden sanctuary,

"Keep him busy," Skye said. She got down low and moved toward the standoff and negotiation. "I'll see how real this shit is. Try not to piss him off."

"He doesn't want to die," Specter said. "You can see it in his body language."

"We can't trust body language," Jason snapped. "Are you nuts?"

Skye watched her footing, stepping over assorted twigs on the ground. She studied her surroundings with every tree she passed, watching for any more men, or Henderson herself.

As she passed an especially large tree, she felt a sudden impact on her face. She crashed forward onto the ground, dropping the handgun.

"You morons," Martha snarled. She looked a far sight from her previous encounter. No longer was she the epitome of a classy, elegant woman that never loses her cool.

Her insufferable smirk and constant talking down demeanor was replaced by a look of unparalleled ferocity that Skye had seldom seen before. Martha stared down at Skye. She had a handgun in her hand. "You're fucking lucky that I'm out." Martha stepped forward.

Skye rolled and got to her feet, kicking the pistol back behind her, further into the woods. She reached up to grab an arrow when Martha charged toward her. She plucked one arrow out of the quiver before she was thrown backwards from the weight of the enraged crime boss.

Skye didn't have time to mentally process the wind being knocked out of her, as she was soon admiring the blue sky above. She shifted the arrow in her grip so she could stab with the arrowhead. She saw Martha loom over her, a crazed look in her eyes. Her right hand reached down out of Skye's sight.

Skye followed where Martha's hand went and saw it extract a knife out of her pant leg. She threw her right hand forward, aiming toward the hand now holding the blade without pause.

Skye was too late.

A flash of pain. Skye looked down at the blade plunged into her chest. She gave another shot at stabbing her victim. This time the arrow found its mark. The arrow entered Martha's wrist and slashed across, leaving a wide gash.

Skye seized the opportunity and raised her leg up. She kicked Martha with all her strength and struggled to get to her feet. A dull ache in her chest showed the injury she had sustained.

"I'll kill you." Martha bared her teeth and held her now bleeding hand.

"What?" Skye saw Duke turn around behind Martha. She reached for another arrow absentmindedly.

"Hey, jackass," Jim jumped out of his cover, now in front of Duke. It was hard to see this as she struggled in a life-or-death contest. A pissed off human trafficker was trying her best to strangle Skye and push her back against the nearest tree.

"You're already dead," Martha cackled, now clearly having had enough. "That blade in your chest was specially made." She had her forearm under Skye's chin, pushing her back against the tree.

It was hard to breathe. Skye finally dropped the bow in the struggle. She locked eyes with the deranged woman. She reached up toward Martha's face.

"It's between your ribs," Martha said, voice barely above a whisper. The smile on her face was not one of happiness, more akin to bloodlust. "All I need to do is twist it, and you're beyond repair. How do you like knowing your life is in my hands, vigilante?"

"Works for me," Skye said. She reached up and dug her hand into Martha's eye, eliciting a horrific scream.

Martha's hands fell to the knife, still lodged deep into her chest. Skye saw the blade twist, but felt no further pain. *Thank God for endorphins*, she thought.

She dug her hand further. Wet warmth covered her hand as the scream kept filling the air. She ripped, tore, and watched as the knife kept moving in her chest. The two were locked in a mortal struggle.

Eventually her effort bore fruit, proverbially speaking. She gripped the gelatinous feeling object within reach and yanked with all her might.

"Why aren't you dead? Duke, get over here? What are you doing over there? For God's sake, get to me now."

"I'm busy. Please wait a few moments," a casual male voice said, clearly not overly exhausted.

Skye couldn't see her boss and the bodyguard fighting as she finally pulled the eye free from its socket. She dropped the now dangling orb when her attacker jerked away.

Martha hopped off. Both hands covered her eyes.

Skye finally reached down and grabbed the knife handle. She pulled it out with great effort and tossed it aside while Henderson was busy. She placed a hand above the wound site, feeling wetness there. *Blood,* she thought. *No shit. I'm bleeding. I've been stabbed.*

"Don't tell me you're done already," Skye said. She tried to get to her feet, but stumbled as Martha finally abated.

"I know that voice," she said. She removed her hands to reveal the eyeball now hanging down. Her voice was enveloped in venom, and she was breathing heavy. "You didn't show up today, did you, Skye?"

"Guess I'll have to take my chances then," Skye said. "Everyone, leave. Now, get out of here."

"Are you crazy?" Ashley's voice was out of breath. "We're in the middle of battle."

"Get behind cover then," Skye said. She used her foot to kick the bow laying nearby and snatched it out of midair. "I'm finishing this. Guardian, get Henderson's car out of here."

"Who are you talking to, bitch?" Martha looked at the battlefield to notice Jim, Ashley, and Duke in the clearing. Jim and Ashley had their swords out while Duke had a knife. "They can't help you now," she said.

"It's not for me," Skye launched herself forward, keeping the bow held out in front of her. She landed on top of Martha and sat above her. She placed her bow over Martha's neck and pressed down, suffocating her.

"You'll kill all of us," Martha choked out. "Don't be a fool."

"Too late for that," Skye said.

The sound of an engine roared to life nearby.

A male voice accompanied the squealing tires. "Watch it." A piercing howl filled the space between metal meeting metal.

"Need help?" A nearby male voice asked. She looked up to see Specter. He got to his knee and held Martha's legs down. "You're lucky I circled around to meet you. I took out three guards that almost killed you."

"Appreciate that, but I think it might be a moot point," she said.

"I don't think so. Your friend Guardian has crushed their plan into shambles."

Skye peeked over her shoulder and no longer saw the limousine anywhere. She glared down at Martha, who was turning shades of red. "Where'd the car go?"

"He took it into the forest. God knows where it is now, but it's away from us. Your boss and other friend are still having their fun behind us, it looks like."

Martha wasn't dead yet. Her hand slapped the earth at her side, violently searching for any means to save her life. Her hand found the discarded knife from her previous assault. She tried again to stab Skye, this time in her side.

"Whoa now," Specter said.

Martha's attack hit home, but unfortunately struck the wrong target. It found its way into Specter's arm.

He let out a cry of momentary pain before grabbing Martha's knife hand, holding it in place.

Her legs kicked up, knees smashing into Skye's stomach as her face turned blue.

The last ounce of strength exited Martha; her hands fell limp as her eyes closed. A strained exhale signaled her exit from consciousness through her pale blue lips.

"No boom yet," Skye said.

"She's unconscious right now. Keep that hold for a while longer and she'll be dead - or slit her throat. Just finish it quick." He looked behind Skye. "Looks like they're done."

Skye kept one hand on her bow and kept it planted against Henderson's throat, while the other went over her shoulder to pluck an arrow from her quiver. "You don't need to tell me twice," she said. She jammed the arrow through Henderson's neck before twisting and ripping it to the side.

A distant explosion shook the very ground.

Specter stumbled getting to his feet and leaned on a nearby tree as Skye wobbled on her knees.

"I'll be damned," Jason's voice said over the call they shared. "They weren't bluffing."

Skye looked at the melee taking place...

Just earlier...

"Hey, jackass." Jim jumped out from behind the tree, keeping the pistol trained on Duke, who was looking back over his shoulder. Jim saw two figures struggling behind Duke but couldn't tell the combatants apart. "Keep focused, big guy," he said.

"Enough of this." Duke lowered his arms and turned to face Jim. "Let's finish this," he said, marching toward Jim.

"Worried about your little hellion back there?" Jim mocked. "I would be too. She's facing a trained killer, but so are you."

"Fool, I don't care for your stories." Duke reached down to his belt line and took out a long knife. He did not slow his approach. "You're out of ammo, just like us."

"Maybe," Jim said, tossing the gun behind him. He reached down to his waistline and hovered his right hand over the blade's handle. "Come to me and see what happens."

Duke obliged Jim's request. His arm was a blur.

Jim raised the weapon and tried to deflect. Unfortunately, trying to deflect a slice from a blade many times smaller was harder than he expected. He jumped back and looked down at his chest to see it sliced diagonally. "Point taken," he said with a smirk. "Let's stop fucking around with this little boy who thinks he's hard."

"Keep talking smack," Duke said. "It'll just make killing you even more satisfying."

Jim kept the sword out ahead of him, pointing at Duke as he backed up. "Nothing wrong with a little trash talk. See, the trick about blade fighting is..." He stopped backpedaling and took a step forward too quickly for Duke to react. He slashed the blade across his chest. "Vest?"

"Vest." Duke did not take the attempted end of his life with passive interest, choosing instead to keep the approach through the one spoken word. He threw his knife hand out first in the blink of an eye, aiming at Jim's leg.

The small weapon found its mark. The knife sunk into Jim's right front leg.

Jim grit his teeth, locking eyes with Duke. He didn't take the assault lying down. He swung his blade again, but Duke was cautious and jumped back after the blow landed, yanking the dagger free with him. Blood dripped from his knife and spattered onto the dirt underneath, adding to the assorted colors of blood, glass, and metal scattered across it.

"Aggressive," Jim said to himself.

Duke turned when he heard footsteps to the side of him to see Ashley charging at him, sword held high above her head.

She brought the killing blow down once she was close, only to be met with nothing but air.

"Wasted your chance, whoever you are," Duke said. "This is simply another day for me." He hopped, showing how routine this was.

"You're calm for someone who's charge is under attack as we speak," Ashley said.

"If they kill her, we all die anyway," Duke said. "There's nothing that can be done about that. For me, it's all about us three."

"Arrogance doesn't prove skill." Jim took a step forward with his good leg and thrust the blade toward Duke, eliciting a hop backward out of the way of the impaling strike. He hissed and stopped in place before hopping back on the one leg.

"It's as good as a one on one now," Duke turned to Ashley. "A woman, huh? If you wish to die, then try me."

Ashley circled around to her right, leaving Jim where he was. "You got yourself a deal," she said as she sidestepped, keeping the blade between them all the while.

Duke refused to turn and expose his back to Jim, choosing instead to sidestep and try to keep them both in view.

Jim used the opportunity to step toward Duke, narrowing the distance. "Come on, tough guy. You're not finished with your first opponent yet."

"There's nothing more embarrassing than someone who doesn't know when they're beaten." Duke spat on the ground. He kicked some dirt up toward Jim.

Jim never winced or took his eyes off Duke. He used his left hand to wipe some of the fresh soil off. He sliced low across his body.

Duke tried to dodge but was too late. The cut was not terribly deep, but it was visible. "Son of a..." he said.

Skye's voice interrupted Jim and Ashley's focus on the ongoing battle. "Everyone leave. Now. Get out of here."

"Are you crazy?" Ashley's voice was out of breath. "We're in the middle of battle."

"Get behind cover then," Skye said. "I'm finishing this. Guardian, get Henderson's car out of here."

"Do it," Specter said. He noticed the disconnect from the phone call. "Guardian, move that vehicle pronto."

"It won't matter," Duke said. He lunged toward Ashley, trying to stab whatever he could.

Ashley was quicker than Jim. Her evasion was successful. She slashed her sword in a desperate bid to fend off her attacker, connecting with a blow aimed at Duke's head.

"Ah," Duke lurched away from Ashley. His glasses fell to the ground, chopped in half. Droplets of blood accompanied them.

"Move," Jason said in their ears.

Ashely used Duke's recoil to run over to Jim and help him over to the side of the clearing. The bus's engine roared to life, and the tires spun again. The car sped past them down the path before turning into the forest. Ashley disentangled herself from Jim. "I got this guy. You stay here." She turned and walked toward Duke.

"To hell with that," Jim said, limping behind her to catch up. "I'm with you." He caught up with her and let her move to the side, keeping his direction. The pain in his leg was amplified now. Walking was difficult, but possible. The constant pain with every movement embedded itself in his mind. He willed his body to work at near full speed.

A few yards to his side, Ashley charged ahead at full

speed. The pair were attacking in a pincer formation, trying to overwhelm their adversary.

Duke chose not to engage in such unfavorable terms. He circled around the nearest car, which was the one they rode in on. He kept the limousine between himself and the pair. "Hurry." He tried the door, only to find it locked.

"Trying to run?" Ashley circled around the car from one side while she saw Jim walk steadily toward the other. "Just fight like your boss back there. She's probably almost dead, you know. You can't afford to lollygag around. Your bomb is out of play. She's in play now."

"Shut the fuck up!" Duke's former calm, collected façade had cracked. His voice was no longer even. It cracked in explosive volume. "You think I don't know that?" He got low to the ground and darted toward Jim.

Jim noticed the movement in time to throw a preemptive swing of the blade. This attack landed as Duke hissed in pain, grasping his injured left hand. "Be a good slaver and die already," he said.

"After you," Duke said. He didn't back away with his wound and instead launched himself into Jim, knocking him backward onto his back.

Jim heard Ashley's rapid footsteps as he positioned his own sword to stab his attacker before that knife could move too much further. He threw the blade forward, only for Duke to grab the blade and direct it away from his midsection with his left hand. His right, containing the blade, was idle. All his attention was directed at the sword trying desperately to end him.

Jim could see Ashley standing above him. She raised her hands above her head, carefully measuring her strike, when the ground beneath them rumbled as an enormous explosion was heard not too far away.

Ashley lost her balance, stumbling in place, trying to stay on her feet.

Jim crawled backwards during the shockwave and kicked Duke as he got away. He struggled to get to his feet, but found he couldn't put any more weight on his injured leg without waves of white hot pain flooding his mind.

He opted to lie on his back, still firmly grasping onto the sword.

Ashley regained her balance and finally sliced downward with a primal yell. Duke scurried away, leaving a part of himself behind. His right hand, to be more specific, was no longer attached to his arm. His knife was laying in the dirt, his hand still desperately grasping onto the blade.

"You're disarmed now," Ashley mocked. "Literally." She thrust the sword down through Duke's shoulder. She pulled the blade out and delivered the coup de grâce. The blade finally ended the battle, having lodged itself firmly in Duke's neck. She pried the blade loose, and the blood flowed as he fell to mother earth to die.

Ashley sheathed the weapon and walked over to Duke to check his body. She found no weapons and moved from the dying Duke to Jim.

"Don't matter," Duke said, grasping the wound. "You're bleeding. Your DNA's here. Soon the entire world will know your identity. When they do, you're going to have a bounty the entire world round. Who are you trying to be? Masked Justice?"

"As a matter of fact," Jim said, being helped to his feet by Ashley, "I am Masked Justice." His grip tightened around the blade as he prepared the fatal strike. "Know you served a monster and share her fate."

"Says the serial killer to the guardian," Duke said. He

looked up at Jim, now towering above him. "You're no better than us. You know that?"

"I don't pretend to be." Jim held the blade high above and delivered the slice that snuffed Duke's life from this mortal realm. He tried to wipe the blade clean as best he could with his hoodie and pointed over to where he thought he'd seen Skye earlier. "Let's retrieve her and leave."

"At least we know she won," Ashley said, looping Jim's arm over her shoulder and helping him walk.

"Guardian, I need to talk to you later tonight."

"Before you chew me out, boss," Jason said. "None of the girls were inside that bus. I got on their radio system after I'd taken control and told them to get out or their contracts were null and void. The explosive inside the bus hurt nobody, except for possibly wild animals."

"You lied, but it was a worthy one," Jim said with an exhale. "I knew you wouldn't endanger their lives needlessly. Well done."

The pair made it over into the tree line. They passed a body immediately to their right, behind the nearest tree. He was dead, clutching his weapon. On either side, behind their own cover, laid more dead men. Further in, they saw Skye laying on the grass along with Specter leaning down to help her up.

The older man pulled Skye up. "Now, where did that go?" He leaned forward, inspecting Skye's chest.

"You old perv," Ashley scolded him. "What are you looking at?"

"I got stabbed earlier," Skye said. "I had a knife here." She raised her left hand and placed it over the fresh injury site. "It hurts, but it's not bleeding." Her right hand had her bow hanging at her side. "I had blood here earlier.

"You have armor on, you idiot," Ashley said. "You have a

bruise. Besides, if you stabbed someone, no shit you'd have blood caking your shirt."

"That explains why I didn't lose much combat efficiency. I thought my endorphins were masking the pain."

"You're lucky. Unlike your boss, it seems." Specter turned with a frown and studied the injured Jim. "Your DNA is here, my friend. Do you have a plan for that?"

"Guardian, Silent, go to the trunk and open it. I have a gas can in there. Douse the place and light it up. We'll call the fire department so this entire forest doesn't go up, but it's the only choice."

Skye brushed past the group and ran toward the car. She saw Jim's trunk pop open before Jason got out of the car, a mask covering his face. He grabbed two cans of gas and handed her one before they got to work dousing the place.

"I don't disagree, but I don't like it," Specter said with a frown. "Let's get out of here. Someone's bound to have heard those shots and called it in. We may only have a few minutes."

"On the double, folks," Jim said as the masked group hurried to the vehicles. "Watch your step. We don't want to track gas back to our cars when they set it alight."

"I need to talk to whoever crashed that bus into my baby," Specter said, seeing his beloved truck displaced. Its front was smashed from the bus's brutal impact and had slid away into a tree from the force.

"It was necessary," Jason said, "but it should still work."

"It'll only cost thousands." Specter tried to open the driver's door. It swung open, wobbling as it moved. "Remind me of this the next time you ask me for help."

"I've got the repair covered," Jim said. "I've also got the mechanic who can do it without asking questions."

"You damned well better," Specter said. He climbed in

the beat up, deformed shell of his former vehicle and quickly left the scene down the dirt path leading to the highway.

Jim hopped in the back of his bullet-riddled car and scooted to the middle of the backseat before leaning over and pulling the rear door shut firmly. "Get it done, and hurry. We're late."

Skye and Jason met after emptying the gas cans. They tossed them back in the trunk before slamming it shut. "I've got this," she said as she reached into her pocket and pulled out a box of matches. She took one out and dragged it across the box, igniting the orange flame. She tossed it toward the near veritable swamp of blood, metal, gasoline, and God knows what else littering the dirt and soil.

The pair, without delay, ran back to the car and got inside. Jason had to enter the driver's seat as he saw the back was full with Ashley, Skye and Jim. The immediate area outside erupted into a sea of flames that quickly spread through the clearing.

Jason started the engine and backed the car up, moving toward the exit. He swung the car around and escaped the ever-expanding flames.

"He's never going to want to work with us again," Jim snorted.

"If you keep that promise, maybe he will," Skye said. She saw Ashley holding a cloth pressed hard against Jim's leg. "That doesn't look good. Have you thought about finding a doctor?"

"It's not like I can go to a hospital," Jim said. "You know that. It didn't hit an artery, I think. I'd have bled out already. It looks worse than it is. I'm not even dizzy yet."

"The bleeding is slowing," Ashley said. "Skye, you call this in."

Jason pulled out onto the highway, illegally crossing traffic and getting in the lane heading back toward Denver's city proper. "Lucky that no one uses this road often. It seems this road's deserted of day. If we're lucky, no one called that in, and we'll be the first caller."

"Quiet," Skye said. She leaned forward between the car's front seats and reached for the glove compartment. "Is there a burner in here?"

"Always is," Jim said, "just to be safe."

"Good," she said. She dialed the number for emergency services and brought it to her ear. "Hello, I'd like to report a disturbance. Yes, it was just outside the city, off Highway 85. Yes, that's correct," she said. "It's by Roxborough State Park. That's correct. Well, I saw smoke and could have sworn I heard a loud ruckus. I think there may be a fire." She hung up the phone. "We need to destroy this."

"Toss it out the window," Jason said. "Even if they find it, they have no clue who's it is."

"Look at my life. Fighting crime and committing the worst crime of all - littering and burning forests down." She pressed down on the window control and waited for the window to lower fully. She tossed the phone outside the window onto the side of the road and rolled it up.

"Cynthia's going to be pissed," Jim said. He tore the mask down from over his mouth.

"More than likely," Ashley said. "I doubt she'll like that her boyfriend took a knife to the leg. I'd be prepared for a lecture if I were you."

"She is the type to explain all the ways you're in the wrong I've found," Skye said. "Not my favorite personality trait, but hey, can't judge taste."

"Aren't you all pillars of support?" Jim inhaled sharply. "Easy," he said.

"There is one more problem we've yet to solve," Ashley said. "We need to stop by a pharmacy, real quick."

"Are you nuts?" Skye asked.

"We can't carry him up there in this condition and not expect his blood to be everywhere. We need to at least wrap it up if we want to remain undetected. It's the last leg of this race. Let's not fuck it up by being hasty."

"Fine, I'm the only one that won't smell like a battlefield or that's not covered in muck." Jason looked up in the mirror at Skye's brown stained clothes. "No offense, but we don't want questions."

"None taken." Skye looked down at her purple attire. "I'm a mess, but at least that bitch is dead, and the girls are safe. Speaking of which, what about the girls?"

"They'll be found when the authorities arrive," Jason said. "They're standing on the side of the highway. Not an ideal pickup area, but it's the only decent idea I thought of on the fly with the constant gunfire."

"At least there's that," Jim said, leaning his head back in rest.

25

"Here's to a job well done." Jim held up a glass filled with clear liquid. He took a big drink and placed the cup down. "All's well that ends well."

"For now," Cynthia said. She was busy ferrying assorted drinks from the kitchen to the table, along with the plates that would soon be needed. "You need to focus on real paying work until that leg heals up. Also, you need to adjust your workouts."

"I get it," Jim said.

"He'll be working out by tomorrow morning as hard as he did before," Skye said. She sat on the sofa, surrounded by Jason and Ashley on either side. "Mark my words. The man is stubborn."

"You're preaching to the choir," Cynthia said. "Don't test me on this. You won't like it."

"I'd just go along with what she says," Jason said from Skye's side. "That's not a battle you choose wisely."

"I'm fine," Jim said. He hovered his right hand over the freshly wrapped wound. "See? It's not bleeding any, and I don't have a fever."

"Then you won't mind coming with me tomorrow to a doctor?" Cynthia asked.

"I'd love to, but that's an operational security hazard," he said. "They'd ask where I got the stab wound from. What would I answer? I was killing the leaders of an international human trafficking ring and her bodyguards?"

"No. I'd pick something more like you were trying to fix an appliance around the house and accidents happen."

"Just fixing the sink and I knock the ice pick off the table onto my leg kind of thing?" Jim asked, trying to suppress a chuckle and failing, causing the rest of the room's occupants to share a laugh.

"That mess could become infected, and then you'd be up shit creek without a paddle. You're going to get some antibiotics, and that's the end. We'll just come up with a story that harms your pride and not your secret identity. No arguing."

"That's that then," Jim said. He looked up at Cynthia. "Help me to the bathroom, would you?"

Skye watched as Cynthia helped Jim up and helped him limp toward the bathroom down the nearby hallway. She turned to Ashley and kept her voice low. "Keep time."

"You don't think?" Ashley leaned back and tried to watch as the pair disappeared out of sight. "They're not going to do anything. Are you nuts?"

"I sincerely hope she is correct," Jason said. His laptop was nowhere to be seen. "I'm more concerned about Specter and his car. I thought he was going to kill me."

"He still might if Jim doesn't pay up like he said he would. Why did you bring the bus into the fray anyway?"

"You know why already." Jason refused to answer and instead looked at the television that was nearly muted. It could barely be heard reporting the daily news - in which their latest escapade was featured.

"Enlighten us and make it official," Ashley said. She reached over and poked Jason in the upper arm. "Come on. Why?"

"Because you heard me in trouble," Skye said after the pregnant pause caused by Jason's refusal to answer. "That's why, isn't it?"

"Who knows?"

"Don't be shy," Ashley said. "That's a fine reason."

"Let's go with that," Jason said. He reached down to the coffee table in front of them and grabbed the remote control. He unmuted the television and the trio watched while their seniors were still absent.

The female newscaster began after returning from commercial break. She and her co-host to her side sat behind a large desk as the news jingle played over the speakers in the darkened room. "A fire broke out earlier this evening, just outside of town. Authorities say that's not all. Apparently a wrecked bus, tire marks, and some kind of exploded vehicle a short distance away were found. Authorities haven't speculated as to what happened, but the fire is still raging. No casualties have been reported, but authorities haven't been able to reach the vehicles we see from our helicopters. Even more bizarre - a group of young ladies were found nearby claiming they were headed toward the airport for a modeling job."

The small square in the screen's corner showed a picture from above, presumably from their helicopter. It looked down on the fire engulfed patch of trees as it raged onward. Long streams of water sprayed onto the burning wood and leaves as the emergency responders fought valiantly against the man-made blaze.

The male news anchor chimed in. "Some pundits have speculated that this resulted from gang warfare that spilled from Denver's city limits, possibly fooling their victims into human slavery. Others guess this is the work of dangerous vigilantes. I can certainly see their reasoning," he said with a shake of his head. "Society is collapsing, and every night there's another attack featuring lunatics."

"No concrete evidence has been released," the female news anchor said. "All we're certain of is an altercation led to the inferno on your screen. We may never learn what happened, as the fire no doubt will erase a lot of evidence. If you want this reporter's opinion, it was done purposely for some nefarious reason. Stay tuned for continuing updates on this story, only on Channel 6 News."

Ashley grabbed the remote from Jason's hand and muted it before tossing the control back onto the table in front of them. "It worked."

"Let's hope there weren't campers," Jason said.

"They'd move away in time," Skye said. "There wasn't a lot of wind today, so if they weren't asleep, they'd have seen it coming - not to mention the smell. Smoke has a distinctive aroma that someone who camps would recognize. They'd bug out quick."

The sound of a toilet flushing and a door opening interrupted them. "That's what I'm hoping," Jim and Cynthia reappeared. He watched the television and read the headline crossing the bottom of the screen that read 'No casualties found so far!'. "It had to be done or I'd be finished. What about that chest wound?"

"This?" Skye asked. She reached up below her neck and pulled the shirt she had on out a little, exposing some flesh that perhaps ought not to be shown.

Jason's eyes bulged before he redirected his gaze as

Ashley smacked Skye.

"What are you doing? Have some shame."

"I'm fine. It barely bled at all and didn't reach any grass. It was stopped by the fabric from the vest and my hoodie."

"Good," Jim said as Cynthia helped him back to his favorite recliner. "Even if you did, it wouldn't matter, judging from that live feed."

"I was wondering something." Jason scratched his head and peeked a glance at Skye.

"Shoot," she said.

"What did you have matches for?"

"Personal use," she said.

"Personal use?"

"Bro," Ashley broke out in uncontrolled laughter, "we're in Denver. One of the first places in the country to legalize weed, and you wonder why Skye would have matches in her pocket?"

"I didn't know you partook."

"Rarely," Skye said. "I prefer to keep my head straight when I know I'll be on the job, but I make exceptions."

"Exceptions?" Ashley had a smile plastered on her face that wasn't leaving soon. "Is that what those are?" She pointed into the kitchen toward a plastic container that was sealed. It contained assorted baked goods that smelled delicious.

"There is nothing wrong with an after-dinner edible," Skye said. "Just start low."

"Not for me," Cynthia said. "I'll take my wine. It's federally legal." She poured herself a glass from the bottle sitting on the table. "You should totally have one though, honey."

"Honey?" Ashley asked. "So, it's official now?"

"Damned right it is." Cynthia sashayed up behind Jim's chair. She took a drink from the filled cup before leaning down and snaking her hand across his chest. "Don't get any ideas. He's mine."

"I'm past that point of my life," Ashley said. "If you want the idiot, he's yours."

"Hey now," he said.

"The idiot is indeed mine."

The sound of the doorbell interrupted.

Cynthia's eyes lit up. She handed Jim the glass and picked up the precise amount of money from a nearby stand. She threw open the apartment door to a teenager holding three pizzas stacked in one of his arms. He had the other out.

"Tasty Quick Pizzas here, ma'am." His voice cracked during the introduction. "That will be $34.43, please."

"I have it here, dear boy," Cynthia said. She took the money she'd prepared earlier and handed it to the young man. She took the pizzas and turned. "Come get these, would one of you?" She somehow closed the door and turned around.

Before she could complain further, Ashley and Jason both took a pizza and carried it off toward the kitchen table. "Just help yourself, why don't you?" She spotted Jim trying to get out of his chair without help. She didn't reach him in time before Jason beat her to the punch, so to speak, and assisted Jim out of the chair and over to the kitchen table she had already prepared for the celebration. Thanking Jason, she made her way over. "As for you," she rested a hand on Jim's shoulder and squeezed, "you know you're injured, correct?"

"I'm fine, sweetie. Seriously."

"Says the man who set fire to that field to cover the amount of blood he lost," Skye said, sarcasm drenching her voice. "Be quiet and follow what she says for once already, will you? That'd be a pleasant change of pace. She only bitches because you don't listen. Who's ready to eat?"

"Give me three of the pepperoni, sausage, ham, and bacon." Ashley handed Skye her plate.

"This pizza's a monstrosity. Meat's fricking everywhere, and greasy as shit. How do you all even enjoy this?"

"How do you like this crap?" Ashley covered her nose and pointed at the pizza Skye had insisted upon. "What even is that?"

"It's called pineapple and ham. What about it? It's less greasy than this crap."

"Let's not argue and just enjoy this occasion," Jim said, reaching out and taking the plate from Skye. He placed it on the table before him and waited until the others had theirs. "That's another job done and quite a few less undesirables chasing after the powerless. Good job, team. Let's eat."

With those last words, all that was audible was blissful eating and occasional conversation.

"Did you guys hear about the latest bill that passed in the house?" Cynthia asked after a bite of the vegetable pizza. "Who am I kidding? Of course you didn't. You were out killing and setting woods on fire."

"Enlighten us," Jim said after a drink of water.

"Ah," Cynthia waved the request off, "this is a party. I'll tell you later."

"Spit it out," Ashley said.

"Police are going to be stepping it up a notch soon enough. The house passed a bill stating that police have a lot more power to stop vigilante justice than they had before. You're going to need to study the whole bill, but it looked bad. You'll probably have to change how you do things. Charlie's hard at work in DC trying to screw you over."

"Not just us," Jim said. "I trust he's been making headway with his other bill?"

"The child protection one? Yes, he has. Though some think it's a gross overstep of privacy that doesn't justify the law. It sounds fine that it'd be able to catch an abuser in the act and all, until you realize that means anyone could watch and listen inside your home. Talk about a violation of our rights. It hasn't passed yet, but it's a matter of time since he's one of America's most polarizing politicians right now. You either love him or hate him."

"I see," Jim said. He finished one slice before clearing his throat. "Then we have homework to do, and we'll need to adjust."

"Part of the newest legislation will impede your little activities too. I'll leave that little detail for you to find out, so I don't ruin the mood totally."

"They'll still have to abide by our fundamental rights. We'll be fine so long as we can peaceably assemble."

"You'd be surprised, but in theory you're right," Cynthia said. "Your boss is out of commission for at least a month."

"That's not a problem," Jim said between bites.

"Swallow and then talk." Cynthia took her nearby napkin and reached up to Jim and wiped his mouth. "Don't act like a kid, darling."

"Aren't you two lovey dovey now?" Ashley teased. "I think I liked it better when she was playing hard to get. At least watching him get smacked was entertaining."

"He'll get a good smack if he needs it," Cynthia said with a smirk. "He's aware."

"Fact of life ever since we were kids. In fact, it's her way of showing her affection." He used his thumb to point at her at his side. "She's never been good at being honest about her feelings."

"Shut up." She slapped his shoulder.

"See?"

"Moving off your dysfunctional relationship blossoming," Ashley said, "where's the music?"

"This is an apartment complex," Cynthia scoffed. "You can't play music in the evening."

"I'm not saying make it so loud they'd hear, but a little music helps relax me." She exited her chair and walked into the living room before stopping by a device. Making double sure the volume was low, she turned the dial, and some old rock and roll flowed onto the airwaves. She returned and sat in the dim kitchen.

"Just make yourself at home in their apartment, why don't you?" Skye asked with a knowing smile.

"You act like that's a new one," Jason said.

"I'm just comfortable here," Ashley said, picking up another piece of pizza.

The three younger ones at the table devolved into a full on conversation, joking, laughing, and talking about inconsequential things like jobs, video games, and their public lives.

Jim turned to Cynthia, tuning out his younger partners' conversation. "This is going to be a wild party, mark my words. When they get like this, it's never simple."

"I envy that," Cynthia said as their guests shared a laugh together. "We both know how this story ultimately ends."

Jim finished the water inside the glass and placed the container on the table. A grim look was on his face, standing in stark contrast to the teenagers populating the room. "It's about the journey, sweet pea, not the destination."

"Sweet pea? Is that really the pet name you're using?"

"I'm just trying it out. Do you like it?"

"Hell no." She gave a demure laugh.

The party lasted well into the night. Cynthia left early, leaving Jim, Skye, Ashley, and Jason once it passed midnight. The remaining were intoxicated, drowsy, or a combination of the two, except for one resident who was in full control of his senses.

Jim looked at Jason, the only member on the sofa still awake. He had Skye leaning on his shoulder. Her eyes were shut, and her chest rose at a steady pace.

Ashley was leaning away from the pair, choosing to lay her head on the opposite side of the sofa with her legs on Skye's lap and her feet on Jason's left leg. Jason had his laptop on his right leg, balanced precariously, reading something.

"Most guys would kill to be in your position, and you're reading," Jim said, his voice quiet.

"I'm just researching the new bill, boss," Jason said. "You know, in case it gets passed somehow. Better to be prepared than caught unaware. It looks a lot like he's trying to loosen county police's protocols against suspected vigilantes."

"Meaning?"

"Meaning they have more tools to catch wind of our identities and what we do. We'll have to tighten up. It says that before this bill heads to the Senate, some big wig is coming to Denver on a special request from Mr. Baskin. What the hell is he sending somebody here for?"

"Me," Jim said. All past semblance of joy was absent from his voice. "He's sending them here for me is why. I never changed my name. He has clearance levels, and I bet he used them to track me down."

"You think he told them who you are?"

"No," Jim said, shaking his head. "He'd have to implicate himself if he did that. He's stirring the pot and wants to see what we'll do is what I think."

"I'm going to kick his ass if he doesn't shut up," Ashley growled. "I'm trying to sleep. Be quiet."

"You heard the stoned girl. Let's get to bed. Will you help me get there?"

"Of course." Jason placed the device on the floor and finally realized Skye's face nuzzled into his shoulder. "Just a minute."

Jim watched the young man try to lift Skye's head without waking her up, then planted his hands on the recliner's arms and pushed himself to his feet. "Forget it," he said once he was out of the chair. "I'm fine. You enjoy that position you've got yourself in."

Jason could do nothing but stare as Jim disappeared down the nearby hallway. He heard a door close and looked at the two sleeping girls beside him. He leaned back and closed his eyes, trying to savor this one moment of peace and happiness he found himself in.

26

"Why are you dragging me out here so early in the morning?" Skye had her head slumping in the passenger seat. The early morning light of the day broke the hold darkness held on the land. She covered her eyes and squinted at the rising sun ahead of them. "What was so important?"

"You said you didn't remember if you handled that burner without gloves," he said. "It's imperative we find it before the police, or there'll be more complications. If the wrong forces locate it, and your prints are on it, then you get a visit from law enforcement. Then we're all under investigation by proxy."

"I see you're careful," Skye said. "Not good for our sleep schedules, but you're the one who told me to toss it."

"I'd assumed you never touched it with your bare hands. That's basic protocol when handling burner devices. You don't want any remnant of yourself on it."

"That's if they find it. Odds are they wouldn't have gotten a trace on it so quickly. I didn't waste time on the call, as you'll remember," she said. "There's got to be another reason."

"Not this time," Jason stopped the car at a red light. "Look out your window. It'd be over there if I'm correct."

"Even if it is there," she said, shifting in her seat with a groan, "what would I do?"

"Kick it under a tire, and we'd be off and away," he said. "Then you resume sleeping or whatever you wanted. Look and this will end faster."

"You're snippy in the early morning." Skye kept her eyes peeled, looking up the sidewalk of the road they were on. "I see it ahead. Stop as soon as you can. Pull over."

Jason followed the directions and stopped the car on the side of the road, amid angry beeps from the motorists behind them.

Skye threw the door open and slammed it shut behind her. Sirens roared behind them as she quickly kicked the device under the car's tire. "Do it now."

Jason hit the gas, and the car lurched over the formerly intact communication device and came to a stop.

More car doors opened, and a male voice spoke. "It was right near here. The signal cut off. This way," he said.

Skye looked over and saw a group of officers walking toward her. She leaned on the car and stared at the ground with a loud moan. "I never should've drank last night."

"It's close. Over here, near this car." Rapid footsteps approached them. "Down here," he said. He kneeled behind the car.

The first voice spoke beside her. "Miss, what are you doing?"

"My boyfriend picked me up to escort me to work since I drank too much last night. I got him to pull over." She looked up at him. "I thought I might vomit. I'm sorry, officer. We didn't mean to cause a traffic disturbance."

"I see." He looked over at Jason and then back at Skye. "Just one second, miss." He looked over his shoulder. "Hey, Jerry. Would it be better if they moved their car?"

"It won't matter anymore. The damage is done. They may as well move and resume their day so we can too."

"Hmm." He turned to Skye and leaned down to view Jason through the open window. "What do you do for a living, job wise, sir? If you don't mind my asking."

"I'm a college student right now, officer." Jason kept his hands stuck to the steering wheel in front of him.

"You two have some terrible luck," the officer said. "Did you feel you ran over anything when you stopped?"

"I did," Jason said. "I prayed it wasn't an animal. Tell me it wasn't a stray dog or cat, please."

"I'm telling you it was more likely to be a rat," Skye said. "Excuse me." She cut herself off by vomiting on the pavement below, outside the car. "Oh," she said, "that feels better now."

"It wasn't an animal, sir. It was a piece of potential evidence in the ongoing case against the vigilantes infesting this city. Do you mind stepping out of the car?" he asked Jason.

"Of course, sir." He unbuckled the seat belt and got out. "If I may ask, why, sir?"

"Just making sure you're not loaded too. It's not that I don't trust you. It's simply your girl obviously had too many last night, and I like to be double certain with people's lives on the roads. Will you take a breathalyzer test?"

"Of course. I was her designated driver last night."

"Good," the officer said.

"Hurry, Tom. We'd like to see if we can get any intel from

this crushing accident today," the geeky looking man with glasses said. He had already collected the remaining crushed bits of the phone in a labeled bag he held in his hands. "There are a few splinters left to find, and they're free to leave."

"Hold your horses," Tom said. He pulled out a sealed device and tore it open before handing it to Jason. "Breathe into that until I say stop."

Jason did until the device beeped.

Tom took it and read the display. "You're good. Now, escort your girlfriend and give her a drink. She needs water."

Skye opened the door and fell inside before slamming the door shut.

"Thank you, officer," Jason said. He stood in front of the door. "Sorry." He looked toward the front tire at the remnants of the shattered splinters of the phone. "Sorry about that, whatever that object was. Have a nice day." He climbed inside and started the engine before pulling off into traffic.

Skye watched the mirror after they left. She saw two of them picking up the remainders of the phone they'd barely destroyed. "How screwed am I now?" she asked.

"Now? You're good," Jason said, "unless they piece that phone back together and somehow get prints, which they're not going to. We're lucky we got there first. Aren't you glad you listened to me and came out with me this morning?"

"Glad enough I could kiss you to show my appreciation. I do not want to try prison."

"Leave that until after you get some mouth wash or something," Jason laughed. He looked over at an annoyed Skye, who started laughing with him. "How did you vomit on command? You didn't drink much last night."

"I drank enough to feel queasy this morning. When I thought the rest of my life could be getting fisted by Suzy in the clink, it gave me that extra push."

"Delightful," he said.

The laughing died down, and Skye cleared her throat. "I was two seconds from being exposed. I have to clean up my act," she said. "Do you mind helping inform me of this latest bill this Charles character is coming up with?"

"I'm already learning it myself. We're going to tighten up our security protocols." He gestured over his shoulder with one hand, pointing behind them. "It'd prevent things like that. The police will become aggressive in the next few months. Things are going to change. We're changing with the times, or we'll find ourselves left behind."

"That won't happen," Skye said. Her eyes were filled with determination as she watched the tall buildings they were passing with every second. "We're going to keep making a difference..."

THANK YOU FOR READING!

The Justice vigilantes' adventure continues in True Justice releasing in 2024. If you'd like to support this work, please feel free to leave an honest review or rating on Amazon. Thanks, and have a great day!

ABOUT THE AUTHOR

Alex J Fischer has been writing for close to a decade, published over a dozen action/adventure novels, and won six National Novel Writing Month challenges in a row.

Alex grew up in a small town in Ohio and still resides there. Hobbies include writing, video games, and watching crime shows.

ALSO BY ALEX J. FISCHER